Miss Gabriel's Gambit

RITA BOUCHER

All rights reserved.

No part of this publication may be sold, copied, distributed, reproduced or transmitted in any form or by any means, mechanical or digital, including photocopying and recording or by any information storage and retrieval system without the prior written permission of both the publisher, Oliver Heber Books and the author, Rita Boucher, except in the case of brief quotations embodied in critical articles and reviews.

PUBLISHER'S NOTE: This is a work of fiction. Names, characters, places, and incidents either are the product of the author's imagination or are used fictitiously. Any resemblance to actual persons, living or dead, business establishments, events, or locales is entirely coincidental.

COPYRIGHT © 2014 Pearl Englander

Published by Oliver-Heber Books

0 9 8 7 6 5 4 3 2 1

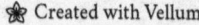 Created with Vellum

To my father, who taught his little girl the Game of Kings and delighted in her first "check mate." Miss you.

CHAPTER 1

An unnatural silence pervaded the dark paneled room at White's. An occasional whisper, a stifled cough and the passing muffled clatter of carriage wheels from St. James Street were the only sounds. All eyes focused on David Rutherford, Lord Donhill, as he seated himself before a small table holding a chessboard with a game in play. He polished his spectacles with his neckcloth before pulling a crumpled envelope from his pocket and reverently broke the seal.

Perching the lenses in their place once more, David scanned the contents of the letter. He reached across to select the lacquered black queen, holding it suspended for a moment, acutely aware of the expectant faces of the small audience of chess aficionados. Then, with a theatrical flourish, David set it on the diagonal opposing the white king. A collective sigh rippled across the room.

"Check," he declared solemnly.

The silence was complete once again as David inspected the board, but it was obvious to himself, as well as to every man who scrutinized the placement of the pieces, that there was no escape possible. Shaking his head bemusedly, David rose, his chair scraping the floor. Like an awakening sleeper, he shook his head wearily, then scanned the room until he lit on the familiar face of Ivan Petrov.

"There is no salvation," David declared, pulling at his rumpled cravat.

"Have I not been saying so," Petrov said, his slow, Russian-accented English emphasizing the mournful tones of his declaration. "Is been apparent for nearly a year now; you were in serious jeopardy. Your opponent is closing trap at last."

"Still, one does hang on to hope," David agreed with a sigh, pushing a shock of unruly, dark hair from his brow. "Nonetheless, Ivan, you are correct. I must confess myself surprised that it continued quite this long."

"Is over," Petrov said, mournfully, his hollow cheeks brushing against absurdly high shirt points.

"Done then. Check and mate," David admitted, toppling the white king on its side in the middle of the board in acknowledgement of his defeat. "The king is dead!"

David's solemn declaration resonated through the room, stirring old Lord Garth from his doze in a comfortably plump leather chair. He woke with a start as the deep bass voice announced the king's demise.

"'Farmer George? Gone?" Garth sniffed, unable to credit his ears. What do they say about the King, young man?" he asked, poking Petrov with a cane.

He looked down his prominent nose at the elderly man. "Is all over, milord," the Russian repeated. "The game is up."

With amazing agility, Garth lifted his considerable bulk from the chair and shuffled off to share the news with his cronies.

Amidst the murmurs of sympathy, David shrugged himself into his loose fitting jacket. For a moment, he stood before the table staring thoughtfully at the array upon the chessboard as if somehow he had mistaken the configuration. But no, it was absolutely as Ivan had said. The outcome had been apparent now for a long time. Still, it was difficult to believe that the game was truly done.

Petrov echoed his thoughts. "Is amazing, David. How long has it been since you are losing chess game? Never in all mine years with you in India have you failed to win."

David smiled as he thought back to the last time he had been trounced on the chessboard. "I was sixteen," he recalled, "My father had brought me to see Philador."

"François-André Philador!" One of the young aficionados gasped in awe, his expression reverent. "The French master who wrote *L'analyse du jeu des Échecs?*"

"The same, the *Analysis of the Game of Chess* was his greatest work, but he made much of his income playing here in England," David recalled, pulling a small notebook from one of him many jacket pockets. "When I first met him, poor Philador was desperately trying to return to his family in France after the Revolution. Robespierre had proscribed him from the country. The man was suffering from gout and extremely glad of the money that my father paid for my tuition, I daresay."

He turned to the last page and carried it to a small escritoire in the corner. With a sigh, he inked in the notation of black's final move, completing his record of the game. "I played with all the impetuosity of youth, feinting and sacrificing. Despite his condition, Philador was ever the master. He bided his time, let me batter myself against his defenses. Then he proceeded to tear me to shreds. I never did defeat him, but I learned a great deal from his style."

"Is difficult to be picturing you playing recklessly, David," Petrov said. "In all these years, I have always been regarding you as model of caution. The many games that we have been playing in India, you have never moved from impulse."

"I have seventeen additional years in my dish now, Ivan," David said, scrawling the word *finis* before blowing the ink dry. "Still, I wonder if a little panache might not have served me better this time than caution. You may examine the record of the game once more if you like. It is all here and you will see that my opponent made audacity into a virtue." David handed his friend the documentation of his defeat before withdrawing to gaze out a nearby window.

As expected, the group of chess enthusiasts clustered round Petrov and the notebook. Normally, David would have joined them as they set up another board to reprise the game move by move. But loss was a strange sensation, in truth, one that he was unaccustomed to.

Even so, this melancholy feeling was not due solely to the loss of a game. David stared out upon the rain drenched street, trying to determine the reason for the unsettled emotions that had been building within him all evening. Outside, umbrellas moved through the twilight downpour like so many darkened moons. The chill of England's spring permeating his very bones, David found himself longing for the warmth and sunlight he had found during his years in India, the vivid colors of silken saris and flowers. By contrast, his native land seemed cold, an empty place.

He wondered if his mood was related to the conclusion of this chess game. One more tie to the past was severed. It was startling to realize that this match by post had been the single constant in his life these past few years. His parents were both gone, leaving him no other personal connections to England. The late Earl, who had held the title before him, was a distant cousin, who had allowed the entailed family manor at Donhill to deteriorate into a moldering pile of rubble, tenanted by vermin and the occasional poacher. David realized that the defeat of his king was far more than the end of a decade-long challenge. It was the closing of a chapter in his life.

"There he is!" Lord Garth declared, waddling into the room followed by a decidedly skeptical-looking George Brummel and Hugo, Lord Highslip, one of the Beau's lesser disciples. Garth pointed a sausage-like finger at the Russian. "'Twas he who said it."

"Ah, Petrov is it?" Beau Brummel asked, lifting his quizzing glass disdainfully.

Petrov nodded nervously.

"Garth tells us you declared the King dead," Brummel said.

"Yes, b...b... but," Petrov stuttered, his English deserting him.

"Ye see?" Garth declared triumphantly. "I told ye, Brummel. Prinny is King now."

"I would not go offering to help choose Prinny's coronation garb yet, George," David interposed, moving back to his chessboard. "Lord Garth is somewhat confused. The king that he refers to is here." He set his toppled king back into its final position. "I have just concluded a rather hard-fought game."

"And who was foolish enough to play chess against you, David?" Brummel asked, rolling his eyes at the blustering Garth. "I trust you won, as usual?"

"Actually, it was my king that went down," David admitted with a rueful grin.

"Never say so!" Brummel declared, surveying the arrangement of pieces in surprise. "I would have wagered that no man on earth could surmount you on the chessboard. Yet, you appear to have been trapped quite handily."

"But the King!" Garth exclaimed once more, clearly annoyed at being ignored.

"Chess, Lord Garth," David said loudly, toppling the piece once more to illustrate. "My king was defeated."

"Oh," Garth said. "No funeral or coronation then?"

"None," David said, keeping his face solemn with effort. "It was but a game. My apologies for disturbing your rest, milord."

"A serious matter, the death of kings," Lord Garth muttered, his jowls shaking in displeasure as he returned to his chair. "Young people make light of everything these days."

"Old fool," Brummel said, as he seated himself at the table. "Still, I am rather glad that Garth roused me from my place, for now that I hear the actual truth, I find the doddering lord's pronouncement about the King's death far more likely than the reality of you losing a game. How did this debacle occur?"

"It is a long story, gentlemen," David said.

"Ten years long," Petrov added.

"Perhaps I ought to sit then, for a ten year story," Brummel declared. "Shall we share a drink? Surely such momentous events deserve an appropriate libation."

A footman scurried off discreetly and soon David, Brummel, Petrov and Highslip were seated round the table, glasses and brandy before them.

"To the death of kings," Brummel proposed, raising his glass.

"Treasonous pups," Lord Garth muttered from his corner, closing his eyes.

"And now, whose hand am I to shake," Brummel said. "Petrov?"

"Not I," the Russian said, stroking his chin. "More likely to be winning at fisticuffs with Mendoza than to be beating David at his game."

"Then where is your opponent?" Highslip asked, pouring himself another tot of brandy.

"Here," David said, pulling a crumpled envelope from his pocket. "It came in this morning's mail. Queen takes pawn to fatally check the king."

"A game by post?" Brummel asked.

David nodded. "It began in India ten years ago, during my soldiering days. My father put me in touch with an old friend of his who was also pawn mad and we have been playing move by move via correspondence the past decade."

"Ten years! Longest game I ever heard of," Highslip declared.

"Indeed, it might have been a bit shorter had I not been required to return to England unexpectedly, to attend to my late cousin's affairs. This letter containing the final move took some time to catch up to me. I spent three months waiting for the *coup de grâce*."

"How tedious," Highslip said.

"I find it most intriguing," Brummel said, casting Highslip a jaundiced stare that dared contradiction. "The wait between moves must have been interminable."

"True," David admitted, eyes alight with animation as he recalled those days. "But for me the wait was part of the excitement. Oftentimes, I would find myself pondering the board in my head, wondering what his next move might be. As the play developed the moves grew bolder. And the endgame! Magnificent! I haven't eaten all day, waiting upon tonight to . . ." David trailed off, flushing. "I am sorry, gentlemen. I tend to forget that chess is not a passion for most people as it is for me," he said, pouring another round.

"Better than many passions I can think of," Brummel allowed. "And far simpler than others. Women for instance."

"Is truth," Petrov agreed, pausing to down his liquor in a single swallow. "In chess, moves are set, rules determined, but women?" He shrugged his shoulders. "They are making rules as they go and changing them mid-game."

"They are inherently erratic," David said, his voice slurring rapidly from the effects of brandy on an empty stomach. "The fairer sex is incapable of logic. Emotion rules the day. That is why I believe that women are unsuited to games like chess where reason is all."

"I am knowing some decent female players," Petrov said. "Mine sister plays excellent game. Always loses, but putting up damned good fight."

"To be fair, women do have some inherent qualities which might be assets in chess," David owned, watching the liquor swirl in the glass before he downed the amber fire. He knew he was drinking far more than he ought, yet the warm, mellow feeling seemed to fill some hollow within. "Their natural disposition to deceit and treachery could make them formidable. Now if it were coupled with superior male logic..."

"Heaven forfend," Brummel declared, laughingly. "I must admit, the very thought of such an unnatural female makes me shudder."

Petrov frowned. "Mine sister is treasure, a jewel," he said in defensive tones, liquor and irritation thickening his accent.

"I am sure your sister is a delightful gel," Brummel hastened to say. "I meant no offense. But what David states is true. Women like your sister can grasp the game, but only on a more rudimentary level. I have yet to meet a woman who can play chess with the skill of any reasonably expert man, let alone defeat someone with anything akin to David's skills at the board."

"Who would wish to meet so perverse a creature?"

Lord Highslip muttered. "No doubt she would be one of those Friday-faced bluestockings."

"You need not fear any such confrontation, Highslip, for no such woman exists," David asserted, his tongue feeling decidedly heavy. "Still, I must admit, the idea is intriguing. A female who could best me at chess!"

"But as you are saying, no such female Goliath is existing, mine friend," Petrov said, raising his glass. "To the fair sex, those incomprehensible creatures," he declared. "Both being delight and demon of our sad existence." He downed the remains of his glass and blinked owl-like at the company. "Speaking of demons, mine cousin Dorothea asks why she is never seeing you at Almack's."

"I shall tell the Countess Lieven that you style her so, Petrov," Brummel said, a wicked gleam in his eye.

"Be telling her what you will," Petrov said with morose dignity. "I am having no need to court Dorothea's favor. Is certain she plans to be marrying me off one way or another. And I am suspecting that she has plans for poor David here. Is talking of him with that matchmaking gleam in her eye. She commands that you are coming next Wednesday."

"I absolutely refuse to be fodder for the matrimonial cannon," David said, sounding much like a petulant child. "I will simply not go."

"You cannot be refusing," Petrov said, aghast at the very idea of such defiance. "You will be making enemy of one of most powerful women in the Ton. Is almost to be like a command from the Tsar, David. She is Patroness."

"I was unaware that a Patroness is the equivalent of Royalty," David declared.

"Damned close to it," Highslip said. "Petrov is right.

You now have a title to secure. You must go to Almack's, else you commit social suicide."

"It would be equally suicidal for him to attend looking like that," Brummel commented, with a raised brow punctuating a look of considered castigation.

"And what is wrong with my clothes?" David asked, rising slowly and leaning over the table.

Brummel suddenly felt a twinge of misgiving. It was one thing to tweak the nose of a man like David Rutherford when he was sober. His intellectual bent and soft spoken ways often caused his friends to forget his sheer physical power. Lord Donhill was as formidable with his fists as he was on the chessboard.

In fact, it was David's prowess with his fives that had cemented the peculiar friendship between the arbiter of fashion and the unkempt newly-titled nabob. At first, Brummel had been inclined to dismiss Rutherford because of his dress, only worthy of notice by the occasional caustic remark. But one night, when they chanced to leave the club together and were set upon by footpads, David had handily dispatched the attackers. Brummel owed the man his life and now, the master of mode whom society styled "Beau," had landed upon a way to repay the debt.

"What is wrong with my clothes?" David repeated in puzzlement, slumping back into his seat.

"Everything," Brummel said, acerbically, hastily determined to take his friend in hand. "Weston would cringe at that coat and I have yet to determine the precise purpose of that sorry slip of rag hanging at your neck."

"You mean this?" David asked, picking up the end of his neckcloth to polish his spectacles.

Brummel groaned. "You are hopeless, David. How will you ever attract the fairer sex if you disdain proper dress? I ought to despair of you."

"Do so, by all means, George," David said. "My valet has long told me that I am a hopeless cause. 'Tis just as well, since my experience has left me no wish to attract eligible members of the predatory sex. Perhaps you might be so good as to convey your negative opinion to the Countess Lieven? In my sorry garb and with my churlish ways, I am surely unfit for the sacred chambers of Almack's."

"Oh, she will have you." Brummel sighed. "The Countess always gets her way. I would wager that you will soon be dressed, trussed and leg-shackled, David. Nothing can save you."

"I have no intention of getting caught in the parson's mousetrap, George," David declared. "Escaped it once by the tip of my tail."

"She was finding another man with title," Petrov explained with a nod. "Woman was tied to be fit when she found David was becoming a lord."

"Fit to be tied, Ivan," David corrected. "I am sorry to disappoint, my friend, But, I refuse to be wrapped up like some prettified parcel. The contents of the package are the same regardless of the ribbons about it."

"But one must make an effort," Highslip said.

"Why?" David asked, blinking as he tried to focus. He knew he was well on the way to being foxed, but the brandy seemed uncommonly smooth as he downed the contents of his glass. "If I were looking to wed, I have shekels aplenty, a decent bloodline, don't look like a leper. That's all the women want, anyway. But I am not seeking to be a lifetime prisoner. I simply refuse to play Lieven's game."

"You cannot forget your newly acquired title, Lord Donhill, although you disdain to use it." Brummel declared, toying with his quizzing glass. "As your history proves the words 'your ladyship' are music to any woman's ear."

"Pah! A mere baron." David waved his hand in dismissal, then poured unsteadily, spilling near as much brandy on the table as in the glass. "'Tis not as if I am an earl, like Highslip here."

Highslip nodded in silent agreement.

"You underestimate your attractions, David," Brummel explained earnestly, "and the skill of your opponents. Courtship is a woman's game, one where your vaunted skills of logic will only work against you."

Petrov tipped back his glass. "You cannot be making your own rules, mine friend," he declared, wagging a chiding finger.

"Why, not?" David asked, his thoughts coming together in a dance of drunken logic. He beckoned to a nearby footman. "Fetch the betting book," he demanded.

The servant returned rapidly with White's record of wagers along with a pen and inkwell. David's shaky fingers moved through myriads of names staking fortunes on the progress of raindrops, the outcomes of horse races and courtships, until he found himself a blank spot. In a faltering hand, David scrawled upon the ledger, then passed the book to Brummel.

"'I, David Rutherford, Lord Donhill will only marry the woman who can beat me in a game of chess,'" Brummel read. "Well, David! It would appear you have assured your freedom forever."

Highslip frowned. "I cannot like it," he said with a sniff. "It is not truly a wager."

"How so?" David queried.

"There are no stakes. What incentive is there for any female to try?" Highslip asked.

"Especially if she knows she is doomed to likely failure and humiliation if she takes up the bet." Brummel outlined the scenario. "And also, we must take into account that his challenger might not wish to marry him?"

"Is absurd! As we say, David is rich as Croesus, titled besides and not so bad in looks," Petrov disagreed. "Is contradiction, Brummel."

"Not when we consider the character of our mythical chess-playing female challenger. She would undoubtedly be a woman of quality. No female of the lower classes would have the ability to become expert at so intellectual a pursuit, especially a game so incongruous to her feminine nature. I posit that our mythical fair Goliath might even have a modicum of taste," the Beau said with a disparaging shake of the head. "His fortune and title provide some enticement, I admit, but not to a Boadicea of the chessboard. No woman of acumen and gentle breeding would give David a second look attired so. I have seen better dressed dustmen on a Sunday."

"I shall add a thousand pounds to sweeten the pot if she wins and turns him down," Highslip declared. "That way if the female does not to wish to wed him, there shall be some incentive to take him on."

"Excellent idea, Highslip. Even though your pockets are to let, I suppose that it is not too imprudent to make such a pledge. It is unlikely that you will ever be required to pay it," the Beau said, his lip curling sarcastically. He touched his finger to his chin in thought, eyes alight with a speculative look as he gazed at David. "But that is not enough. Every effort must be made to fashion this wager into a truly sportsmanlike proposition. Therefore, I give you, Highslip, the charge of dressing David appropriately for the length of the Season."

"Surely that would take a veritable miracle worker," Highslip protested.

"I would only entrust someone with the most exquisite taste for the task, Hugo," Brummel said, smoothly.

Highslip preened himself at the compliment. "Why thank you Brummel, I do try to keep up the standards. It is just . . . well . . ." He regarded Rutherford who sat, elbows on the table, chin in hand, necklinen soaking in splashed liquor. The earl shrugged his shoulders eloquently. "It seems almost the undertaking of Sisyphus."

"A most noble effort, Highslip. For the sake of sport," Brummel said, inclining his head graciously. "I, of course, shall be available should any advice be required." He added his scrawl beneath David's recording the full details of the wager. "I daresay, you shall be transformed David and no one can quibble at the boundaries of the bet. Nonetheless, you may now enter the sacred portals of Almack's in utter safety, for surely the woman does not exist who could trounce you on the board."

David frowned, not at all sure if he wished to act the role of clay in Brummel and Highslip's hands, but he shrugged that thought aside. With the terms of the wager set, he was safe from the harridans and harpies. "Now that my future is secure, gentlemen," he said, rising unsteadily to his feet, "shall we raise a glass to the one who actually did rout me? My worthy opponent, Sir Miles Gabriel."

"May he rot in hell," Highslip said sullenly.

David dropped his glass in astonishment, its contents spewing across the table. "What was that, Highslip?"

"Sir Miles? The old scoundrel stuck his spoon in the wall nigh on a year ago," Lord Highslip said.

David relaxed visibly. "It is ill to speak so of the dead," he scolded. "Even though the Sir Miles you speak of must be some other man, for this was posted just three months ago," he said, taking off his spectacles and holding the letter close to his eyes so he could make out the wavering scrawl. "Miles Gabriel of Northumberland. His estate is named the Crown Beeches."

"Aye," Highslip said. "And there he was buried, February before last. My estate marches with his. The old man was always toying with a chessboard. Don't know of any other baronet named Miles Gabriel in those parts."

David shook his befuddled head, trying to clear his thoughts. "But that is impossible I have his letter."

Brummel took the paper from Rutherford's hand. "December 10, 1810," he read. "How very extraordinary, David. It appears that you have been playing chess with a dead man. And more's the shame of it, he has beaten you."

. . .

Sylvia Gabriel paused as she descended the stairs. It was well into mid-morning and the delightful effect of sunlight streaming through the stained glass rosette above the door to the elegant Berkeley Square townhouse held her momentarily entranced.

When she was a child, the shimmering reds and golds and greens had always seemed to her like the rays of some faerie's wand coloring the delicate Chippendale pieces in the elegant foyer with wondrous magic. Unfortunately, the exquisite pieces were soon to be swept away in the path of Aunt Ruby's refurbishing frenzy.

A petulant call from below roused Sylvia from her reverie.

"Sylvia. Are you dawdling again?"

The young woman hurried down the remainder of the steps as her aunt bustled into the foyer.

"Inferior quality, poorly stitched," Ruby Gabriel muttered, her lips pursed in her usual look of perpetual discontent as she tugged off her gloves. "You shall have to return them to the shop tomorrow and demand a refund, Sylvia. Did you mend the tear in my wrap?"

"Yes, Aunt Ruby," Sylvia replied, handing her the delicately embroidered shawl. As her aunt examined the repair critically, Sylvia held her breath. It had taken the better part of the morning to reweave the filmy threads and conceal the tear. Anyone else would have gifted the ruined garment to a servant, but Ruby Gabriel was known to pinch a penny until it screamed for mercy. Apparently she was satisfied as she wordlessly returned the shawl, presenting her back so that her niece might drape it upon her.

"Excuse me, Madame." Boniface, the butler, gestured toward a pair of footman, "They are ready to clear the sitting room. Where do you wish the old items situated before the replacements arrive this afternoon? As you are no doubt aware, the attics are full due to the late Sir Miles' efforts at renovation."

"And an unfashionable muddle my husband's brother made of that!" Sylvia's aunt muttered. "Not a stick in the latest mode, requiring me to do it all over again! The chamber off the garden will have to do for now."

"But Madame, there is barely sufficient room to-" Boniface began.

"Barely is enough," Mrs. Gabriel said dismissively as the clock in the hallway chimed the hour.

"Now where is Caroline?" Mrs. Gabriel asked, her florid face darkening with a frown. "We have bespoken time with the modiste. Sylvia, go and see what is keeping the girl," she demanded.

Sylvia gratefully grasped at the excuse to be gone before her aunt found reason for yet another petty scold or worse, to demand that her niece accompany them on their expedition. As Sylvia hastened up the stairs, she prayed that her cousin was ready to depart before Aunt Ruby's formidable temper crossed the border between annoyance and fury.

"Oh, thank heavens you've come," Caroline wailed as soon as Sylvia entered the bedchamber. "I cannot locate my celestial blue bonnet and my maid is nowhere to be found. I do not understand what happened to it, for I am sure it was at the corner of the wardrobe shelf."

"Daisy has the afternoon off, Caro. Now there is no time to dawdle, let us find the bonnet and hurry you away," Sylvia said, an unintentional sigh escaping her.

"Poor Sylvia! Mama is in one of her moods and she has been venting it upon you again, hasn't she?" Caroline asked. "Unlike the servants, you never have any time off."

"It is enough to overset anyone, bringing a daughter out in her first London Season," Sylvia said, peering into one of the myriad boxes that lined the wardrobe's extensive shelves.

"That is no excuse for the way that she treats you," Caroline observed, angrily. "Why it was bad enough when she did not replace Miles' governess and set you to tutoring him, but since we have come to Town, I am shamed to say that she has been treating you almost as if you are in her service and not an upper servant at that."

"It is good to be of some use, Caro," Sylvia said quietly. "Far better than being a burdensome charge upon the family. Besides, I enjoy teaching young Miles. He is quite clever for a boy of nine years and very eager to learn."

"Only because he adores you, Syl. I cannot count how many governesses and tutors our precocious Miles sent packing before he inherited the title and we came to live at Crown Beeches. Still, I cannot see how you bear mama's treatment. You should be coming with us to Bond Street, visiting the modistes and shops. It is outrageous that our uncle's confounded Will has brought you to such a pass," the young girl said, tossing a hat carelessly upon the floor. "And disgraceful that my mama is too purse-pinching to stand you the cost of a Season."

"To what purpose, Caro?" Sylvia asked, picking up the bonnet and smoothing out the pink silk ribbons, replacing it carefully in its box before taking up the search once more. "I have no portion, not a pennypiece left to my name. Indeed, it is fortunate that Uncle Miles set aside a fund for William's tuition at Oxford, else my brother would be in the bumble-broth with me."

"But you are so beautiful. Surely you could find a husband," Caroline protested. "Even in the plainest of gowns, you turn heads everywhere we go. You could be like one of the Gunning sisters. Why, they both wed dukes and 'tis said that the Duke of Hamilton was in such haste to wed Caroline Gunning that he used a brass hoop from the bed curtains as a wedding ring. Both the sisters were empty of purse."

"That was well over fifty years ago, Caro," Sylvia said, smiling at the girl's enthusiasm. "I would imagine the way of the world has changed. Men no longer marry a pretty face without it being attached to a healthy dowry." *As well I know*, she added silently. "But now, where could that dratted bonnet have gone? Which shelf did you say?"

"The middle," Caroline replied.

"Then I shall have it for you in a trice," Sylvia said, plunging into the wardrobe once more and emerging to wave the absent hat triumphantly. "My abigail was always missing things upon that middle shelf, for there is a hollow in the cabinet that allows things to slip to the back."

"This was your room?" Caroline asked, her face flushing in mortification. "Oh, Syl. I am so sorry."

Sylvia shook her head, annoyed that she had been so remiss in that slip of tongue. "I do not grudge it to you, widgeon, and do not worry yourself, for you will find it devilish chilly here if the family chooses to winter in town. Let us hope that, by then you will be married."

"With a husband to keep me warm?" Caroline giggled.

"Caro, do not let your mother hear you speaking so vulgarly," Sylvia warned. She tied the ribbons beneath the girl's chin. "Now fly, else your mama might take it upon herself to come seeking you. I can just imagine what she will think of the mess that this room is in."

"Daisy will take care of it when she returns," Caroline said with assurance, giving her cousin a light kiss on the cheek. "Bond Street, beware, for I am on my way."

Sylvia laughed as Caroline flounced out the door, but the smile faded as the sound of her aunt's shrill tones wafted up the hall and she caught the mention of her own name. As she quietly closed the door, Sylvia had little doubt she was being blamed somehow for Caroline's sluggishness.

From the window, Sylvia watched as the footman handed Caroline and her mother into the antiquated carriage. Once the lumbering vehicle turned the corner, Sylvia let the curtain drop and sat heavily upon the bed looking at the wallpaper of sea-green silk. Was it only six years ago that she and Uncle Miles had chosen the pattern?

It had been so exciting. They had come early to

Town, before Aunt Ruby was due to join them as chaperone for Sylvia's Season. For all her travels abroad with her parents, Sylvia had never truly seen London and Uncle had taken her to visit all of its attractions, the Tower, Astley's Royal Amphitheater, the opera. But then, he had become ill and they had returned to Crown Beeches.

For a moment, Sylvia allowed herself to wonder what would have happened if she had been allowed that spring in London. So many girlish dreams had been put aside since then, visions of a marvelous man who would see beyond her face and figure into her very soul, value her for what was within.

Perhaps it was fortunate never to have been given that opportunity, she thought, for foolish dreamers make the most stupid mistakes. It was frightening to think how close she had come to giving herself to an illusion, a man who, when he viewed her naked of her fortune, had turned away without a backward glance. She sniffed, brushing the tears of self-pity from her cheek.

"Syl?" A voice called. The door flew open after a perfunctory rap and a young boy came running into the room "Boniface said that you might be in here. Why are your eyes red, Syl?"

Sylvia sought refuge in a rebuke. "No gentleman comes racing into a room like that, Miles. You shall exit and enter the room properly. Immediately."

Miles thrust out his lower lip defiantly.

"Immediately, young man," she commanded. "For if I have to wait too long for your compliance, I doubt we shall have any time to play chess this morning."

The boy's belligerence disappeared and he ran out the door, closing it loudly behind him. Sylvia glanced at the mirror and dabbed a bit of Caro's powder over the tell-tale redness as Miles knocked loudly.

"Who is at the door, pray tell?" Sylvia asked.

"'Tis I, Sir Miles Gabriel," the boy declared, deepening his voice. "May I have your highly esteemed permission to enter the chamber, Miss Gabriel?"

"Enter, kind sir," Sylvia said, dropping a mocking curtsy as she opened the door. "Sir Miles."

Miles bowed stiffly and Sylvia was hard set to match his air of false dignity. Her lower lip began to tremble, but Miles' face remained perfectly placid. When he took her hand, serving it a smacking wet kiss, Sylvia burst into laughter.

"I win!" Miles declared with a chortle. "I outfaced you."

"Indeed you did, you wretched boy," Sylvia conceded. "However did you manage to keep your countenance during that performance?"

"By doing just as you said. I thought of something extremely serious- Mama in one of her fits of temper," the boy said, watching dismayed as his cousin's face fell. "I'm sorry, Syl. Was that why you were crying?"

Sylvia shook her head. "You are too curious by half, Miles. I have a mind to declare you a cheater, for my hand is wet as a mop. That kiss could not fail to discompose me. Now, come, let us repair to the schoolroom and get to our lessons."

Miles groaned. "I didn't cheat."

"No youngling, I should not have accused you wrongly, for I must say you are becoming almost as good at keeping a straight face as your namesake. Dear Uncle Miles always said that the ability to keep your opponent from reading your visage was the most important gambit of all."

"And I am good?"

"Very good," she said fondly. "Now, we do Geography today and as our subject is India, I shall tell you the story of what occurred between my Papa and a

Rajah who wagered a chess set made of gold and silver."

"Truly?" Miles asked.

"Truly," Sylvia answered, raising her hand in avowal. "The pieces were carved of lapis and ivory and I shall finish the tale before the lesson if you are upstairs ahead of me." With those words, she hitched up her skirts and raced up the wide staircase. The boy, with a whoop of dismay at her head start, scrambled swiftly to catch up.

CHAPTER 2

The Sikh moved with silent steps, his spotless white turban and jacket, a vivid contrast to the dark velvet of the curtains. With a mercuric motion, he pulled the draperies of the bedchamber open, letting a flood of sunshine into the darkened chamber.

The figure on the bed stirred, pulling the covers over his eyes with a woeful moan. "Damn you, Harjit. Have you no respect for the dying?"

"It is not imminent death that plagues you," Harjit Singh replied with the familiarity of an old servant. "But the effects of a surfeit of liquor upon a man who rarely indulges. If I disturb you, it is only upon your orders to wake you without fail before ten of the clock."

"There is no need to shout." David's muffled voice begged from under the covers. "Belay those orders, close those curtains and allow me to die in peace."

There was a choking sound, something of a cross between a cough and an arrested groan. Harjit arrived at the bedside with the washbasin just as David cast up his accounts.

"There now," he said as he placed the bowl aside to wipe the sweat from his employer's brow. "With your stomach purged, you shall be feeling much improved, I think. Here, drink this."

The cup of brew that had somehow materialized in the Sikh's hand smelled noxious and looked twice as vile as its odor, but David downed it at once, willing to try anything that would dull the dreadful hammering in his skull. He lay back on the pillow, utterly drained, feeling a flush of heat as Harjit's concoction spread through his body.

"I have had such strange dreams, Harjit," David murmured weakly as the pounding receded. "There was a curious wager..."

"Regarding chess and your marriage," Harjit supplied as he tossed the contents of the bowl out the window into the garden below. His lips curled slightly upwards. The gardener had been quite vocal in his remarks about "'eathen furriners.'"

David sat bolt upright, wincing at the pain in his head. "Then it was real."

"Indeed, I had the whole of it from Petrov Sahib's groom, who delivered you early this morning. Lord Highslip has already sent a note round that you are to meet him at Weston's establishment at precisely two this afternoon. I am to confer with his valet for instruction in the art of properly dressing a gentleman."

"Why in the world did George put me in that man-milliner's hand?" David groaned and closed his eyes.

"Prudence. Far better that someone else undertake to dress you than Brummel himself," Harjit explained, as he tidied the room. "It would not do at all if the Beau's own protégé were to fail in the realms of fashion."

"Do you expect me to fail?"

"I have long believed that there is a component of your *homai* that is inimical to fine clothing," Harjit replied, his brow raised thoughtfully. "Still, you have given your word to abide by the terms and you are not a man to deliberately fail."

David threw the servant a baleful look. "You are most pleased by this, I take it, Harjit Singh. Ever since you entered my employ you have been bullying me to enter the ranks of the fashionable."

Harjit bowed. "I only do your will, Rutherford Sahib. If you had no desire to dress in a manner suiting your rank, who am I, your humble servant, to thwart your wishes?"

"Humble, humbug and 'Sahib' my stockings," David said, putting a cautious foot on the lush carpet. The world whirled for a moment and settled into a somewhat normal perspective. "Get me my clothes, oh humble servant, but do not try to trick me up like some Bond Street lounger just yet. I have a few hours of comfort left before Highslip suits me, boots me and styles me and damme, I shall enjoy them. The brown jacket, Harjit!"

On his way to the wardrobe, the servant's step faltered. "Not the dung-coat of many pockets," he begged. "It is an offense to the eye, the execrable handiwork of a dog's son who masqueraded as a tailor. Do you so hate me, milord, that you thus humiliate my skills before the world?"

"I do not know why you malign that garment so, for it is wonderfully comfortable and I have as many places as I might require to carry my things. And I'll wear the buckskin breeches as well," David added, taking wicked pleasure in Harjit's woeful expression. "And do not call me 'milord,' Harjit."

"You are a most contrary individual," the Sikh said, surprised at the man's vehement tones. "Why do you not wish me to address you properly?"

"Because there will be no such nonsense between us, my friend," David said with a frown. "You have given your loyalty and friendship to David Rutherford, not some trumped up lordling. I cannot tell you how many people have been falling over themselves to fawn upon me in these months since I inherited my distant cousin's empty title and the huge pile of debts that accompanied it. Now that I am a new gilded lord, I have suddenly become worthy of their notice. No, Harjit, do not 'milord' me, for now that I have lent myself to this accursed wager and the sartorial predominance of that popinjay, Highslip, I may have need of someone to remind me who I truly am."

"As you wish," Harjit said, presenting the brown woolen coat as if it were made of some vile substance. "But it is a pity if you believe that this wretched discard from an offal heap reflects your true self," he mumbled under his breath.

Within a half of an hour, David was tooling his high perch phaeton though Mayfair. As he skillfully threaded his team through the dense traffic, he heartily wished that the Gabriels had remained ensconced in the hinterlands of Northumberland. Surely his duty and determination to pay proper condolences to the family would have been considered paramount to a trip to the tailor, and provided a splendid means of avoiding his first steps of the journey down Brummel's road to fashion.

Unfortunately, Lord Highslip had been quite certain that the Gabriel family had recently come to town for the Season. As David dismounted from his vehicle, he could see that the Earl was correct. An elaborate polished brass knocker in the shape of a rook was fixed on the door, indicating that the residents of the Berkeley Square address were at home.

David almost laughed aloud at the footman's indignant expression as he opened the door.

"Trade entry is ..." The rest of his statement was

forestalled by a proffered piece of pasteboard. To give the servant his due, he recovered rapidly, deciding to credit what he read above what he saw.

"Milord?" he asked, hesitantly, "how may I assist you?"

"I come regarding Sir Miles," David said, becoming somber as he stated the purpose of his call. Even though they had never met, he would miss Sir Miles dreadfully. At the back of his mind, David had always looked forward to the day that they would face each other across the board. The realization that it would never be so and the game was ended forever was almost beyond bearing.

"Sir Miles?" the footman said, brightening. "I shall bring up your card to him immediately, milord. Do you care to wait in the drawing room?"

As the look of confusion cleared from the servant's face, David's spirits soared. It seemed that Highslip's pronouncement regarding Sir Miles' death was merely a wretched error. *Should have known better than to trust the judgment of a besotted man*, David thought, as the footman hurriedly showed the guest into the empty library and bade him to be seated in a well-stuffed leather chair. David smiled, anticipating Highslip's dismay when he was confronted with his blunder. 'Twould confound the pompous idiot indeed to find that he had mistakenly declared his old neighbor dead and buried.

David chuckled, looking about him at what was obviously a man's room, its furnishings chosen more for comfort than a feminine eye for fashion. No Egyptian chaises or lacquered chinoiserie here; just walls of shelves, overflowing with leather-tooled bindings. He rose to run his fingers over the plethora of books on chess, opening a text in what appeared to be Arabic at random, only to shelve it when he spotted the latest edition of Allgaier's treatises on the game. But David rapidly found that he could not concentrate on the German chess master's ramblings and he returned the book to its place.

Restlessly, he roamed the room, trying to anticipate what he would say. Over the years, he had dreamt of this meeting, rehearsed it in his mind, but all the well-thought-out phrases now seemed silly. Sir Miles' letters had been an anchor in David's life, with their sound advice, warmth and wry wit, holding him steady amidst the turbulence. In the chaos of the past decade, that wisdom had become a source of order in a world where the rules were few. His sole certainties were the sun rising and the next move in the game.

Near the window was a simple wooden chessboard and David noted with satisfaction that the configuration exactly reflected the inevitable denouement of last night's move, the king lying on its side in abject surrender. Suddenly, he felt calm. How foolish to act as if Sir Miles were some stranger when there was perhaps, no one on this earth who knew him half so well. He stared into the fireplace, watching the tongues of flame lick the coals, as he remembered the man's letters, every single one of them read and re-read almost to the point of perfect memory. Certainly, there was no need to be nervous.

"Milord?"

David whirled at the sound of that soft voice to confront a vision. At first, he wondered if his drunken dreams were still plaguing him, for no real woman could be so exquisitely beautiful. A plaited crown of blond hair framed a face of the kind that Botticelli had adored. Eyes the color of a calm green ocean regarded him from beneath a dark lashed fringe. Porcelain cheeks began to glow a delightful red, as ripe-cherry lips began to thin into a frown. David tried to recall himself, but could not help letting his gaze linger on the delightful contours of her lush figure. Even the concealing folds of her shapeless black merino gown could not entirely mask a woman who might serve as a model for temptation personified.

Sylvia took a deep breath, trying to control her growing anger and decided to return the stranger's rude gaze measure for measure. It had been a mistake to come down in answer to the peculiar summons, she could see that now. Far better to have sent the footman to seek out Boniface than to subject herself to providing a spectacle for this slack-jawed pretender! Lord Donhill, indeed! Even as a novice to the fashionable world, Sylvia could see that the garments on the man's tall, muscular frame looked as if they had been pieced together by a tailor with more cheek than skill.

Since her uncle's death had unexpectedly demoted her from the respected daughter of the house to a poor relation dogsbody, Sylvia had learned that there were those who might consider her fair game for dalliance. She waited for the visitor's thunderstruck expression to transform into the leering lust she had come to expect from the men who equated poverty with vulnerability, but his shabby lordship surprised her.

"I must apologize, Miss . . ." he said, his expression shifting to an appealing smile.

"Gabriel, milord," Sylvia said, schooling her countenance to blandness, she resisted the desire to tell him to tuck his apologies into the pocket of his hideous coat and leave. Caution and habit caused her to evaluate the situation logically.

While his dress was less than fashionable it was definitely clean and well-kept. Among the top tiers of the Ton, most masculine foibles were tolerated if not celebrated. There was, therefore, the distinct chance that this was one of those instances where eccentricity rather than poverty was at play. In either event, if the man truly did have a title, Aunt Ruby would be most furious at missing this unlikely lord's call, much more so if she found that her niece had turned him away.

It would be a sin beyond forgiveness if Sylvia were to offend any man who might be viewed as a likely suitor for Caroline, especially a noble one. Still, if Sylvia's cousin was his lordship's object, why had the footman insisted that the visitor had come to call on a mere boy of nine?

"Miss Gabriel," David said, feeling more than a little ashamed at putting Sir Miles' kinswoman to the blush. "I hope that you will forgive me for my uncommon rudeness, but to be blunt; I was startled. I assume that you are aware of your uncommon looks. It is somewhat unsettling to be confronted with a living image of a seraph this early in the morning, particularly when one has spent a somewhat iniquitous night."

Sylvia found herself relaxing somewhat at his jocular tone and his disarming honesty. She felt an absurd longing to straighten his cravat and sweep that thatch of coal black hair from his eyes until, in a gesture of chagrin, he brushed it aside himself. A shaft of sun streaming through the windows touched him as he removed his spectacles, polishing them absently on that woeful neckcloth of his. Those green-flecked brown eyes put Sylvia in mind of rich earth at tilling time. A peculiar sparkle seemed to light his face, making him seem almost like a little boy who has been caught at some mischief. Despite his unexpected charm, Sylvia reminded herself that it might prove to be a serious error to let down her facade.

"Indeed," Sylvia replied. "I have no sword, milord, so I fail to see how you could mistake me for an avenging angel."

David looked up in surprise. *Comeliness and insinuations of wit?*

He returned his glasses to the bridge of his nose. It was only years of reading the countenances of those who challenged him across the chessboard that allowed him to detect a hint of quickly concealed tempest in those sea-green eyes. Other than that fleeting telltale, her exquisite face was fatuously blank, seemingly devoid of expression.

Had she sized him up and dismissed him because of his casual attire? It would not be the first time that he had been cut because of his sartorial heedlessness, but nonetheless, he felt a strange stir of disappointment. A pity that Miss Gabriel seemed to lack the humor and spirit that would have animated those chiseled features. As it was, she seemed no more than a pretty, but dull piece of living statuary.

"I have come to see Sir Miles," David said, his voice formal once more.

"He shall be down shortly," the stone angel said, in a toneless voice.

David cast about for some topic to fill the growing silence. Perhaps the weather? The latest *on-dit*? But then he did not know the latest *on-dit*, so it would have to be the weather. Surely that would not be too much for a woman of even limited intellect. In David's narrow experience it was almost a certitude that women endowed with superior beauty were shortchanged in the attribute of intelligence. Once beyond the set topics of climate and gossip they inevitably foundered and sank in the seas of more intellectual conversation. He was about to comment on the delights of the sun after so much rain when relief arrived and the door was thrown open. However, instead of the elderly Sir Miles, a young boy of about nine burst into the room.

"I'm done with my lesson, Syl. Now may I meet Lord Whatsisname?"

"Lord Donhill, Miles," she reproved, turning to their guest. "May I present Sir Miles Gabriel."

The boy made his leg. David returned the greeting perfunctorily before looking abruptly to the window, hoping to conceal his shock and disappointment as the web he had woven of ephemeral hope and fancy was torn to shreds. It was clear now that Highslip had been correct. The old baronet was dead. A few moments passed before David dared to turn his face again. Fortunately, the years of chess play had given him infinite practice in commanding his features. However, he could not quite control the betraying tones of roughness in his voice.

"I am sorry to disturb your studies, lad," he said extending his hand. "I was expecting your uncle, truth be told."

"Uncle Miles died over a year ago," the boy said sympathetically. "Surely everyone knows that."

Although his features were now impassive, Sylvia had seen Lord Donhill's face before he looked away; the pain in his eyes had mirrored the ache in her own heart. Despite Uncle Miles' multitude of eccentricities, Sylvia had loved her uncle dearly and it was clear to see that Lord Donhill too, must have held the late Sir Miles in great esteem. Her curiosity roused, Sylvia was about to question Lord Donhill but to her surprise, he bent down before the boy, squatting until the two were eye to eye.

Sylvia smiled at the sight of that awkwardly bent lanky frame, her reserve thawing entirely. It was a rare adult that realized how intimidating a grown man's height could be to a child. Lucky indeed, that Lord Donhill did not favor fashion, for a pair of skin-fitting breeches could not have stood the stress of the powerful thighs that were limned by the tautened fabric.

"I lived very far away," David said. "In India. Your uncle and I were good friends, but we had never met face to face."

"I never heard of no Lord Donhill." Miles asked cocking his head in an inquiring pose. "How can you be friends if you never met?

By post, Sylvia thought, an uneasy cold feeling spreading through the pit of her stomach as she digested his words. She felt much as if she had swallowed one of Gunther's famous ice confections whole, her mind racing giddily as she considered the unlikely possibility that the consequences of her deceit were coming to roost on her doorstep. However, the more she tried to convince herself that her fears were foolish, that David Rutherford had often declared that he would never leave India, the more certain Sylvia became that her worst nightmares were about to come true.

"I have only recently become Lord Donhill, just as you are a relatively new-made Sir Miles. My name is David Rutherford," he said, taking off his glasses and polishing them in a forlorn gesture before slipping them absently into a pocket.

The pronouncement of his name cut the last thread of Sylvia's clinging hope and she felt herself spinning down into the abyss of her own making. Somehow she had always pictured her uncle's correspondent as an older gentleman, close to Uncle Miles in age. Still, would that have made her actions any less improper?

Sylvia doubted that Aunt Ruby would see it in that light, much less forgive her scapegrace niece were she to hear the tale in its entirety. Deliberately, Sylvia cleared the confusion from her mind, concentrating on the problem arrayed before her. Knowing David

Rutherford, the truth would undoubtedly be the best solution.

"Famous! I've heard all about you," the boy exclaimed. "You play chess nearly as well as cousin..."

"Miles," Sylvia interrupted quickly. "Would you ask Boniface to see to some refreshments for our guest?"

"Why not just ring?" Miles asked, but he was forestalled by Sylvia's quelling look. "I'll go get him," he mumbled. "Can't just say you don't want me to listen, can you?"

Once more, David found himself alone with the stone angel.

"I am sorry, milord. Had I known your identity, I would have spared you this," she said. "However, the footman is a new one and he quite insisted that you wished to speak to my young cousin."

There was a curious tone to her voice, one that he almost would have styled warmth. Curious, he patted his pockets in search of his spectacles.

"Sir Miles spoke quite fondly of you, milord," Sylvia said choosing her words carefully. "Your letters and the game were a joy to him, particularly in the last months of his illness. Even when he could no longer play at his best, he bade the game continue."

The brass knocker rapped impatiently and a babble of voices echoed in the entryway. Surely Aunt Ruby and Caroline had not returned so soon! Sylvia felt a growing tide of panic at the unmistakable high pitched nasal whine of her aunt's orders to the staff.

Sylvia rapidly considered her options. If she were to tell him the whole now, without any preamble, there would certainly be questions, questions that would take far too long to answer. Discovery would be inevitable, since Aunt Ruby would be upon them in a matter of moments. There was only one possible move.

"I know it was most improper, milord," Sylvia said

in a rush. "My younger brother William could not bear to leave the game unfinished and it was he who continued the play in the months of Uncle's illness until his passing. In a way, playing on afterward was his tribute to a man who was most dear to the both of us."

"I would certainly have acceded to continue the game," David said, feeling a rush of annoyance.

Sylvia hung her head guiltily. In truth, she had feared that he would put an end to the play upon hearing the news. "Your last letters had mentioned some business difficulties," she said weakly, praying that William would forgive her for the lie that she was putting in his dish. "I believe my brother meant to spare you the additional burden until you were on your feet once more. However, I soon realized that it was wrong to keep the news from you. I, myself, sent a letter informing you of Uncle Miles' death."

"Unfortunately, I never received your letter. I suppose that, like my other correspondence, it will catch up with me in time. After all, I only received your brother's final move last evening. And if the final moves were his, I must commend him upon his *tour de force*. I declare, I did not see my doom upon me till almost the very end," David declared. "Is he at home?"

"No, milord," Sylvia said. "He is down at Oxford."

"He plays splendidly," David reiterated. "Nonetheless, Miss Gabriel, I do not enjoy being made to look a fool. The truth would certainly have spared me some mockery, although I cannot say it is any less humbling to lose to a callow youth than to a man who has passed from this earth altogether. I knew that Sir Miles had been ill, of course, but I am sorry to say that I paid it too scant attention."

His wistful tones caused Sylvia agonies of guilt. "Milord, do not blame yourself. My uncle's health was never of the best. Until his last months, he deliberately minimized the severity of his circumstances."

The sound of footsteps treading heavily up the stairs reminded her of her danger. Aunt Ruby would be angry, so very angry if she heard the whole of her niece's deceit. "I know that it was wrong to deceive you, milord, but I beg you, do not hold it against my brother and do not tell my Aunt Ruby, I pray you. She and William do not get on well and I fear if she hears of this she will cause him no end of trouble. Please, milord."

"He did me no real harm. If you feel so strongly, I shall say nothing," David agreed, moved by the sincerity of her plea. *So, the stone angel does have a heart after all*, he thought as he fumbled for his glasses once more to better view the effect of emotion on that marble face.

Just as he found the proper pocket, the door flew open. When he saw the sight framed by the doorway, he wished that he had left the lenses off.

"Milord! We did not expect callers when we are so soon come to town," Ruby Gabriel said coyly.

David would not have believed that a matron of her years could simper so, but simper she did, pulling a young chit in tow. Like a ship of the line, floating amidst an ocean of unbecoming ruffles and furbelows, the woman plunged forward into the sea of introductions and neatly maneuvered her daughter to the side of the prize. To her credit, the girl seemed rather reluctant to be put forward, but her mother was a force too strong to resist.

"My daughter, Caroline Gabriel, milord," Mrs. Gabriel declared.

As she advanced, David edged back slowly until his knees met the edge of a chair. Masterfully cornered, David bowed and planned his defensive position.

"Delighted, Miss Gabriel," he said.

MISS GABRIEL'S GAMBIT

"Would you take some refreshment, milord?" Mrs. Gabriel said in tones more commanding than inquisitive.

David knew that if he seated himself, he was lost. A change of tactic was definitely in order, a strategic retreat. "I am sorry, Mrs. Gabriel..." but he was forestalled in mid-sentence by a look from Miss Sylvia Gabriel, the green eyes eloquent, pleading.

"Niece, why have you not yet seen to our guest?" the termagant aunt demanded, directing the girl an annoyed look that could not be misinterpreted. If he departed suddenly, the stone angel was in the broth, there was no mistaking.

David felt his irritation melt into pity. It would cost him little to remain for a brief visit and do the pretty. If that would stay the shrew's anger then he would do it, he resolved.

"Miss Gabriel has been a most gracious hostess," David interjected. "I believe your staff is preparing even now."

"Make certain that they don't dawdle," Mrs. Gabriel directed

Sylvia Gabriel left the room, casting a grateful glance behind her.

"I do hope that you will forgive my foolish niece for presenting my son," Mrs. Gabriel said with a frown. "The simpleton girl should have realized that you would not be seeking an interview with a nine-year-old boy."

"Actually, it was your footman who assumed it was the child I wished to see," David said stiffly, somewhat confused by the strength of his irritated reaction to the woman's disparaging tones. "It was a natural mistake on your servant's part and I cannot claim to be sorry of the error. We had an opportunity to speak of the late Sir Miles, who was a dear friend."

Mrs. Gabriel digested this information with a grimace. So, it was not Caroline that he had come to call upon. "Still, Sylvia should not have put herself forward so, but then, what can one expect from a girl who was raised almost entirely by a bachelor uncle? The child has not the vaguest idea how to go on in society."

"Indeed," David said. "Then your task is formidable, Madame, for I understand that introducing a young lady to polite society is a vast undertaking. To care for both your daughter and your niece will be a double effort."

Mrs. Gabriel's florid face flushed even more and David noted absently that her stocky neck was nearly as red as a rooster's comb. Just then, further conversation was forestalled as the butler entered with cakes and ratafia. Sylvia, however, did not reappear and David found himself wondering about the girl's place in the household scheme. Although he usually did not concern himself with matters of dress, it was clear by contrast that her clothing was far inferior to the garments of her cousin and aunt. He would wager that they each wore a year of Harjit's wages on their backs. Sylvia had been garbed simply.

Finally, the butler withdrew.

"My niece's circumstances..." Mrs. Gabriel began.

"What Mama is trying to say is that Sylvia is not to come out with me," Miss Caroline declared, finding her voice at last. "And I think..."

But David was not destined to hear what the girl's thoughts were upon the matter. Her mother finished the sentence, giving her daughter a glowering glance of warning.

"It is a pity, milord, that poor Sylvia's prospects are at such a pass. Sir Miles was the oldest of his family and a confirmed bachelor. My dear departed husband was next in line, so my son Miles inherited the title. Sylvia is the daughter of his youngest brother, John."

"John Gabriel?" David queried.

"You have heard of him?" Mrs. Gabriel asked, surprised.

David nodded. "Truly, I wonder that I did not make the connection long ago. John Gabriel was one of the foremost chess players of the previous century. Why, 'Gabriel's Gambit' is one of the premier attacks the game has ever known. He was the brother of the late Sir Miles, then?"

"Yes, although they were separated in age by nearly a score of years, John was as chess mad as his oldest brother. I can only thank my stars that my dear Horace was spared the malady," Mrs. Gabriel declared vehemently. "For I can tell you that chess has caused a great deal of misery in this family. That ne'er-do-well John dragged his family all over Creation in search of the perfect game and of course, Miles, my other brother-by-marriage, was always staring at the board. 'Tis no wonder that Sylvia has not the foggiest idea of how to get on in the world. Do you know that he actually requested that no proper period of mourning be observed? As if we would be so lost to propriety to bring Caroline out only a few months after his death!"

The chair creaked as she leaned forward to emphasize her point . "Bad enough that Miles had no notion of suitably educating the girl, but to so utterly ruin her future! I vow, he must have run quite mad in his old age, with his crazy Will full of chess mutterings."

Despite his annoyance at Mrs. Gabriel's malicious tongue, David found himself intrigued. "Chess mutterings?"

"Sylvia and her brother had a fortune, you see, of which our uncle was sole guardian," Caroline broke in. "Precious objects and things that their papa had collected in his travels as well as large sums of money, but upon Uncle's death, not so much as a *sou* was found."

"Precious objects? Fiddle! Chessboards and trinket trash more like! If only John had been prudent enough to leave his children in my care!" Mrs. Gabriel declared with a sniff. "However, I suspect that poor Miles had lost it all upon the Exchange and that idiotish Will was only a way of trying to excuse himself. To think that Sylvia is destined to remain forever on the shelf."

"Sylvia believes that the treasure is all hidden away somewhere and that the chess puzzle that Uncle set in his Will contains the key," Caroline added.

"Nonsense," Mrs. Gabriel said forbiddingly, deterring her daughter by taking firm hold of the course of the conversation with a quelling stare. "Sylvia is hoping that wishes will turn to horses; for, of course, no stone has been left unturned in search of the money or this so-called treasure! But I am sure that Lord Donhill has heard enough of your poor cousin's problems. Caroline, why do you not tell Lord Donhill of our plans to refurbish the house? Caroline has chosen the most delightful furnishings, a la chinoiserie, for this room, milord. I vow, I cannot match her taste."

"I find that difficult to believe, Madame," David said, repressing a shudder. Once the subject of modish decor was exhausted, the topic was forcefully turned to the doings of various members of the Ton. Luckily, as the woman prattled on endlessly about people that she obviously did not know, there was no need for David to do little more than nod in what he hoped were appropriate places. He pondered the mystery of the chess puzzle until he was roused by the mention of Brummel and his fashionable eccentricities. A surreptitious glance at the china clock upon the table showed that the hands were at half past one and he sent a grateful thought heavenward. Downing the last of his ratafia in a gulp, David rose and made his farewells, suddenly pleased that he was promised to Highslip, Brummel and the tailor at two.

...

"'Tis most unfair!" Miles exclaimed, kicking at the leg of a schoolroom stool. "'Twas me Lord Donhill came to call on and there was cakes!"

"I know, Miles," Sylvia said soothingly, as she pulled a book from the shelf. "But we have both been sent upstairs and there is little we can do about it. Now, let us get back to our geography."

"No," Miles declared with a pout, stamping his foot. "I won't."

Sylvia sighed. There was no dealing with the boy in this moody state and, in truth, she could not blame him. She understood his feelings well enough. She, too, had been summarily dismissed.

There had been no need for Aunt Ruby to articulate the warning in her eyes. Sylvia was not to return to the drawing room. She had little doubt that despite her obedience to her aunt's unspoken wishes, the woman would ring a peal over Sylvia's head. Still, it could be far worse, Sylvia thought, replacing the book of maps upon the shelf and going to the door of her chamber.

The governess' room was far more luxurious than most quarters of its kind. A thick carpet covered the floor and Sylvia had furnished her nook with the delicate Chippendale that her aunt had cast off in favor of more stylish accoutrements. The large attic windows commanded an incomparable view of Berkeley Square. The corner window overlooked the garden.

Nonetheless, when Sylvia had found that she was to share the nursery with Miles, it had been a bitter blow. At least, in her uncle's Northumberland home, she had been able to hold on to some shred of pretense. There the servants still deferred to her as mistress, a matter of no small irritation to her aunt. In the shelter of Crown Beeches, she could still believe that the money would be found and her position restored. According to her late father's Will, since she was past her majority, she would be completely free of any guardian's control.

Now that they were in London, however, only the sympathy of Boniface, her uncle's old butler, and her cousin Caroline, kept her from the general lot of governesses. Neither fish nor fowl nor good red herring, those poor women usually wandered the netherworld between upstairs and below, finding respect in neither.

No, Sylvia corrected, there was one other major item that separated her from the realm of service. Aunt Ruby paid her servants, however poorly. As an impoverished relation, Sylvia received nothing but cold charity.

Even now, Sylvia speculated, Aunt Ruby was pouring the entire sad tale into Lord Donhill's sympathetic ears. "Poor Sylvia, cheated by her wicked uncle, cast upon our mercy . . . " What utter rubbish! The shilling-squeezing woman had not spent so much as a tuppence on either Sylvia or her brother since it was determined that their money had disappeared.

Shutting the door behind her, Sylvia threw herself upon her bed, blinking back angry tears. Bad enough to be made into an object of pity, but Aunt Ruby had made her opinion of Uncle Miles' clear and had no compunction of casting his reputation to the winds, But poisoning David Rutherford against him? It was an affront not to be borne.

She turned onto her back, staring up at the cracks in the ceiling. There was no help for it. It would be foolish beyond permission to storm downstairs to throw Aunt Ruby's barley-water charity into her face. Besides,

Sylvia tried to convince herself, it was undoubtedly better this way. If Aunt Ruby behaved with her usual lack of grace, Lord Donhill would probably take his leave forever. There would be no further questions about the culmination of the correspondence chess game.

Strange, how that thought left her feeling utterly bereft.

You should be relieved, she berated herself. *The deception is over.* There would be no more stealthy searches through the mail, hoping to intercept David's letter before it came to Aunt Ruby's hands. Yet, all she could do was mourn, as this last link to a happier past was severed. The game was ended and there would be no more.

When Uncle had become too ill to write, Sylvia had known that she should have informed his opponent. However, over the years, she had come to know and respect David Rutherford. Indeed, she began to think of her uncle's correspondent on a first name basis. Sylvia had often read David's letters aloud to Sir Miles and they had laughed together over David's wry observations about life in the army and later, the difficulties of making a fresh start in a foreign land. His vivid descriptions of the East had reminded Sylvia of those wonderful years that she and William had spent in India with Mama and Papa.

Then, at the end of each letter, there was always the next move. When they were in London, Uncle Miles would stand before the gold and silver board, lifting the designated lapis piece as if he were some high priest performing a sacred rite. Afterward, they would ponder the possibilities together, racing to the shelves to consult the chess texts, arguing strategy, history and their opponent's intent until the wee hours of the morning. It would take days of debate, until at last, they had chosen their own next move together.

Ten years. It was hard to believe that so much time had passed. She had been a mere girl in plaits when the game had begun, but Uncle had made her a part of it from the start.

Her father had recognized her native talent, nurturing it until he and Mama were killed in a carriage accident. Uncle Miles had recognized the comfort his young niece found in the love of the game that he had shared with his brother. Her uncle had helped her to hone her skill until she eventually had surpassed him. Indeed, in his last days, he had joked that David was playing a far wilier opponent than he realized, for no male could ever hope to follow the twists of a female mind.

And now, the precious board with its inlaid squares was gone, disappeared along with all the other treasures into some secret cache. Sylvia could not bring herself to believe that her uncle had misspent her fortune. She hoped that, despite Aunt Ruby's venom, David would come to the same conclusion, even though the two men had never had the opportunity to meet.

Uncle Miles had come to view his chess correspondent in the light of a close friend. Perhaps that was why Sylvia had always assumed that David was a much older man. As it was, Sylvia judged that David looked to be about thirty, though beyond those spectacles, his eyes had seemed older with wisdom and kindness.

"Syl?" A questioning whisper came from beyond the door. "May I come in?"

Sylvia rose and smoothed her skirts. "You may, Miles," she called.

The boy entered, hanging his head. "I'm sorry, Syl. 'Tain't your fault, I know."

"No need to worry, Miles," Sylvia said. "The truth is, we are both a bit blue-devilled."

"Truly, it must be worse for you. Fancy meeting the 'India player' after all this time," Miles said, glad at being so easily let off. "Did he find a way out of your trap?"

"No," Sylvia said, smiling with triumph. "He called it a *'tour de force.'*"

"Must have shocked him to the marrow, being trounced by a girl," Miles said. "Wish I could've seen his face."

"He does not know, Miles," Sylvia said, her forehead furrowing as she was assailed by her conscience once again. In the months after her uncle's death, David's letters had been her lifeline. She had read them again and again. The very thought that this sole source of comfort might cease had driven her to deceit. Since she had usually acted as her uncle's secretary, the handwriting in the letters had undergone no change. Sir Miles' style of address was simple to mimic. Even during her uncle's illness, the replies to David's letters had been as much Sylvia's own as the responses to his chess moves.

Now, as she looked at the boy's puzzled face Sylvia realized that there was little choice. She had told young Miles about the correspondence game because of their shared passion for chess, never dreaming that the "India player," as Miles called him, would ever set foot in London. Now, the child would have to become a party to the deceit. "I told him that William took over the play," Sylvia said.

"William?" Miles scoffed. "Your brother don't know a pawn from a pennypiece. Might as well've told the India player I was the one who brought the game to the end."

"You are quite skilled, Miles," Sylvia said. "But by no

means are you on level with Lord Donhill. He might have wished to put you to the test and then, we surely would have been caught out. William is at Oxford and unlikely to appear and put me to the lie."

"Don't see why you didn't tell him the truth. Now that would have set the cat amongst the pigeons," Miles said, his eyes shining. "'Specially with that wager of his!"

"Wager?" Sylvia asked.

"Jack the footman got it from Lord Donhill's tiger," the boy informed her eagerly. "I heard when I went seeking Boniface, accidental of course. Know you don't hold with gossiping, but this is famous. Seems last night his lordship got utterly cup-shot."

"Miles," Sylvia warned. "I do not wish to hear you using vulgar cant language. And if you are about to tell one of those dreadful stories that you glean from the servants, I do not believe that I wish to hear the rest of this. Now let us return to our lessons." Even though she was bursting with curiosity, she turned and walked back to the schoolroom.

"Syl," Miles groaned, and followed her, tugging at her arm. "'Tis awfully important. In fact, you could even become Lady Donhill."

"Are you ill, youngling?" Sylvia smiled at his earnest face. "Ought I to be concerned? Because you are sounding quite daft."

"Lord Donhill wagered that he would only marry the woman who could beat him at chess," Miles proclaimed. "And you've *already* trounced him once. There's a purse of a thousand pounds besides. Oh, Syl, you have only to tell him and he'll be forced to honor his wager."

"That is ridiculous, Miles. Who would make so foolish a bet?" Sylvia asked, even though she knew it entirely possible. Her own father had taken outrageous chances, hazarding fortunes on the outcome of a game that he rarely lost. "Besides, even in the unlikely event that the gossip is true, the game was not entirely mine. I was only fourteen years of age when David Rutherford's correspondence with Uncle Miles began ten years ago."

"Aren't you the one always telling me *'it's the endgame that counts?'* You beat him once. *That was you!*" the boy insisted. "And you could trounce him again in an instant. He's rich as the Golden Ball and a lord besides. Take him up on his challenge!"

"Miles," she said, taking the boy by the shoulders. "Even if Lord Donhill made so foolish a wager and I were so forward as to win his challenge, it would be unfair to press him to keep a vow made in a moment of drunkenness. He was Uncle's friend and I consider him mine as well."

"But you would be the best kind of wife," Miles protested. "You're a bang up to the mark chess player and you don't even scream at snakes."

"High praise, indeed," Sylvia said with a laugh, "But he would not love me and love is the most important part of a marriage."

"Love," Miles sneered, wrinkling his nose in disgust. "You sound just like Caroline and those novels she reads. 'Love this, love that, love, love, love!' Sighing like a mooncalf all the time."

"Someday, Miles, you will understand."

"I hope not," Miles declared vehemently. "A wager's a wager. What if some other female steals a march on you? I'd hazard it in a tick-tock!"

"I rather doubt it," Sylvia chuckled. "There are not many chess players of either sex who could match David Rutherford," she said. "Besides, what would your Mama say if I should play him and lose? You know how she hates chess and thinks it no fit game for ladies. If she did not think me the rankest of amateurs I doubt that she would even tolerate a board in the house. Challenging a man for a wager, I venture, would put me entirely beyond the pale."

"But you could *win* it, Syl," the boy declared once more, and would have persisted were he not distracted by a sound from below. Sylvia was relieved as he ran to the window.

"Look, Syl," he called, beckoning her to the glass. "Look at those matched greys... ain't they fine?"

Sylvia watched as David leapt lightly into his vehicle. The sun glinted on his silver handled whip as he chanced to look up. Saluting the waving boy with a flourish, David took up the reins. Sylvia backed away, flushing in shame that he might have seen her gawping like some country greenling.

"Ain't nothing behindhand about those horses," Miles said, waving enthusiastically until the carriage was out of sight. "If it were me, I'd challenge him in a minute."

Sylvia sighed. "No, Miles...and I hope that you will not betray me. If your Mama should find out what I have been about, I have no doubt that she would cast me out on the street."

"Not me! You know I'd never cry rope!" Miles said, stoutly, offended at the very suggestion. "Still..."

"Sylvia!" There was no mistaking that shrill voice and with a sympathetic look, Miles scampered to a seat, taking up a book just as the door swung open to admit his mother, puffing with the exertion. It said much for the level of her annoyance that she had ventured the climb up the nursery stairs.

Sylvia closed her eyes for a moment, bracing herself for the tirade that was sure to come and for some reason, David Rutherford's face came to mind. As she listened with feigned meekness, Miles' words echoed in her head. "I'd hazard him in a minute."

Sylvia had always thought those Minerva Press heroines, who timidly submitted to fate with stoic resolution, were fools. It was humbling to realize that she was no less of a ninny, at heart. In all likelihood, she could best David Rutherford. But no matter what senseless wager he had made, Sylvia hoped that she would never serve a friend so poorly. Still, as Aunt Ruby's whine hummed in her ears, such fine feelings were but cold comfort.

CHAPTER 3

A puff of clouds drifted in the sky above Green Park, momentarily obscuring the weak spring sunshine. Sylvia held the reins of her horse loosely as it ambled along.

"I do not know how you bear Mama these days," Caroline said, her lowered voice barely audible above the slow clip of the horses' hooves. She glanced behind to satisfy herself that the groom and her brother were beyond hearing. "She behaves as if it is your fault that the house is almost empty of callers. Mama keeps harkening back to the time before you were about to make your curtsy to the Ton."

"Poor Uncle Miles had no notion of how to respond to the flood of invitations and the visits," Sylvia recalled. "He wrote begging your Mama to come rescue him."

"Lady Harwell called the other day," Caroline said with a sigh. "When she found out that the Miss Gabriel of the house was not you, she could not leave fast enough."

"Lady Harwell was a particular friend of my mama's," Sylvia said apologetically. "If my Season had gone on as planned, years ago, she had expected to assist your mother with my introduction to society. You must not fault yourself, Caro. I was an heiress then and most of those callers were lured by the siren call of my shekels, hoping to steal an early march in their campaigns to secure my fortune."

"Even so, it is unbearably sad that Uncle Miles became ill and you were forced to return to Northumberland before your Season," Caroline declared, sympathetically. Seeing her cousin's distress, she turned the subject. "Lord Donhill particularly asked after you yesterday."

Sylvia's fingers tightened upon the tack, her knuckles whitening, but her voice remained controlled. "Lord Donhill came to call?" she asked, feigning a casual air.

"Oh yes," Caroline said absently, looking up at the sky. "Dear me, look at those grey clouds above the trees. Lord Donhill called while you were out matching that lace for Mama. Do you think it will rain?"

"The lace that she sent me to return in the end," Sylvia said in clipped tones. Obviously, Aunt Ruby had expected that David Rutherford would visit and deliberately sent her niece on a useless errand.

"He seemed somewhat disappointed to miss you," Caroline said, tearing her attention from the sky momentarily. "And you would not believe the change, Syl. Lord Donhill is now all the go, a veritable pattern card of fashion. Although, I must say that he was not nearly so fine as his friend, Mr. Petrov. You should have seen him. I tell you, Sylvia, he is the most handsome man I have ever seen in my life, so dashing and so charming. His manners are most delightful."

"Yes," Sylvia said, stifling a sigh. "Lord Donhill would do well for the dressing."

"Lord Donhill?" Caroline drew her horse to a stop, looking confusedly at her cousin. "Why, it is Mr. Petrov of whom I speak. Lord Donhill is far too old; he must be well past thirty," she declared. "For all Mama's prosings about his wealth and title, I would not marry him, even if he had not made that strange wager."

Sylvia laughed at her seventeen-year-old cousin's vehemence. "A veritable Methuselah," she declared, feeling strangely relieved although she could not say why. "So, Lord Donhill has become a Bond Street beau."

"Not quite, his cravat was rumpled and askew," Caroline said, urging her mount forward once again. "It is all part of that infamous wager of his. Mama was quite distressed when she heard of it."

"So, it is true," Sylvia said. "His wife will have to win him in a chess match."

Caroline nodded. "And a purse of a thousand pounds if she should be so foolish as to forgo him. According to the latest *on dit*, half the females in London are engaging chess masters although Mr. Petrov says that any woman who would hope to best him is befuddled in the brainbox. In fact, Ivan declares that Uncle Miles was the only man he knew who ever beat him."

"So, you call him 'Ivan,' do you, Caro?" Sylvia said, trying to turn the subject from its hazardous course.

But Sylvia's effort only caused her cousin to color slightly, and ramble on. "You get along well enough on the board with Miles, but I am so glad that you declared yourself an indifferent chess player, else I believe Mama would have you tutoring me," Caro continued.

"Lord Donhill is no stripling and a far more formidable opponent than your brother," Sylvia said quickly, his image coming sharply to mind. Somehow, his deplorable mode of dress had made him no less handsome. She wondered sadly if her aunt would ever allow them to meet again. "It is quite unlikely that any come-lately to the game could best him."

"I suppose," Caroline said, with a toss of her head. "Still, I am glad he is ineligible as a suitor because of his wager. I much prefer Mr. Petrov. Mama merely tolerates both him and Lord Donhill both because any caller is better than no callers at all."

A stiff breeze began to blow through the branches of the trees causing Caroline to clamp her hat firmly to her head. "It will rain, I just know it and my new *chapeau a la' militaire* will be utterly ruined. Perhaps if we turn back now?" she wailed, reining in her mount once more.

Miles rode up just in time to hear his sister's declaration. "Aw, g'wan," he moaned. "You made of sugar, Caro? A little rain never hurt anyone."

Sylvia controlled her frisking animal with a light touch as she added her voice to Miles'. "I doubt that it will rain anytime soon, Caro. See, the sun is coming out once more."

"I am positive that it will rain," Caroline said, with a pout. "And the ostrich feathers in my shako will be drenched. We shall have to go home immediately."

Sylvia took a deep breath and nodded her head at the groom. "I suppose . . ." she began.

"Go home, yourself!" Miles yelled, cutting Sylvia off. "You selfish beast. Invite yourself along for our ride, riding slow as treacle to show off your new habit, but that ain't enough for you, oh no, Miss Caroline Care-for-no-one! Angry that there ain't anybody about so's you can preen yourself, conceited looby!"

Sylvia knew that she ought to rebuke the boy for his rudeness, but from Caro's flush, she knew that Miles had struck upon the truth. She had wondered at her cousin's sudden eagerness for exercise.

"A fine one you are to talk, Master Rudesby," Caroline retorted. "You would rather see a small fortune ruined than forgo your ride."

"Ain't just my ride," Miles said. "'Tis Sylvia's too and if it were up to Mama, she would never go anywhere but on your foolish frippery errands. You know if you take the groom home, there's nothing for it but we all have to go back. Who told you to wear the silly hat anyway? Makes you look like Wellington's sister, with a nose you could hang a lamp upon."

The groom began to cough violently and the girl's brown eyes fairly snapped in fury. Once more, Miles had scored on a sore point. Unfortunately, Caroline had inherited her mother's prominent proboscis. From the look of the girl's clenched fists, Sylvia feared that Caroline might actually come to blows with her brother. Apparently, so did Miles, for the boy dug his heels into his mount and was off across the field.

"I shall chase him down," Sylvia said as she caught the groom's inquiring look. "You stay with Miss Caroline under those trees that we just passed. You should be safe from any rain there, Caro."

Caroline gave her cousin a tight-lipped nod. "Mama says that you ought to whip him and I am beginning to find myself thinking her almost right. He is growing quite insolent."

Sylvia did not trust herself to reply, afraid that she might say that Miles had given his sister as much as she deserved. Sylvia cantered off in the direction that the boy had taken, fairly certain that Miles was heading for his usual favorite spot out toward Buckingham House. Still, once she was out of sight, she deliberately slowed her horse's pace, determined to enjoy some semblance of an outing despite Caro's tantrum.

Sure enough, Sylvia found her young cousin waiting for her upon the wide open field.

"Syl!" he called, waving at her cheerfully. "I hoped that it would be you coming after me."

"You were very naughty, Miles," Sylvia said, mustering as much anger as she could. "You should not have provoked Caro so."

"Someone ought to," Miles said, walking his horse toward her. "I daresay she has become the veriest prig since we came to Town. She sounds more and more like Mama every day. Besides, didn't you get to ride?" He smiled mischievously.

"At what cost?" Sylvia asked as she dismounted. "You know very well that this morning's events will get back to Aunt Ruby one way or another."

"I'm sorry, Syl. I didn't think of that," he said.

"Well," Sylvia said, relenting at the boy's crestfallen expression. "I ought not to say it, but I was glad of the ride."

The two walked their horses together in companionable silence for a moment, delaying their return, when suddenly, a magnificent mare raced into the clearing. Astride her was a man in white, his costume contrasting vividly with the animal's coat of stark black.

"Cor!" Miles whispered in awe. "A Hindoo!"

"No, Miles. 'Tis a Sikh. You can tell by..." But before Sylvia could finish her sentence, a large, spotted dog burst from the brush in a blur of speed, nipping at the heels of the mare. The horse reared in fright, kicking at the mongrel with flaying hooves while his rider struggled to retain his seat.

To Sylvia's dismay, the Sikh flew from the saddle, landing in a crumpled heap at the edge of the woods while his mount galloped away in terror, pursued by the cur.

"Miles, go get the groom and Caro, quickly," Sylvia ordered, helping the boy up into his saddle.

"I shall go after the horse," Miles declared as he caught up the reins.

"You shall not!" Sylvia commanded in a voice that

brooked no contradiction. "Not when a human being needs help. Now, off with you." She swatted his horse's rump and leaving her own mount to graze, raced toward the fallen man.

She knelt down beside the Sikh, noting in relief that he was still breathing, but other than chafing his hand, Sylvia was totally at a loss. She had never tended anything more serious than a scrape. He moaned and stirred slightly and Sylvia was reassured.

"Do not worry," she said in Hindi. "Soon someone will come. Soon."

The liquid brown eyes flew open. "The horse?" he whispered. "I must seek my master's mare," he declared, attempting to raise himself, but he closed his eyes once more as dizziness overcame him.

Sylvia rose to her feet, praying that Miles would soon arrive with the groom, but instead the dog burst from the bushes once more, racing toward her. Frantically, Sylvia looked about her for some weapon. In desperation, she snatched up a fallen branch and placed herself between the animal and the man lying senseless upon the muddy ground. The dog stopped short, ears flattening against his head as he growled at her menacingly.

"Get away!" she screamed, waving the stick. "Go home!"

But the hound only bared its teeth in reply and lunged forward.

"Spots!"

Sylvia heaved a sigh of relief as the dog turned and raced toward a short, heavyset man who was striding out of the woods. As he came closer, his shabby attire and tattered boots became apparent, but his uncouth appearance was far less fearsome than the speculative look on his face as he drew near.

"Well, well. What have you brought to ground here

m'boy?" the man said eying Sylvia with a lascivious leer.

Sylvia shivered as his words confirmed what his expression had told her. She was little more than prey. A glance at the prostrate Sikh made clear that there was no hope of help from that quarter. As Spots' master devoured her with his gaze, Sylvia prayed that Miles would put in a quick appearance. Until then, Sylvia swallowed hard as she brought up her makeshift club once more. There was only herself to rely on. In a timed match, sometimes delay was the only means of winning.

"No need for that, m'beauty," the man said with a gap-toothed smile. "You be gathering up whatever coin you and your man servant might be carrying. And mebbe I'll take just a liddle kiss to thank me for calling the 'ound off."

"If you do not leave immediately with your dog, I shall have you hauled before the magistrate." Sylvia declared, her voice shaking.

"I'm quakin' in me boots," he chortled, sneering at the threat. "Would ye like t'see Spots do some o' 'is tricks? Y'ev already seen 'is best. Got 'im trained to bring down any rider likely to 'ave a goodly purse on 'im. Put down yer stick, missy."

Miles, where are you? Sylvia wondered desperately, her heart racing as her attacker advanced, the unpleasant sound of his laughter sending a shiver of foreboding up Sylvia's spine. Raising her weapon high, she prepared to swing.

"Spots!"

At the sound of his master's voice, the dog lunged forward, jaws snapping. Sylvia felt a stab of white hot pain as sharp fangs raked her fingers, causing her to release the branch and clutch her throbbing hand.

The man laughed as Sylvia backed away, stumbled

and fell to the ground. Through the haze of pain and fear, she saw a gleam in the Sikh's sash. Her right hand was useless, but she reached with her left to pull at the jeweled handle of the ceremonial *khanda* that all Sikh men wore. The wicked blade gleamed in the sunlight as she pushed herself to her feet, awkwardly swiping the air before her.

"Now you son of a mangy bitch, now I shall spit you and your accursed animal on one blade," Sylvia waved the weapon wildly, hoping that her attacker would not realize that she had not the foggiest notion of how to use the dagger. She hurled Hindi curses at him, howling and dancing about like a madwoman. "I shall send you to your vile ancestors," she threatened. "I am Kali, the she-demon!"

The man started to back away, but the dog was unimpressed. Perhaps sensing the core of fear at the center of Sylvia's lunatic display, the animal lunged at her once more only to veer sharply to the side as the report of a pistol echoed through the clearing. Whining piteously, the dog returned to his master, who clutched at a suddenly spreading redness about his shoulder. The wounded man turned and ran, stumbling into the woods, the dog following close on his heels. There was the sound of hoofbeats as a horse sprang from behind Sylvia in pursuit of the animal and his master.

Sylvia's legs seemed to melt beneath her; she sank to her knees, weak with relief. The residue of fear left her scarcely able to breathe, her heart hammering as if it would beat itself from her breast. The *khanda* slipped to the ground as she clutched at her aching hand.

The Sihk's eyes had opened and he was regarding her in confusion. "A beautiful warrior defends me," he said in Hindi. "Is Kali now an Englishwoman?"

Suddenly, she heard a twig snap behind her, but before she could turn, a hand touched her shoulder. Her fear returning full force, Sylvia attempted to twist away, throwing herself flat upon the ground to grab at the fallen *khanda*, unwittingly taking her new assailant down with her. Stones dug into her stomach as she fought to free herself from the weight upon her back. Her throat produced nothing but a ragged choking sound as she tried to scream.

"A warrior indeed. Easy, easy, Kali," a familiar voice said. "Calm yourself. He is gone."

Abruptly the weight shifted, then disappeared. The restraint removed, Sylvia rolled, grabbing the dagger as she staggered to her feet. Breathing raggedly, she attempted to focus through the haze of terror.

"You can put the *khanda* down now," David urged softly, cursing himself for a fool. He should have known better than to come at her from behind and startle her so. Primal fear had pushed her beyond reason. The feral instinct for self-preservation dominated those green eyes. "The cur and his dog are gone and there is no need to cut my Weston coat to shreds, however you might deplore the fit."

Reality penetrated the curtain of shock. Her arm slowly dropped to her side. The blade slipped from suddenly lax fingers with a soft thud as its point embedded itself in the muddy ground.

"Much better," David said with relief as he watched the awareness return to her face. "You are safe, Kali. Foolishly brave, with that temple dance of yours, but you are safe now."

She stood watching him in a trembling quiet, far more disturbing than any tears or female frenzy. David moved toward her, uncertain. His senses urged him to gather her into his arms, to hold her, comfort her. But he feared that any move on his part might drive her into panic once more. So, as the moments passed, all he could do was watch and wait for the inevitable onset of hysteria

"You ... called me ... 'Kali.'" Sylvia whispered, her voice coming out in something of a croak. "If you heard that much ... milord, why in Heaven's name ... did you not chase the devil off sooner?"

"Unfortunately, with all your moving about it was difficult to get a clear shot," David said, his face splitting into a relieved grin at this unexpected scold.

"Capering about like a lunatic was the only defense I could muster," Sylvia admitted. "I can barely carve a chicken."

The attempt at humor was surprising. A most remarkable woman. How had he ever thought her deficient in wit? Although her voice and demeanor were still strained, she had yet to give way to sobbing or weeping. "You gave a masterful performance, Miss Gabriel. Most frightening."

"Was I, indeed?" she said, taking deep ragged breaths. "Sh- shall I consider the stage then?"

"I am sure that you would put Mrs. Siddons upon her mettle," he said, trying to keep his voice soothing.

"You should see to your servant," Sylvia said. "He took a bad fall."

When David made a tentative move in his servant's direction, Harjit shook his head. "I am well enough," he said, rolling to his knees.

"Would I match Mrs. Siddons' excellent Lady MacBeth, do you think?" Sylvia asked, starting to shiver. "The morning has grown chilly, don't you agree?"

"You would make an excellent murderess, but a most untidy one," he said, deliberately emulating her tone of gallows humor in an effort to erase the terror from her eyes. Her face was still stark white and her words were almost coming in gasps now. Her teeth were starting to chatter violently. He had seen much the same reactions in soldiers after a battle, when they came to the realization of the consequences that might have been. Peeling off his jacket, David draped the garment over her trembling shoulders.

Sylvia pulled the jacket close about her, grateful for the warmth. In her still-agitated state she found the scents of horse and man that rose from the fabric to be curiously comforting. Even the frantic thump of her heart seemed to slow. "You milord, are something of a mess yourself," Sylvia declared, smiling at last.

Despite a coating of dirt on her cheek, there was something about that smile that made his heart skip a beat. "That is most unfair of you, Lady Macbeth, or should I say 'Kali?' You are responsible for my roll in the mud. But then, there are some, including Harjit Singh here, who claim that untidiness is my natural state," he said wiping ineffectually at his breeches and noticing the familiar scarlet shade of . . . "Blood!" he exclaimed. "You are bleeding, Miss Gabriel."

David laid gentle hands upon Sylvia in an effort to discover the location of her wound. She stood quiescent as he examined her, finally finding the source of the bleeding.

"'Twas where Spots scratched me I believe," she murmured. "'Tis nothing."

"Your pardon if I differ, Kali." He gently spread the hand upon his, shaking his head, his insides clenching at the sight of the jagged bite-wound. A rapid fumble through his pockets revealed no trace of a clean handkerchief. With impatient hands, he managed to unwrap the linen stock from his neck, using an end to wipe away the cake of mud and blood.

"Neckcloths do have some justification for existence after all," he reflected. "It appears far worse than it is," To his dismay, he saw a worried look in her green eyes. "It will heal Sylvia, I promise you. The dog only nipped you, although I am concerned that you may carry a scar due to this day's work."

"It is not my hand that troubles me, milord. It is…" Her eyes perused him from head to foot, disturbed by the fact that she had ruined his elegant clothing. He was half covered in mud from the lawn of his shirt to the tip of his Hessians. "I am so sorry about your garments, milord."

"My clothes?" David said in surprise. He had been more than certain that it was the prospect of the scar that was the source of her serious expression. "Do not give them a thought, Lady Macbeth. Why, it will be but a small matter to clean them. 'Out damned spots!'" he intoned, as Petrov rode up leading Harjit's horse.

"'Out damned spots' indeed! Oh!" Sylvia began to giggle helplessly

"While you are standing here quoting your Shakespeare, the evil one got away. I am losing him in the woods. His partner who was holding horse ran when he sees me," Petrov said as he dismounted. "Poor girl, she having the hysteria, no? Is my opinion that you should have been shooting to kill villain, David."

David looked at Sylvia, who was chortling so hard, that the tears were beginning to fall. "It would seem so," he said.

"No," Sylvia declared, between giggles. "Spots was the name of that wretched dog."

But David did not smile as he cut away a clean section of the neckcloth with the *khanda* and carefully wrapped the wounded hand. "You are right, Ivan. I should have killed him," he said, with quiet menace as he looked at Sylvia's blood streaked habit.

"Could have been worse," Petrov said. "Just as well you were not killing the rogue, though. In this country, magistrates are getting involved, such simple matters are becoming too messy." Suddenly, his face lit with a smile that transformed his mournful visage. "A pun! I am understanding now. 'Out damned spot,' from the Shakespeare play, no? Hamlet?"

"Macbeth," David corrected absently, as he finished binding the wound.

Harjit rose to his feet, salaaming toward Sylvia awkwardly. "You have been wounded in my defense, young miss," he said, softly in Hindi. "I am in your debt."

"It is not to me the obligation is owed, but to Lord Donhill. In truth, it is I who am the greater debtor, for it was more than my life he saved. I suspect my honor was at risk as well," Sylvia replied in the same tongue, regaining her composure at last.

David looked at her in surprise, flushing at her praise. "You speak Hindi?"

But before Sylvia could give the obvious answer to the question, Petrov saw the full extent of the damage to David's attire and let out a despairing wail. "By my grandmother's last tooth, David. Look at you! Your riding jacket," Petrov cried. "Is mud upon it. You use your neckcloth for bandage. Your knees are bloody, ai! Muck and grass stains will be remaining upon your breeches forever."

"Cut line, Ivan," David said, casting him an annoyed glance. "You are not my nursemaid."

"Highslip will be having mine head," Petrov declared tragically, his accent gaining added flavor with emotion. "Your new riding costume is shumbles, all within an hour. You are having to change before we meet Brummel for breakfast, David. Then off to Weston's for you, mine friend."

"That is *shambles*, Ivan," David said, smiling. "And I shall be damned if I set foot in that pin-pusher's parlor again. If you do not cease this arrant nonsense, I swear that I shall find the first mud puddle that I may, dip my boots in it and splatter you as well."

Petrov recoiled in horror, as if the dirty pool were imminent. Sylvia let out a peal of laughter, causing the men to look upon her in shocked surprise. It was an infectious sound, neither light nor musical, but a wholehearted invitation to mirth. Soon, both David and Petrov were clasping their sides and even Harjit's lips were stretched in a broad smile.

"Holoo, Syl," Miles called, galloping across the field, followed in the distance by Caroline and the groom. "Is everything all right? Caro would go slow... didn't want to lose that confounded hat," he said disparagingly as he slid from his horse.

"Is a most charming hat, a crime to lose so beautiful an adornment," Petrov declared, smoothly, as he helped Caroline dismount. "Entirely suitable to your loveliness."

Caroline's annoyed expression disappeared. She gazed into the Russian's worshipping face as she spoke. "You see, dear brother," Caroline declared, the very picture of sisterly sweetness. "I told you there was no need to gallop neck or nothing. Sylvia did not really need us at all."

...

Despite his declaration that he would risk damnation rather than another encounter with Weston, David Rutherford was once more consigned to purgatory at the tailor's hands. After their belated breakfast, Petrov added his pleas to both Highslip and Brummel's adamant demands. Thus, Lord Donhill found himself swiftly transported yet again to Bond Street and stripped to his small clothes. The damp chill bit at his bare legs as he stood, fearing to move in the pin-infested half-finished garments. Rain drops fiercely pelted the windows of the Bond Street shop, but David was far away, thinking of Sylvia.

When they had delivered her home, the girl's aunt had given her the devil of a time, rebuking her niece as if the vile attack had been her own fault. It was all that he could do to hold his temper, knowing there was nothing that he might say that would help her. David was roused from his reverie by the sound of raised voices.

"I say, the yellow!" Highslip declared, picking up a bolt of silk, his eyes alight.

"With his skin? Are you mad?" Brummel declared in emotional tones. "It would cause David to look hopelessly sallow."

"But surely a touch of color..."

"Darker shades are far more becoming," Brummel declared, his gaze stony.

"Please," David groaned. "We have been at this for the better part of an hour now. I feel like a veritable pincushion. My limbs ache and my neck is stiff from standing like a piece of pasteboard. Can we go home?"

"Now, now, milord," Weston said, as he entered the fitting room, carrying a bolt of deep blue fabric. "We shall be finished shortly." The master tailor proceeded to unwrap a length for Brummel's inspection much in the manner of a magician producing a miracle from thin air. The Beau rewarded Weston with a pleased nod.

"Excellent," Brummel said, fingering the cloth critically. "This blue is just the ticket."

David blinked in disbelief. "But it is nearly the exact shade of the one we examined half of an hour ago."

"'Nearly' is insufficient," Lord Highslip declared, shaking his head disapprovingly. "A gentleman's sartorial splendor must be perfection in itself. Why, I spend well above an hour each morning refining the appearance of my neckcloth."

"I can well believe it." David snorted derisively. "Ouch!" he yelped, as Weston stuck him with a pin.

"My apologies, milord," the tailor said, twitching the sleeve of the garment into place, "but you do persist in moving. These broad shoulders require careful fitting for the proper result."

"I can barely move a muscle in your damned jackets," David said, looking murderously at his tormentor, half-suspicious that the man had pricked him on purpose. "All I did was shrug my shoulders and the thing came apart. Do not make this one so tight and I do not see why you cannot give me a few pockets here and there!"

Weston looked at Brummel and shook his head. "I cannot, Mr. Brummel. I simply cannot do it," he said, casting his eyes heavenward.

"I shall speak to him," Brummel said, watching as the tailor left the room muttering in dismay. The arbiter of fashion turned toward David, who was shrugging off the half-finished garment with hasty relief.

"You agreed to the wager," Brummel began, in much the same tones one would use to chide a recalcitrant child.

"I pledged to dress properly," David declared, pushing his spectacles further up upon his nose. "I did not expect to submit to torture."

"If you would not persist in ruining your garments," Lord Highslip said in a sneering voice, "you would not require so many trips to the tailor. Ripping coats to shreds with a shrug, mud on your riding costume, blood on your linen…"

"The mess was unavoidable," David said, looking at the earl belligerently.

"A gentleman does not soil his hands in that manner." Highslip sniffed.

"I suppose I should have left the lady to her own devices!" David replied.

"Highslip!" Brummel stepped between the two men. "Would you stop behaving as if David did the damage deliberately? Before he left us, Petrov himself testified that the ruin was necessary."

David gave Highslip a satisfied smirk.

"However," Brummel continued. "You must replace the injured garments, David, with clothing of equal quality and stop abusing Weston. The man is an artist of the highest order and you must treat him with care."

It was Highslip's turn to curl his lip.

"Now, while we wait for Weston to return, tell us a bit more about the incident this morning," Brummel cajoled with dolorous expression of a tutor trying to divert two uncommonly belligerent boys.

David hesitated.

"Come, come," Brummel urged, "it is most gallant of you to protect her. Even so, the story will be bandied up Bond Street and down Drury Lane before the sun sets, I would wager."

"No more wagers for me," David groaned. "One is more than sufficient."

"You might as well serve us up the name," Highslip demanded. "After all, it's no less than the chit's own fault for acting the Amazon."

Brummel silenced Highslip with a warning glare. "As Petrov so rightly told you, this is too remarkable a tale not to make the rounds," Brummel reasoned. "The servants will inevitably talk, David. Moreover, if the girl's relation is the gorgon your friend describes, then you may be sure the story will be told with enough relish to flavor it as scandal broth. However, if *I* disseminate the *on dit* in a flattering light…"

"You are very sure of your credit, George," David said.

"My friend, you have yet to learn that gossip is the very coin of society and the power of my purse is far from modest," George said, turning to the mirror to make a slight adjustment to his own neckcloth. "Now give me the name of your Amazon and I will go forth to dispense this news as if it were the veriest gold."

"I would not style her an Amazon, George," David said. "She was however, most courageous and undoubtedly the most beautiful woman I have ever seen."

"And what is the name of this vision?" Highslip asked derisively. "Were you wearing your glasses?"

David glared at Highslip. "Her name is Miss Sylvia Gabriel, the late Sir Miles' niece."

"It is unlike you to speak in such superlatives, David," Brummel said, intervening once more. "I shall look forward to making her acquaintance during the Season."

"It is doubtful that you shall have the opportunity," David said with a frown. "The girl has no dower to speak of and her aunt means to keep her under wraps."

"A shame, if she has half the beauty you say," Brummel said.

"Indeed, he does not do her justice," Lord Highslip said softly, a strange look stealing across his face. "Sylvia is perfection, an Incomparable in every way."

"You know the girl, Highslip?" David asked.

"I do," Highslip said. "My estates march with her uncle's land in Northumberland. I was well acquainted with Sylvia. In truth, we had something of an understanding."

"Did you?" David queried, the very idea somehow disturbing.

Highslip nodded, his eyes narrowing in anger as he spoke. "Sad thing when mere money comes in the way of true love. I am certain that Sylvia regrets her choice. She could have come away with me."

"You proposed a runaway match?" Brummel asked, his eyebrows rose in surprise. Lord "High in the Instep Highslip," as they styled him, was a notable stickler for propriety. It was hard to credit that he would so much as put a toe beyond the pale of proper behavior.

Highslip nodded. "Not strictly honorable I know, but such was the depth of my feelings. I think that if she had loved me well enough, we could have gone to Gretna. Unfortunately, my regard was not returned."

David looked at the popinjay peer with a leery eye. Something about his story did not quite ring true. Still, there was no telling what a woman might do. His own mother was a prime example, marrying his father when his cousin, the Earl, seemed ready to turn up his toes and then complaining bitterly when the old man unexpectedly recovered and lived on for decades.

In his experience, fond sentiments were given much lip-service, to be sure, but money and position were all that mattered in the end. Lucre won over love every time. Perhaps Sylvia had thought to entertain Highslip's suit for his title and, David granted grudgingly, the earl's looks were above the common.

Still, David found it difficult to believe that Sylvia Gabriel had heartlessly jilted Highslip. There was a gentle strength about Sylvia that would not countenance such behindhand behavior. Moreover, David could not help but think that Miss Gabriel had been uncommonly sensible to avoid a lifetime sentence with the elegant earl.

"I, for one, account avoiding Gretna to the girl's credit," Brummel declared, pursing his lips. "A woman of valor, beauty and reason! Damme, 'tis a crying shame that the most interesting female of the Season seems doomed to remain in the shadows. The chattering chits that it has been my misfortune to meet make me yawn with boredom. Unless . . ." he cogitated aloud, a slow, sardonic smile dawning. "Such courage should not go unrewarded."

"And what do you have in mind, George?" David asked, uneasily. "Miss Gabriel's aunt is dead set against presenting her niece. While Caroline is well enough to look upon, Sylvia casts her cousin completely in the shade."

"Ah," said Brummel, "but that is precisely her merit, David. We shall contrive to make Miss Sylvia Gabriel fashionable. So fashionable, in fact, that her dear aunt will find that she cannot do without her."

"It will not serve," Highslip protested. "Sylvia has no dowry."

"Beautiful women have been known to wed without the benefit of gilding," Brummel stated. "What better reward for bravery than a husband, eh? Gentlemen, I hereby declare that Miss Sylvia Gabriel is the most desirable woman in London. Now, I shall go seek Mr. Weston."

David was able to hold back until Brummel quit the room, then he burst into such a fit of laughter that his spectacles slid dangerously to the tip of his nose.

"You think he jests?" Highslip asked, tight-lipped with annoyance.

"He must be joking," David said, the room reverberating with his bass chuckle. "The sheer presumption. . ."

"To the contrary, dear Donhill. Nothing could be simpler. Within the week, I would wager, Sylvia Gabriel will be the reigning Incomparable and there is little that anyone can do to prevent it."

CHAPTER 4

*D*avid soon found that Highslip had spoken no less than the truth. Brummel played his pawns in polite society with the finesse of a master. A few casual words in the correct ears and soon, Sylvia Gabriel's name rolled upon every tongue. Her bravery was applauded, her beauty extolled and rumors of a mysterious lost fortune were carefully cultivated until the Ton was in a veritable tizzy, craving an encounter with the unknown paragon.

At the house on Belvedere Square, Mrs. Gabriel was at a loss to cope with the sudden flood of interest in her empty-pursed niece. She banished Sylvia to the nursery, claiming to the crowds of callers that the poor girl was overset by her ordeal. Caroline was pushed forth into the distinguished company. But it was plain, even to the doting Mrs. Gabriel, that once the visitors found that Sylvia was not to be seen, they were not disposed to linger despite Caroline's many charms.

Knowing the attention of the Ton to be as fleeting as a child's, Brummel moved rapidly. The sun had not set twice since the incident at Green Park, when, with David and Petrov in tow, the Beau presented himself at the Gabriel's door. The tide of callers was at high crest;

the large saloon filled to capacity with nary an empty chair to be had.

Yet, when Brummel and his party were announced, vacancies beside the hostess mysteriously appeared.

As the Beau did the pretty, a curious hush settled over the room as all awaited the pronouncement of the oracle of fashion. The atmosphere was much like the air of anticipation around the pit before a cockfight, for Mrs. Gabriel was obviously a prime target for Brummel's famed sarcasm. Despite her irreproachable bloodlines, her clothing with its surfeit of fripperies was quite tasteless and her mannerisms bordered on the vulgar. It seemed certain that the reigning monarch of the mode would rip the encroaching female to shreds.

Unfortunately, they were destined to be disappointed on that score, for Brummel confined himself to polite inconsequentials. However, those who knew him best recognizing the gleam of devilish intent behind the Beau's otherwise bland expression. There was entertainment yet to come.

"How, unfortunate that your niece continues to be indisposed," Brummel declared, his smile chill. "I confess myself deeply disappointed, for I came expressly to congratulate her upon her brave actions."

"Bishop checks queen," Petrov whispered under his breath. "He informs that the girl has his interest."

With his elbow, David nudged the Russian to silence.

"You are acquainted with my niece?" Mrs. Gabriel asked with a croak of surprise.

"Only by dint of her excellent reputation, as yet," Brummel allowed. "But I am looking forward to meeting her once the Season begins. As we all are." He scanned the crowd demanding their accord. "One can only hope that she will soon recover, so that we may express our admiration."

David watched in amusement as the visitors bobbed their heads in agreement, like a collection of well-dressed puppets. As for Mrs. Gabriel, her jaw dropped, agape as the mouth of a child's nutcracker. David imagined that he could hear the grinding of gears as she split the shell of Brummel's statement to reveal the kernel of his intent.

The Beau skewered the woman with his eyes, while he applied his final stroke of calculated social pressure. "I must confess my admiration for you, Mrs. Gabriel," Brummel declared, inclining his head in a gesture of approval. "In truth, I know of few relations would be kind enough to stand their kin for a Season, even a woman of your vast resources. You do, after all have your own child to launch. Rumor has it that your daughter is wholly in accord with sharing her debut with her cousin. Beauty and family possessed of a generous spirit!" He regarded Caroline, like a priest pronouncing a benediction of approval.

"Game is ending, mine friend," Petrov mumbled, watching with delight as Caroline colored delicately, flattered at Brummel's notice. "His opponent is cornered. Check and mate."

Petrov was undoubtedly correct, David realized, as he marked that Mrs. Gabriel too, was flushing, albeit far less prettily. She could not escape Brummel's maneuver without seeming the most miserly of mushrooms, accounting mere money of more import than familial obligation. Denial of her imputed generosity would mean the loss of Brummel's tacit endorsement and likely, Society's censure. It was time for his move on this tandem board.

"I am sorry George, if you misunderstood..." David began.

"Misunderstood? Do not say so, David?" Brummel said, raising his quizzing glass. "Do I mistake the matter, Mrs. Gabriel?"

Mrs. Gabriel had no choice but to smile and acquiesce weakly. "The poor darling would have none of it, at first," Mrs. Gabriel lied. "I vow, the girl is so proud, don't want to take as much as a farthing from me, her own aunt. Nonetheless, I have decided that she ought to have a Season, despite the fact that she don't have a pennypiece to her name and that she is fully four-and-twenty."

The woman's eyes narrowed in self-satisfaction, having in one sentence assured that Sylvia would present no serious competition to Caroline. Sylvia's beauty and courage might be universally praised. Adulation cost nothing. Ultimately, the serious suitors would go to the girl with the dowry rather than the poverty stricken spinster. Indeed, David noticed more than one look of consternation amidst the general murmurs of approval.

"Draw?" Petrov questioned.

David shook his head. "No, from the look in George's eyes, he has another move yet."

"Is that so?" Brummel asked, making a show of wiping his quizzing glass before placing Mrs. Gabriel under the scrutiny of his lens once more. "I had understood that your niece is something of an heiress."

"Indeed she *was*, once," Mrs. Gabriel pronounced with no little relish. "But when Sir Miles passed on, not a trace of the fortune was found. Not that my brother by marriage misspent it, mind. I believe he invested badly on her behalf," she hastened to add as she saw the dawning of disapproval among her audience.

"Or as you mentioned, it may be squirreled away in hiding somewhere," David added, fortifying Brummel's position.

"Indeed," Brummel said slowly. "So there is the distinct possibility that the money will be found."

"It would be misleading to say so," Mrs. Gabriel declared, speedily attempting to dampen such speculation. "Heaven knows that we have tried to locate the treasure, but the late Sir Miles' Will was a model of confusion. I believe the poor man was out of his head with all his mutterings of 'fool's mates' and other such chess terms."

"Ah, if the clues are in chess jargon, then my friend Lord Donhill might be able to help. He breathes, eats and sleeps the game," Brummel said. "And he certainly owes your niece a favor, for 'twas his servant that she saved."

"The man is playing two boards, David. You also are a pawn, I am thinking," Petrov said softly, his lip twisting wryly. "Is check mate again."

David nodded in discomfited agreement. Although he had given some thought to Sir Miles' last testament, and would gladly examine it, he could not like being so publicly committed to a cause that might very well dash Sylvia Gabriel's hopes. From the speculating looks being cast his way, it seemed that Miss Gabriel's marital prospects would be largely determined by his success or failure.

"It was most foolhardy of her! Especially to put herself at risk for a mere servant! The girl ought to have waited for help," Mrs. Gabriel pursed her lips in disapproval. From the nods among her audience, there were more than a few who agreed.

"Unfortunately, Mama, there was no time to wait for rescue." Caroline countered with just the right tone of polite disagreement. "I believe that Mr. Brummel has the right of it. My cousin is a heroine, stepping into the breach as she did!"

"This cousin is having courage and wit, using the

Beau's opinion as shield for her own," Petrov observed quietly to David. "Loyalty, brains and beauty, is much to be admiring of her."

As if guided by some inner clock, Brummel arose at the correct time, bowing over Mrs. Gabriel's pudgy fingers as he bade his farewells. In a mere twenty minutes, he had accomplished most of his goals. Sylvia Gabriel had been elevated to the ranks of eligible maidens, although her fortune was phantom and her person seen by but a few. David waited knowing that Brummel had no intention of relying exclusively on the likelihood of locating the lady's inheritance. There was one last parting shot he had promised to attempt.

"You have my admiration, Madame," Brummel proclaimed, pouring liberally from the butter boat. "Your generosity is beyond compare. Even though your brother-by-marriage is at fault for your niece's difficulties, you were not obligated to provide for a Season and her marriage."

There were some in the crowd who gasped aloud, stunned by Brummel's sheer nerve. The implication was clear. Not content with the mere promise of a Season, the Beau had opted to inveigle for the pledge of a *dot* as well.

But this time, Mrs. Gabriel held her ground. "I only wish that I could provide dear Sylvia with a dowry. My own Caroline was, of course, extremely well provided for by her late papa, but it is all I can do to give Sylvia an entree into society. Of course one may only hope that Sylvia's fortune will be recovered." Her complete skepticism regarding the likelihood of the event was more than clear.

Brummel took the setback in stride. "Indeed," he reflected. "Stranger things have been known to occur. I bid you farewell, most-munificent Madame."

"Pooh," she declared, waving her hand in dismissal. "'Twas the least I could do."

"And you may be sure, it will be the absolute *least* she can do," David muttered darkly to Petrov as Brummel led them triumphantly out the door.

. . .

For Sylvia, the days that followed seemed like travelling in the midst of a whirlwind. Over Miles' protests, she was yanked from the nursery and dragged on a rapid tour of shoddy shops and second-rate seamstresses, for true to David's prediction, Mrs. Gabriel was doing the very least she could.

Yet, despite the inferior quality of the establishments, the mediocre modistes exerted themselves once they heard the name of their customer. Here too, Brummel's efforts had borne fruit. Word had spread and the gossip was worth far more than mere gold.

The patron saint of English fashion had given Sylvia Gabriel his blessing and any seamstress with even a soupçon of ambition knew that this was an opportunity to shine. A damaged bolt of green silk was purchased at a pinchpenny price. An exquisite, but unpaid-for riding habit was altered.

Bit by bit, by dint of skillful cutting, a snatch of concealing embroidery, inspired stitchery and styling, flaws were disguised, rips were remedied and defects transformed into accented embellishments. The aspiring seamstresses were eager to introduce their wares to the modish world and exerted themselves to produce garments that would garner the notice of the Ton. Sylvia was outfitted in a plethora of bargains.

Moreover, Mrs. Gabriel's determination to deprive her niece of the frills and furbelows that adorned Caroline's clothing worked in Sylvia's favor. The simplicity of Sylvia's gowns only served to accentuate her classic beauty and the dark colors that Mrs. Gabriel chose to contrast her niece's age with Caroline's youthful pastels, lent Sylvia an air of sophistication and distinction.

Any pleasure that Sylvia might have drawn from her new finery, however, was nearly destroyed by her aunt's incessant groaning at even the paltriest of expenses. Every shilling spent on Sylvia was begrudged. The delivery of every garment elicited a litany of grievances. Somehow, Sylvia was blamed for the turn of events that necessitated this depletion of her aunt's purse.

Still, even Mrs. Gabriel's constant grumbling could not completely surmount Sylvia's excitement as their carriage crept up Pall Mall to number Fifty...Almack's.

As the lines of carriages disgorged their well-dressed passengers, Sylvia felt a thrill of anticipation. Although Almack's was often denigrated for its stale cake and inferior orgeat, it was the dearest dream of every well-born maiden to enter the assembly rooms' portals, to dance every dance and perhaps, find true love treading a measure to the strains of the orchestra. Even though her head told her otherwise, Sylvia's heart still felt the force of those long-ago girlish dreams.

Nonetheless, Sylvia told herself that she harbored no delusions of finding love. Without a dowry, a decent suitor was less than likely, as well she knew. Idly, she wondered if she would encounter Hugo, Lord Highslip at Almack's. One of their callers had mentioned that he was in town. Although she had known him as "Hugo," since childhood, there was something about him that had always caused her to be mindful of his title, as if the earl's diadem had been forever fixed upon his head.

With half an ear, Sylvia listened to her aunt's list of strictures yet once again. Sylvia was not to put herself forward, not to smile overly much, not to talk too frequently or dance too boisterously. In short, she was adjured to fade into the shadows.

It seemed that no matter how Sylvia comported herself, the evening would provide her aunt's mill of displeasure with a bounty of grist to grind. As their conveyance edged to the entry and Aunt Ruby set forth more boundaries of behavior, Sylvia thought glumly that she might better have remained home to play chess with Miles.

Thoughts of chess led inevitably to thoughts of David Rutherford. Would he be at Almack's, she wondered, conjuring up his face in the semi-darkness of the coach? The very prospect of his presence caused her spirits to rise.

Chiding herself for her foolishness, Sylvia decided that it was most unlikely that David would appear at the Marriage Mart's primary temple, especially since he had gone to such lengths to protect himself from having to pronounce his "I do" to the parson. The terms of his notorious wager gnawed at the edge of her mind. *You could take him*, a teasing inner voice whispered. She shoved those treacherous thoughts aside immediately.

"Sylvia! We have arrived. Why are you daydreaming?" Aunt Ruby asked, her annoyance patent as she compared her daughter's looks to those of her niece. Somehow, Sylvia had contrived to make her gown look far better than it had seemed in the shop. Although it had not appeared so in the fashion plate, the dress was adorned with elaborate easing, accentuating the column of her neck and the whiteness of her shoulders. Sylvia had coiffed her hair in a simple psyche knot and a natural glow of excitement precluded the need for pinching cheeks.

Mrs. Gabriel gave a pat to her turban and composed her features, knowing there was no remedy for Sylvia's unwanted company. Since Brummel's visit, vouchers for Almack's had arrived with gratifying speed. Invitations to routs and balls were piling upon her desk. The Beau's patronage and the Ton's curiosity had paved the road to social acceptance. Although Mrs. Gabriel would not deign to acknowledge it, Sylvia's presence was a small price to pay for the cachet.

Still, the woman decided to take her own measures to make certain that Caroline was not completely eclipsed by her beautiful cousin. Fortunately, gossip had provided her with the perfect nostrum to dose away any guarded delight that Sylvia might feel. She would inform the child, for her own sake of course, lest she be disappointed by unwarranted expectations.

"Sylvia," Mrs. Gabriel said, her voice barely audible below the noise from within. "I feel that I must tell you that somehow word of your ended engagement to Lord Highslip has become public."

The girl blanched. "B . . but how?" she stammered.

"I have no notion," her aunt informed her, "but while you are no longer suitable to be his wife, I would not have you interfere with Caroline's chances to be a countess. Do you understand?"

"Of course, Aunt Ruby," she whispered, trying to quiet the turmoil within. As humiliating as it might be to think that all of Society might know of Highslip's rejection, she prayed that Caro would not be tempted by the title of countess. Although the girl was something of a widgeon, her cousin had enough sense to see the foppish earl's façade.

Or did she? Heaven knows, Sylvia herself had been fooled, even though she was older and had deemed herself far wiser.

. . .

The strains of music wafted from the nearby ballroom as Lord Highslip attempted to tweak David's neckcloth back into proper placement. "I cannot understand it, Rutherford," Highslip said in exasperation. "At first, I thought that the problem lies with that valet of yours. I can only conclude at this point that he is not at fault. Regardless of who has the dressing of you, the result is inevitably the same. Within the space of a few moments, your shirt points have wilted."

"I am sorry, but I tend to sweat," David said, his apology blunted by his belligerent tone as he squirmed like a little boy beneath Highslip's grasp.

"Gentlemen do not 'sweat' and even were they so vulgar, perspiration is no excuse," Highslip drawled dismissively. "However, if that were all, I would not be dissatisfied. Look at your neckcloth, man."

Obediently, David looked down his nose at the snowy folds, holding up a bit of the linen and crumpling it in the process. "It is still there. I have not taken it off."

"Would that you had," Highslip muttered. "When we left your rooms, it was tied into a perfect, crisp Mathematical, now it is beyond repair. Have you been using it to polish your spectacles again?"

"No, I swear," David said raising his hand in affirmation. As he brought it down, his fingers ruffled consciously through his hair, throwing the artfully styled Brutus arrangement into careless disarray. "My spectacles are safe upon my nose."

Highslip groaned as he watched this wanton desecration of his sartorial protégé's painstakingly produced coiffure. Stepping back, the earl eyed David with growing dismay. "Your linen is askew again and somehow, between my coach and the assembly rooms, your coat has gotten wrinkled. I cannot fathom how that is possible. And your stockings!" he moaned. "There is a splatter of mud on your left ankle. I would vow on my mother's grave that we have not been near a drop of mud and we have not had rain this week past."

"Your coach, perhaps?" David questioned, his eyes lighting with devilish pleasure as he deliberately goaded the dandy,

"Always immaculate," Highslip said, thrusting out his chin pugnaciously. "I have yet to encounter a speck of soil in any of my conveyances, yet dirt seems to be attracted to you as if you are a veritable magnet. Were it not for my promise to Brummel, I swear, I would wash my hands of you."

"Indeed, you might be well advised to do so. Is that a speck of dust I see on your left sleeve?" David asked making as if to touch the cuff in question.

Highslip backed away. "I confess, I would not be surprised if you were contagious. Well, I have done the best I can. I doubt that Brummel himself could do better."

"Think you so, Highslip?" Brummel asked, raising his quizzing glass in disdain. Pursing his lips, he eyed Rutherford in patent disapproval. "A marked improvement, David," he said, slowly. "But then anything would have been an improvement."

Highslip reddened at the implied criticism.

"Not another sermon on the importance of being well-dressed, I pray you, George." David tugged at the linen that hugged his neck like a veritable noose. "I swear the first Adam was a fool when he put on those blasted leaves in Eden. I am sure that had he realized it would lead to the neckcloth, he would have been content in his nakedness."

"No, you heathen," Brummel declared with a bark of laughter. "I have not come to preach to you, merely to tell you that Miss Gabriel has arrived. I may deplore your taste in tailoring matters, Donhill, but your eye for the fairer sex is impeccable. I must admit I was concerned that she could not be the paragon you described. However, there is no need for me to create her an 'Incomparable,' for as Highslip stated, she is one without my intervention."

As he entered the ballroom and saw Miss Gabriel crossing the floor, David could not help but agree with Brummel's assessment. The unusual green shade of Miss Gabriel's gown accentuated her porcelain coloring and the candlelight glinted in her hair, burnishing it to the color of new-minted gold. Yet, despite her outstanding looks, her face lacked animation and for a moment, he was reminded forcibly of their first meeting.

Once again, her countenance was a study in marble, closed and emotionless as she turned her head mechanically and looked upon the assemblage. Then, those green eyes met his and David saw beyond the mask that she effected. Her anguish was obvious, as was the likely cause.

Mrs. Gabriel's glowering looks were all too easy to interpret. Although she was making a poor attempt at hiding it, the woman's jealousy of the attention that her niece was garnering was patent. Miss Gabriel was in obvious need of rescue and David abruptly determined that he would act the part of her champion.

However, he soon found that he was not the only would-be knight on the board. By the time he had crossed the floor, he found her besieged by a crowd of young swains, eager for an introduction.

"La, Lord Donhill," Mrs. Gabriel said tapping him on the arm with her fan. "I declare myself surprised to see you at Almack's of all places."

David suppressed a wince. The woman wielded her fan like a club and the logic of her statement was no less of an assault. Why had he come to the very place he had vowed to avoid like the plague? The terms of the wager had not required that he endure the crowd of eager mamas, callow youths and simpering misses. Where had his wits gone? David wondered.

He had endured hours of Highslip's high-handed management, been primped, polished and appareled under that popinjay's paw and for what purpose? Certainly, Mrs. Gabriel seemed singularly unimpressed by the marked improvement in his appearance. Indeed, by the short shrift the matron had given him, he deduced that Miss Caroline Gabriel had no potential for chess. Even as he made an attempt to reply to her sally, Mrs. Gabriel turned her attention to Lord Highslip, who had made no wagers impairing his eligibility.

"Caroline, darling. Look who is come! Lord Highslip," the woman proclaimed loudly as if the earl was long-lost kin, rapping him soundly on the arm. "Our dear neighbor."

But even had she knocked him on the noggin, Mrs. Gabriel would have been unable to direct Highslip's attention to Caroline, for it was clearly Sylvia who claimed his gaze. While David was long accustomed to reading faces, he was hard put to name the expression that passed across Sylvia Gabriel's countenance. Was it regret, he wondered, that she had whistled a titled suitor to the wind? As for Highslip, his usually bland mask slipped for barely a fraction of a moment, but it was long enough for David to perceive the raw desire burning in the earl's eyes.

"Beautiful, as ever, Sylvia," Highslip declared at last, a slight hesitation in his drawled compliment.

"Am I, indeed, Hugo?" Sylvia asked, her tones cold and clipped.

David wondered at the air of tension between them, the crackle of feelings imbuing the atmosphere with an electricity of emotion. Even Mrs. Gabriel could detect the silent undercurrent, for her color was becoming alarmingly beet in hue as the earl continued to stare.

"May I have this dance, Miss Gabriel?" David found himself asking, looking toward Mrs. Gabriel for permission to take her niece to join the forming set.

With a glowering nod, Mrs. Gabriel gave her assent, while Highslip gazed angrily after them.

"I account myself lucky to steal you away, Miss Gabriel," David said, trying to fill the awkward silence.

"Is he still staring after me, milord?" Sylvia asked under her breath, a pasted smile upon her lips.

David glanced in Highslip's direction. "No, Miss Gabriel," he said softly. "He has recovered himself and is currently engaged in a conversation with your cousin." The girl relaxed visibly, the tension in her posture easing as the orchestra began to play.

"'I feel almost a Bartholomew Fair freak,'" Sylvia said, thinking aloud. "It seems as if every eye is upon me. 'Tis hard enough to bear without Hugo acting the fool."

David stiffened. Although Highslip's behavior had been inappropriate, surely her rejected former suitor deserved more sympathy. "Men have forever been making fools of themselves over beautiful women, Miss Gabriel, so you are scarcely a freak," David said, ruefully recalling hopeless infatuations in his past, when he had been without title or purse. "Brummel has pronounced you an Incomparable. Is not that type of attention gratifying?"

"Think you so, milord?" Sylvia asked. Although his voice was even and his smile was pleasant enough, her reading of his expression detected the unfavorable set to his jaw, the glint of reprimand in his eye. Surely he could not fault her for the uncommon notice that she was receiving? "I did not campaign for the title, sir and now that I have been granted the moniker, I am certain that it will only cause me grief."

"There are some who would put marriage in the grievous category, but I have never met a female who looked upon it so," David said. "We had supposed that between your uncommon looks and Brummel's approbation, you would certainly be able to snare some man."

"*We?*" It took all of Sylvia's skill to keep her visage calm, but she could not keep the snap of anger from her voice. The events of the past days were suddenly becoming clear. "So, my sudden popularity has not come *ex nihilo*. Who is counted among this cabal of 'we,' milord?"

David fingered his neckcloth uncomfortably as he tried to extricate himself from the results of his foolish disclosure. "It was Brummel's idea, actually," he began clearing his throat. They were parted momentarily by the pattern of the dance and he prayed that her anger would wane somewhat by the time they rejoined. However, that was not the case. Although a placid facade was fixed on her face, her eyes were spitting sparks as they linked arms.

"I ask you again, who else is in on this plot of yours?" Sylvia asked, in tones of poisoned honey.

"We had only meant to help you, Miss Gabriel," David explained weakly. "Your desperate situation . . . I uh, mean."

"'My desperate situation,' as you call it, has only been made more untenable by your interference," Sylvia whispered, nodding briefly toward the corner that her aunt occupied. "Look you and tell me what you see."

"Well," David allowed, "her expression is somewhat annoyed. Now she is speaking to Caroline."

"Who is obviously not dancing," Sylvia lamented. "And, knowing my aunt, I will be to blame for it."

"I am sure that your cousin will find a suitor, Miss Gabriel," David said, feeling a pang of guilt as he realized the likely truth of her conclusions. "As you shall."

"I know you meant well, milord," Sylvia said. The hangdog look in his eyes reminded her forcibly of young Miles' aspect when one of his brainstorms had gone awry and her indignation abated. "However, do you honestly believe that I could find a worthy suitor who would overlook the absence of a dowry?"

David looked at her, astonished that she should have any doubts on that point. Yet, Miss Gabriel did not seem to be fishing for compliments. Her manner was entirely serious. There was an underlying bitterness in her words that told him she had reason to believe her statement.

"A man may admire a showy piece of horseflesh, milord, but if it has little else to recommend, he will not buy it," Sylvia stated flatly, aching inside as she recalled her past hurt and disappointment. "At present, Lord Donhill, my looks are more a curse than a blessing. My appearance bars me from seeking a respectable position, for what woman with husband or son would be blind enough to hire a governess with a face that tempts men to indiscretion? Gentle birth shields no on from those who would take advantage. In all likelihood, I will forever be dependent on Aunt Ruby's charity and then, perhaps my brother's should he have a household of his own."

It was a statement of fact, not vanity. David marveled that she had actually considered the possibility of employment and felt saddened that his old friend's niece had come to such a pass. Although his compliance with Brummel's plan had initially been half-hearted, he now pledged himself fully to Miss Gabriel's assistance.

"What do you want then, Miss Gabriel?" David asked.

"My freedom," Sylvia replied at once. "To be quit of Aunt Ruby's grudging assistance."

"Marriage would do that. Not all men are mercenary." David pointed out. "You would be beyond your aunt's authority."

"And completely under the catspaw to another's will. A different form of servitude perhaps," Sylvia said. "'Tis the same thing to be white's pawn as black's - the moves are limited without resources."

"What if you could be queen?" Amused by the reference to the game, David continued the chess analogy. "With complete freedom of the board." But before Miss Gabriel could reply they were separated by the figure of the dance again. She moved gracefully, executing the steps with airy precision before she returned to his side.

"To be a flesh and blood queen requires a treasury, milord," Sylvia said with a regretful smile. "Unfortunately, mine seems to have been permanently misplaced."

"Then I must find it, Miss Gabriel," David declared.

"I have tried for this year past," Sylvia reminded him. "Even Aunt Ruby has tried, for then she could be rid of responsibility for me and my brother. She is convinced that the blot on Uncle Miles' name has cast my cousin in the shade. We have all been searching for the treasure."

"Ah," David said smugly. "But my knowledge of chess is far superior. I am sure that those clues your uncle left will be far more intelligible to a master of the game than one with limited skills."

"I doubt it. The clues are too confusing, even for a master." Her candid declaration elicited a startled expression from Lord Donhill. Horrified, Sylvia realized her error.

But David recouped for her. "Ah yes, your brother. I am sure he searched high and low. But perhaps a fresh perspective might serve."

Sylvia let his supposition stand. "Perhaps. I hope that you will forgive my frankness, but I feel that I almost know you, Lord Donhill. Uncle often read your letters to me and it is almost as if you are something of an old friend."

"Surely not an *old* friend," David bantered, as he circled round her and bowed in answer to her elegant curtsy.

"Primeval," Sylvia replied, a teasing light in her eyes, as they came together once more. "I had envisioned you as a grizzled ancient, balding, with a Moorish cap upon your head, the tassel waving to and fro as you pondered your moves."

"And you, my girl, were described as a mere member of the infantry. A terror in plaits who prattled incessantly," David declared, recalling Sir Miles' brief mentions of his niece.

"So in your mind, I remained eternally in the nursery, just as you were my uncle's elderly, faraway crony," she mused. "Strange, the elaborate pictures that our imaginations create from mere assumption, usually far better than the reality."

"To the contrary, Miss Gabriel. I find myself preferring reality," he said, surprising himself with his own sincerity. "An intelligent, beautiful woman is infinitely better than a chattering schoolroom minx."

"Why, that is by far the best of compliments, milord," Sylvia said, a smile banishing her serious expression. "No man has ever credited me with a brainbox before. Most males do not look beyond my face."

"Then most men are fools, Miss Gabriel," he said, looking into the depths of her eyes. The candlelight imbued them with a topaz light, making them glow with a lambent flame.

The tempo of the music increased and they changed partners. There was no further opportunity for conversation until David reluctantly brought Miss Gabriel back to her aunt's side. It was easy to see that the girl's evaluation of the situation was on the mark, for the look that her aunt gave her would have done credit to Medusa.

"I hope that you did not find Sylvia's ways too forward, Lord Donhill," Mrs. Gabriel said, favoring him with a pasteboard smile. "I fear my niece has not yet learned that her countrified conduct is inappropriate for town."

"Indeed, Mrs. Gabriel, I found her irreproachable. Your tutelage does you credit," David commented, larding on flattery liberally. "In fact, I would be grateful if your daughter would favor me with a dance."

He could almost hear the gears grinding in Mrs. Gabriel's head as she considered the request. Although his monstrous wager made him ineligible, he would do well enough as a dance partner. Moreover, as Brummel was his bosom friend, it would not do to give him offense. After a moment, Mrs. Gabriel nodded graciously.

David was delighted to find that, except for her unfortunate nose, Caroline did not resemble her mother in the least. Freed of Mrs. Gabriel's crushing presence, the young woman chattered freely, flitting from topic to topic with the abandon of a conversational butterfly as the steps of the dance joined and parted them. She required no more of David's concentration than an appropriate nod or two, as he mulled over Sylvia Gabriel's situation. He owed it to the memory of his late chess partner to solve the mystery and clear his name. Unfortunately, he had discovered that Sylvia's aunt was correct in her presumption there were many who gave credit to the rumors that the late Sir Miles had frittered away his nephew and niece's inheritance.

David found himself wondering about William Gabriel, Sylvia's brother. Perhaps a visit to Oxford might be in order to determine what moves he had made to seek the treasure? After all, two brilliant chessplayers pondering the same problem were far better than one. However, David was brought up short in his contemplations by a question from Miss Caroline Gabriel.

"I beg your pardon, Miss Gabriel," he said, noting her look of annoyance.

"You are just like Sylvia, ever listening with half an ear," she said with a pout. "I wondered if your friend Mr. Petrov ever attends Almack's?"

"His aunt, the Countess Lieven, is a Patroness, so I am sure that he does make an occasional appearance," David replied. "I believe that he had an engagement for a chess game at White's this evening."

"Chess," Caroline made the word a sigh. "How I hate that game, milord. It has ruined my dear cousin's life. Oh my!" The girl bit her lip and her brow wrinkled in worry.

"Whatever is wrong? Have I trod upon you, for I confess that I am not the best of dancers?" David asked.

"Oh no, milord. It is far worse, I fear. Lord Highslip has returned once again with your friend Brummel. It is too bad that the earl chooses to make a cake of himself, like this. Poor Sylvia, if he continues in this vein it is bound to add credence to the dreadful talk that has been making the rounds," she said, shaking her head sadly.

Indeed, a glance confirmed that Highslip had returned to Miss Gabriel's side and was behaving like a veritable moonling.

"Really," Caroline said in exasperation. "One would think that the wretch would be ashamed to approach her, after all the damage that he has done."

"Whatever do you mean, Miss Gabriel?" David asked, his full attention upon her now.

"I really ought not to say," Caroline declared, pursing her lips. She lowered her voice conspiratorially. "When Highslip found that all of Sylvia's money was gone, he jilted her. It broke her heart and I fear that she will never recover from her unrequited love."

Although David was surprised that Miss Gabriel would confide her cousin's secrets to a near-stranger, he made no attempt to stem the flow of gossip.

"It is too bad of him to be making an exhibition of her and exploding her reputation to flinders. Especially when he made it clear last year that he had to marry to fill his purse," Caroline whispered indignantly. "And after she had defied Uncle Miles' wishes in the matter by continuing to entertain the earl's suit! It was a bitter blow for Sylvia, I suppose, to find that Uncle Miles had been correct about Lord Highslip's character all along."

"And they were engaged?" David asked, encouraging further revelation.

"The banns had not been read, nor had announcements been made," Caroline allowed. "Uncle Miles would not countenance it. He insisted that Sylvia should spend some time in London before making it all official. However, according to her papa's Will, my cousin was due to come into control of her affairs and Uncle could not have stopped her then."

"Rather unusual, for an heiress to be given free rein so young," David observed.

"Mama was mortified when she heard of it, but by then Uncle Miles was gone and so was Sylvia's fortune."

Caroline gave Highslip a fulminating glance. "Only the family and Lord Highslip knew of the matter. So, when the earl cried off, we had thought it buried and done, but apparently, that is not the case. Lady Jersey just taxed me with it. Although I told her that Lord Highslip ended it, I fear that she did not believe me. I know the man is your friend, but he is the only one who could have spread this malice."

The measure of the music required them to exchange partners and Caroline was brooding in glum silence by the time she returned to David's side. The girl had given him ample fare to chew upon as they circled the room together. There was little doubt in David's mind that Caroline Gabriel's account of the affair was more faithful to truth than the earl's. David's regard for the dandy dropped from minimal to nil. Highslip sought to place Sylvia Gabriel in the role of jilt when it was he who had done her the injury.

After David returned Caroline to her mama, he pondered his moves. Ambling about in a desultory manner, David caught snatches of whispers. Even seemingly favorable comments about Miss Gabriel were tinged with the green of jealousy. A hasty consultation with Brummel confirmed the worst. The story that Miss Gabriel had entertained Highslip's suit then high-handedly spurned him was gaining wide circulation.

"I would like to do Highslip's neckcloth up good and tight," David declared.

Brummel shook his head. "That would remedy nothing."

"What can we do?" David asked.

"Very little, I am afraid," Brummel admitted with a shrug. "There are far too many tabbies who are envious of Miss Gabriel's looks. All we can attempt is to tell the true tale, but even then, I suspicion that the winds of gossip will not blow in her favor."

"I fear we have done her no good, George. With such talk going about, I doubt that she will be able to find a suitor as we had hoped," David said looking mournfully at Sylvia. "I ask you, was there ever such a fool as Highslip? To jilt any female is contemptible, but to forsake a woman like Sylvia Gabriel is an act of sheer stupidity. Any man of intelligence would take her in a trice, even if she had only a shift to her name." The thought of Sylvia in a shift flashed through David's brain and the room grew suddenly warm.

Brummel smiled knowingly. "There is one way to teach the dog a lesson, David. Find her fortune and Highslip will be well-served for his perfidy."

David grinned in understanding. "Bad enough to lose the girl, but if the fortune was there all along . . . I am quite certain it will send him into apoplexy. I shall do it!" he declared, pulling off his spectacles to polish them excitedly.

"Your linen," Brummel reminded.

David looked shamefacedly at him. "Sorry, George. Shall I attempt to retie the thing?"

Brummel waved his hand in dismissal. "Might as well try to resurrect the dead," he declared. "'Tis too far-gone."

David hurried off to speak to Sylvia regarding her uncle's Will.

"Far-gone, indeed," Brummel murmured softly. "I sincerely hope the lady plays chess."

CHAPTER 5

"Perhaps I ought to go back to Crown Beeches," Sylvia said, putting aside her tambour frame and going to the window. A curtain of rain fell, pounding in heavy drops against the pane. "The whispers have gotten worse, I fear. The chill looks that I get almost make me shiver."

"On the contrary, Syl," Caroline said, leafing idly through Ackermann's fashion plates. "You get the warmest of looks from the male contingent. 'Tis just the females that wish you to China or someplace equally distant. There are none that hold a candle to you, cousin."

Sylvia looked at Caroline sharply, but could detect no trace of resentment upon her face or in her voice.

"I am no beauty. I know that," Caroline said with a smile. "But I am well enough to look upon and my dowry lends enchantment."

"Mr. Petrov seems to think so," Sylvia said, returning to sit beside her cousin.

"Pooh, he thinks of nothing but his chessboard," Caroline declared, nonetheless, she blushed.

"Not when he called the other day," Sylvia pointed

out. "Those dark, mournful eyes of his were fixed upon you all the while."

"Yes, Ivan's eyes are..." she sighed and shook her head.

"*Ivan*, is it now?" Sylvia teased.

"You know full well that he only accompanied Lord Donhill to discuss Uncle's Will," Caroline complained. "'Tis only the chess puzzle that fascinates him, I fear, not my *beau yeux*. Mr. Petrov follows Lord Donhill like the tail to a hound."

"Unfortunately, we had no chance to talk of the treasure, the parlor was so crowded," Sylvia said glumly.

"With all your suitors," Caroline said, laughingly.

"Do not call them so, please." Sylvia shook her head.

In a teasing voice, Caroline ticked off the names on her fingers. "Lord Entshaw seemed quite taken with you and I thought Mr. Colber's eyes would quite pop out of his head as he contemplated your décolletage."

"Lord Entshaw, puts me in mind of a balding slug, fifty if he is a day, with hands that are forever straying. Your mama was in alt at his condescension, for slug though he may be, he is a titled slug." Sylvia grimaced. "As for Mr. Colber, his staring is but a trifle compared to Hugo's gaze. Last night I could feel his eyes following me about the room. Everyone could not help but remark it. It was most discomfiting. I really should leave, Caro, go home to Crown Beeches."

"You cannot let Lord Highslip chase you from town, Syl," Caroline said, putting her magazine down to take her cousin's hand. "If it were not so monstrously annoying, it would be quite romantic. It seems if Highslip cannot have you, he seeks to assure that no one else will."

Sylvia looked at the girl in surprise. Although Caroline was not known for the depths of her perception,

Sylvia considered her cousin's pronouncement with growing concern. During Hugo's courtship, Sylvia had accounted his excessive jealousy as a sign of his regard, now she wondered if Caro's conjecture had hit the mark. Certainly, it would explain the earl's *outrè* behavior as well as the rumors that had suddenly become rife. As much as Aunt Ruby disliked her, Sylvia could not credit that the woman would deliberately spread information that would cast such serious aspersions upon a member of her own family.

Even in his youth, Highslip had always been uncommonly possessive, issuing dire warnings about trespassing upon Highslip land to the local children, often enforcing his rules with his fists, Sylvia remembered.

From the recesses of memory, she dredged up an incident, recollected, in the main, because of the great agitation that it had caused Uncle Miles. It had occurred soon before she and William had come to Crown Beeches. In an effort at economy, Hugo's father had sold a hunter to Sylvia's uncle, one that his son had greatly prized. However, before the horse could be sent to its new owner, Hugo rode off upon it, neck or nothing, bringing the animal back utterly ruined. The stallion had to be put down.

Back then, she had dismissed the tale as an overblown rumor, but now, Sylvia felt a cold finger of fear running up her spine. Unfortunately, if Hugo had deliberately set out to ruin her chances, there was little she could do. "What rubbish," Sylvia declared, as much to herself as to her cousin. "It sounds like the plot to one of those novels that you devour, Caro."

The girl grinned sheepishly. "Actually, it is from *The Viscount's Vengeance*. Edward - he's the hero - attempts to thwart the heroine's marriage to an Italian nobleman who is really a loathsome fiend. Would you care to read it?"

"I doubt that it would be instructive in my case," Sylvia said wistfully as she took up her needlework again. "Since it is unlikely that anyone shall wish to wed me, especially with Hugo behaving so untowardly."

"A posy arrived from Lord Donhill," Caroline said, attempting to cheer her cousin. "It arrived before Mama went up to rest."

"I saw it, and one was sent for you as well," Sylvia said. "Lord Donhill is merely being kind."

There was a knock.

"Enter," Caroline called, picking up her fashion plates once more with a sigh. "I suppose that you are right about Lord Donhill. After all, neither of us are likely to attempt to checkmate him and wed him."

"Then we may both enter in complete safety, Petrov," David said, as he and his friend were ushered into the drawing room. "It seems everywhere I turn these days; I face importunate ladies with chessboards at the ready. Why only yesterday, I was challenged by a widow who was near twice my age and certainly three times my girth."

"And what did you do, milord?" Caroline asked with a coquettish smile.

"Quaked in my boots and prayed to the spirit of Philador," David said, the twinkle in his eyes belying his somber demeanor. "But I need not have worried, the woman was the rankest pawn-pushing amateur, as most females are."

Sylvia busied herself with her embroidery, taking in deep breaths and keeping her tongue between her teeth. Still, it was difficult to resist the temptation to call the chess master to account for his denigrating braggadocio. "You have brought this plague upon yourself, milord. I suppose you shall have to bear the consequences."

"Unless some woman is being up to task," Petrov said, seating himself near Caroline.

"Those challenges are diminishing." David laughed as he took the chair close to Sylvia. "It would seem the fairer sex has more important matters to occupy their pretty heads...fashions, fripperies and other such folderol."

"Do we?" Sylvia asked. "Am I not speaking to the man who is now a slave to fashion as a result of a foolish wager?"

"She is having you in check, David." Petrov chortled.

"Let us not forget the task at hand," David said, casting his friend a fulminating look. "My apologies for calling so early, but there seemed no other way to have private speech with you," he explained. "I have come to fulfill my promise. If you will but set your uncle's puzzle before me, I shall attempt to solve it."

It was difficult for Sylvia to maintain her annoyance in the face of his enthusiasm. David's wet Hessians were dripping on the Aubusson carpet. His dark curls hung damply across his forehead. He reached up for his neckcloth, hesitated and then pulled a handkerchief from his pocket to wipe fogged glasses clear. Sylvia smiled as she noted this testament to Brummel's influence sighing inwardly at the unshuttered effect of those eyes. She found herself caught in their depths, unable to look away. It unsettled her until he set the spectacles on his nose once more.

"Do you have your uncle's Will?" David asked.

Sylvia blinked and shook her head. "No, I am afraid not. However," she hastened to add, seeing his disappointment, "I do know the clues by heart." She set the embroidery frame aside and closing her eyes in concentration, she began to recite.

"Yea, dance with a fool, I shall not allow,
Silly Sylvia to wed him anyhow.
For though I may be buried and dead,
No fool's mate shall ye take to your bed.
When you seek to tread the matrimonial measure,
You shall recall these words with pleasure.
King's pawn black, king's pawn white,
Bishop's move black and black's move knight.
Knight to rook's forth move again,
Queen to rook's fifth, bishop's mate at end.
Seek the board and step at leisure,
And you shall uncover the Rajah's treasure."

She opened her eyes to find David staring raptly at her. "My uncle was a far better chess-player than he was a poet, I fear."

"I would say so," David said, scrambling to recall the words of the poem, having been utterly distracted by the woman who recited it. "'The Rajah's treasure,' I suppose, is the fortune your father amassed from his play in India?"

Sylvia nodded.

"And the 'fool's mate,' is Lord Highslip?" David guessed. Sylvia's blush was a confirmation.

"Uncle objected strongly to the match. He told me that I ought to give other men a chance. In fact, his last requests stipulated that the family travel to London immediately for a Season and that no mourning should be observed."

"Mama deemed it so *outré* a demand that she gave up a substantial financial incentive to repair to London right after the burial," Caroline added.

"Perhaps Aunt Ruby was right. She claimed Uncle was out of his head when he made the Will, for he had always been something of a stickler for proper behavior," Sylvia speculated. *Which was why he never wished it known that I am a mistress of chess,* she added silently. *Even Uncle deemed chess no proper woman's game.*

"Failing to mourn properly would have gained nothing but condemnation," David agreed. "And the chess puzzle seems somewhat out of kilter."

"I was sure that he was referring to one of the eight classic 'fool's mates,'" Sylvia mused. "Except that black takes precedence and white has only one move." Sylvia flushed as she realized that David was looking at her. "Coming from a family such as mine, milord, one cannot help but absorb something of the game. I was my uncle's secretary for several years and he taught me a bit," Sylvia said, hoping that her hedging had satisfied him.

"I would have expected as much, both your father and uncle being premier chess-players," David said.

"They were indeed," Sylvia said, seizing the opportunity to turn his attention from herself. "Papa devoted his life to the game, travelling all over Europe, the East, even the Americas, searching for worthy opponents. He would win and lose fortunes."

"John Gabriel!" Petrov interjected. "Winning, without question."

Sylvia nodded. "He rarely lost a game, even when it would have been more politic to do so. One Pasha nearly had him beheaded for daring to trounce him, but we escaped. Mama disguised him as her maid, hiding him in a chador and veil." She smiled at the recollection of her dignified papa in skirts.

"Truly?" David asked in surprise.

"The costume is in the attic somewhere, I believe, among my parents' things if you do not credit me. We travelled everywhere with Mama and Papa. The family was rarely in the same place for more than a month," Sylvia said. "There were so few players that could match Papa, you see. He always had to move on to fresh competition."

David heard the traces of wistfulness in her voice. "It must have been a strange life for a child."

"It was certainly unusual" Sylvia agreed. "There were times that I wished for a proper home, but I do not think that either of us, my brother William or myself, would have really wanted to miss the adventures we had."

Her eyes were far away as if focused on those distant lands and her lips curved upward dreamily, as she recalled those days, but the smile disappeared as she continued.

"However, Mama . . . it was extremely difficult for her. We lived like nomads, constantly packing and unpacking. I think that she almost hated the game. When I was very small, I recall playing with the pieces and Mama knocked them out of my hand and began to cry."

"But why did your mama tolerate it then?" David asked. "Surely they had funds for a home in England?"

"She adored Papa and she was his anchor. He often said that she made his life possible. He loved Mama, but I think that she always believed that he loved the game more," Sylvia said. "Chess was my mother's greatest rival. I heard her say once that she wanted to come first. Every woman wants to be above all else in a man's life."

Her eyes glistened with unshed tears and David wondered if she were thinking of Highslip, who had put money before love. Was Caroline correct? Was her cousin still nursing a broken heart despite the fact that the man had been proven an utter blackguard? It was easy to understand why Sir Miles had gone to such extreme lengths to protect his niece from Highslip and David's resolve was firmed. Brummel was correct; locating her fortune would be the ultimate revenge for the suffering that Highslip had inflicted upon her.

"Due to chess, you have endured much Miss Gabriel," Petrov observed. Is amazing to me you do not hate the Game of Kings as much as your mama did."

"Oh no," Sylvia declared, "'Tis not the game that causes the difficulties, 'tis the player. It makes no matter if it is Faro or the Fancy. Some people allow themselves to become obsessed, to allow a game to dictate all aspects of their lives. My father was merely one of many such people."

Did she number him among the obsessed, David wondered? After all, he had never allowed chess to control his life. Or had he? The wager? It was a distinctly disconcerting thought. He chose to change the subject.

"Shall we get back to the matter at hand?" David asked, polishing his spectacles, avoiding her frank gaze. "Call me David, please," he requested, pushing the wire frame back up his nose. "After all, as you pointed out last evening, we can be considered old friends."

"Very well, David. And you too, may use my given name," Sylvia agreed. "Where shall we begin? I suppose I need not tell you that the moves in Uncle's poem were tried on every chessboard in Crown Beeches. We even ripped some apart in the hopes that we would find some hidden compartment within the squares, but there was nothing."

David thought for a moment. "Clearly, it was your uncle's intent that you come to London in short order after his demise. Have you searched the chessboards here?"

"Aunt Ruby had most of the larger ones transported to the country to be examined," Sylvia said, "although, I can think of a few she missed. I have come to believe that Uncle wanted us to leave Crown Beeches because he wanted me to get away from Hugo - Lord Highslip, I mean."

"But what if the treasure is here?" Caroline asked, excitedly. "Could that be why he wanted us to make such unseemly haste to London?"

"Both it might be," said Petrov. "Your uncle, he was most fond of fork attacks."

Caroline gave him a puzzled look.

"Is when one piece can threaten two," Petrov explained. "Smashing two birds with one rock."

"Ah, I see. Two birds with one stone!"

"Just so!" Petrov beamed joyously at Caroline.

Within a few hours, the four of them had hunted down and examined every chessboard in the house. From the lacquered Chinese chessboard of jade and silver in the study to young Miles' wooden board in the nursery, every square was closely examined, played upon in the manner prescribed by the late Sir Miles' rhyme, using all eight variations of a fool's mate.

"Never fear, I will have it repaired," David promised, surveying the sad remains of Miles' chessboard. The inlaid squares had seemed to conceal a hollow and so, they had taken it to pieces. "Is that the last of them?"

"'Cept, the little one in your room, Syl." Miles remembered.

"'Tis but a small pocket set that was my father's," Sylvia said, going into the room and bringing out a teak and mahogany case for them to view. She opened it to reveal a well-used tiny board with peg pieces. "As you can see, there can be nothing concealed in it."

"Your cousin is sleeping in the nursery, Caroline?" Petrov asked in astonishment.

Caroline flushed in embarrassment and Sylvia went over to take her hand.

"It is none of Caro's doing, you may be certain, Mr. Petrov. I am naught but a poor relation now," Sylvia said, trying to smile. "And so, it seems, I am destined to remain." She turned abruptly toward the window, unwilling to let the others see her disappointment. Despite her doubts, a small seed of hope had grown. Now, as it withered and died, the future stretched out before her like an endless desert.

A footman rapped at the nursery door. "Miss Caroline, Miss Sylvia, Mrs. Gabriel requests that you return downstairs immediately if you are done with your tour of the house. Leastways, that's what Mr. Boniface told her you were up to."

"Thank you, Robbie," Caroline said to the servant, "and thank Boniface as well for his quick thinking. We shall be down in a trice." She put an arm on Sylvia's shoulder. "I shall tell Mama that Miles required your attention, Syl. That should give you a few moments to compose yourself." She kissed her cousin on the cheek and started out with Petrov and David, but in the hallway David hesitated and went back to the nursery.

"Don't worry, Syl," he heard Miles say. "'Tis only another twelve years and then Mama can't tell me what to do no more. I been thinking, if I got to marry somebody, might as well be you. You can play chess and you fly a kite better than any girl I know, don't cut up stiff at frogs neither."

David moved closer and watched unseen as Sylvia knelt beside the boy and gathered him close.

"High praise, indeed! I thank you most kindly for your generous offer of your hand, noble sir," she said, hugging him to her. "We have missed our usual Friday morning kite fly in Green Park. Shall we go next week? I fear it cannot be earlier."

"Can we Syl? That'll be famous. And just remember, you needn't worry about Mama. You can stay with me, till we get married," Miles added, squirming slightly. "If she tries to get another governess, I'll run her off. See if I don't."

Reluctantly, Sylvia let him go and looked up to see

David standing in the doorway. "You needn't have waited for me, David," she said softly. "I shall be fine. As you no doubt heard, I have received a most honorable proposal."

"Indeed, I did," David said, offering his hand to the boy. "You are a very discerning young man, Miles. Ladies who do not cut up stiff at frogs and go kite-flying every Friday, are the rarest of breeds."

"Why don't you marry her now, if you want?" Miles said, cocking his head sidewise in thought. "Won't be able to do it myself for few years."

Sylvia's tear-stained face broke into a smile. "Trying to fob me off already, you young scamp! You cannot trade wives about like marbles and besides, Lord Donhill cannot marry anyone, unless he loses his wager."

"But Syl!" Miles began to protest.

She spoke quickly to staunch him, knowing that the boy could easily spill her secret. "Even if I could trounce him, Miles," she said, "I would not, you know. I could not abide a life dictated by a game. I saw what it did to my mama, how it hurt her. People's lives are not pieces to be lost and won by skill or luck. I want to be loved fully, to always be first in someone's heart."

"Guess you'll just have to wait for me, Syl," Miles said, cheerfully. "Want me to put your board away?"

Wordlessly, she handed Miles the small chess set and he scampered out of the room. She rose and saw an angry frown upon David's brow. She groaned inwardly. Obviously, he had taken personal offense from her words.

"I did not mean to rebuke you, David," she said, trying to contain a growing sense of annoyance. She had spoken no less than the truth.

"You did," David contradicted stiffly. "Females understand nothing about wagers, about honor."

"And men do?" Sylvia said, her head shaking in disbelief. "I am full to the gills with the protestations of men and their strange concepts of honor. A titled man may woo a woman for her purse, that is honorable! Yet a female who courts a man for money is an adventuress. A man may mount a mistress! Yet a woman who seeks pleasure outside of marriage is a doxy. My uncle hides my money…"

"For your own protection," David said, his jaw tightening. "To prevent you from wedding a greedy, penniless fribble."

"And am I well protected now?" Sylvia mocked, her eyes narrowing. "An unpaid governess, a free maid of all work! Dependent upon my aunt's most *gracious* charity for the remainder of my life because I am a female and deemed to be too weak-minded to make sensible decisions! However, unlike myself, you, at least, were given some choice, Lord Donhill. But you have selected your own doom, to remain alone all the rest of your days. Because of your wretched honor you will stick to a stupid vow, made in an hour of drunkenness. I cry fie upon such honor, milord!" She whirled and left the room.

David stared after her in disbelief. The girl had obviously been overset by disappointment. Still, as he went slowly down the stairs, her derisive words echoed after him.

"Did you enjoy your tour, Lord Donhill?" Mrs. Gabriel asked as he returned to the parlor.

"Lovely place, isn't it?" Observed a familiar voice from behind.

David turned to face Lord Highslip. The elegant earl smiled superciliously and David felt a surge of anger. How dare he come here, after what he had done to plague Sylvia? It was not to be borne.

"You are improving," Highslip noted with a patronizing sniff. "I am forced to admit that your neckcloth appears almost decent."

"Does it?" David asked, reaching out to grasp the delicate folds of Highslip's linen in a squeeze. "I have always wondered how you tie this. A Mathematical, is it not?"

"Was!" Highslip snapped, his lower lip jutting in annoyance. "You have quite ruined my neckcloth, sirrah. 'Tis lucky indeed that I know you to be untutored in civilized ways. Were anyone else to do that, I might call them out."

"You need not accord me any special privileges if I offended you," David said, his voice dangerously smooth.

Petrov sprang up and grasped David by the shoulder. "You will not be starting duel in Caro's drawing room," the Russian murmured softly as he steered his friend toward a chair.

"Lord Highslip is telling us that you have been starting something of a fashion," Petrov said, with a quelling look. "The betting books are being full of wagers, men saying they will not be marrying ladies who cannot out-fence them or out-shoot them or out-do them in some other way."

"I say, 'tis wicked," Mrs. Gabriel said, her jowls shaking as she scowled at David in annoyance.

"I must agree, Mrs. Gabriel," Highslip said, his lip curling derisively. "Marriage is a most felicitous state, a blessing to be rejoiced in. Hiding behind a wager is the height of foolishness."

"I am so glad you think so!" Mrs. Gabriel declared, chortling in delight. "Do you not agree, Caroline darling?"

"Of course, Mama." Caroline nodded obediently, looking down at her lap to hide her mortification.

"She is such a good gel. She sews, milord and her voice is so fine..."

"Maybe she should be opening up her mouth so he can be looking on her teeth," Petrov muttered glumly as Mrs. Gabriel loudly prattled her list of Caroline's fine points. "I am changing mine mind. Go, be grabbing his neckcloth again and I be your second, or better, I grab."

"I cannot understand why she receives him," David mumbled. "The out-and-outer has all but spoiled her niece's chances and yet she entertains his suit for her daughter."

"Is simple. Rook outranks pawn and English earl bests nephew of Russian Grand Duke," Petrov whispered somberly.

Sylvia stood by the door, eyes wide with shock when she saw Highslip sitting in her aunt's parlor. She would have turned to leave, but Aunt Ruby's eyes gave a silent command.

"Sylvia, have you finished with Miles' lessons?" Mrs. Gabriel asked, emphasizing the girl's inferior standing in the household. "Why do you not join us? Lord Highslip has come to pay a call upon your cousin."

Sylvia felt as if she had been transformed to a mechanical toy, her limbs obeying her in jerky movements as she took the vacant chair by the door and picked up her embroidery. Although Hugo addressed barely a word to her, she could feel his eyes with their hungry burning gaze upon her. She plied her needle heedlessly, creating a tangled mess amidst the delicate pattern as she prayed for time to pass.

"Did you know, Lord Highslip, that dear Sylvia has several suitors?" Mrs. Gabriel remarked archly. "Lord Entshaw has sent the most remarkable flowers and Mr. Colber has been most particular in his attentions as well."

"Entshaw is old enough to be her grandfather,"

Highslip said, his voice suddenly cold. "And Colber is but the grandson of an upstart tradesman, surely you do not entertain those suits."

But Mrs. Gabriel was oblivious to his disapproval. "Beggars cannot afford to be choosy, milord. I am sure, being a sensible girl, Sylvia will do the wise thing. Is that not true Sylvia?"

Sylvia looked up, her chess training standing her in good stead. Not by so much of a quiver of her lip did she betray her humiliation. "You are correct, of course, Aunt Ruby. Oftentimes, we are not given much of a choice."

Although her voice was steady, David could feel Sylvia's silent misery and felt the rebuke in her words. Her face was stark white against the blue of her morning gown and she returned her eyes to her needlework. His anger simmered as Lord Highslip conducted his sham courtship of Caroline, casting covert glances all the while at Sylvia. It was clear that Mrs. Gabriel did not hold him to account for his actions. In fact, she was doing all she could to promote her daughter as a potential countess.

There was no stopping the ticking of the clock and much as David hated to leave, both he and Petrov had stayed well beyond what was proper for a morning call. Petrov's face was like a thundercloud and once they left the house the Russian burst into a torrent of words.

"What is being his game?" Petrov exploded. "He woos one while making goat's eyes at the other."

"Sheep's eyes, Ivan," David corrected as took up the reins of his silver high-perch phaeton.

"Sheeps, cows, goats! Is no difference. Animal is animal and Highslip is animal!" Petrov said, climbing in beside David. "I must be rescuing the girl!"

"I quite agree, but what do you propose, Petrov?" David asked, slapping the reins to urge the horses forward. "We cannot force Mrs. Gabriel to bar Highslip from the door."

"There is only being one possible move," Petrov declared, his dark eyes smoldering. "Marriage!"

"You would marry Miss Gabriel?" David asked, his heart sinking. It was a perfect solution. Petrov was of a good family and had well-lined pockets, an excellent match for a woman in Sylvia's circumstance. Yet, the very notion of Sylvia wed to Petrov caused a melancholy that was almost a physical pain. "I had no notion that you were so fond of her."

"I am thinking David, that maybe you are being blind, even with your glasses. I am loving her from the first minute I see her," Petrov said, smiling bemusedly, his brooding face alight with a whimsical joy. "Her voice is like angel's, eyes like doe and her face, is reminding me of mine own dear mother."

David recalled the portrait of Madame Petrov that hung in Ivan's rooms, but could remember absolutely no resemblance to Sylvia. Ivan's mother had dark hair and a rounded face with a hooked nose exactly like her son's exactly like . . . David burst into laughter.

"I am not seeing what you are finding funny," Petrov declared, deeply offended. "Situation is being very serious."

"I know, my friend, I know and I wish you happy. It is Caroline you speak of?"

Petrov looked at him incredulously. "You are thinking I talk of Sylvia. *Bozhe moi*! Is Caroline for me from the start." Petrov fell silent, and his expression became quizzical. "I am finding myself pitying Caroline's cousin." The Russian began. "She is pretty girl and Lord Highslip could be ruining her chances I think."

"Yes, she is very beautiful," David said, recalling Sylvia's face, aglow with excitement as they had searched for the treasure. "Perhaps it was foolish to get her hopes up, Ivan. If we cannot find her fortune, it would be a bitter blow."

"Poor girl," Petrov said, shaking his head sadly. "Is shame if she is forced to be marrying man like Entshaw or Colber."

"She shall not!" David said, glaring at his friend.

But Petrov merely shrugged. "Is she having choice? Unless you are finding her fortune David, is nothing for it."

"Brummel said that the rumors would, like as not, blow over soon. The broth of scandal grows cold quickly," he mused, an ache spreading in his chest as he thought of Sylvia wed to that toad Entshaw or the mushroom Colber. He pushed his spectacles up upon his nose, peering intently ahead as if the lenses could somehow discern a solution to the conundrum.

Petrov shook his head. David tried to read his friend's odd expression. Over the years, David had seen the panoply of the Russian's emotional palette, but there was something on his visage that was beyond interpretation. Sympathy? Sadness? But it was more. "Maybe the written copy of the full testament contains some clue?" David ventured.

Petrov shook his head. "Might be. Is shame the girl does not play chess, I am thinking."

Suddenly, David knew what stirred in Petrov's eyes.

It was pity.

CHAPTER 6

As Brummel had predicted, the attention of the Ton was soon diverted by other far juicier scandals than a long-ago jilt. Nonetheless, as the days passed and the dazzle of Brummel's patronage lost some of its gilding, Sylvia became merely a lovely face without a prayer of a fortune.

David was no closer to solving Sir Miles' conundrum than he had been before. The late baronet's man of law had only one scrivener who was as old as Methuselah and uncommon slow. Hopefully, the sizable *pourboire* that David had promised would add some speed to his scrawl.

As he greeted the porter at the door of White's absently, David wondered what his next move ought to be. Surely, he had to do something, for he was in large part responsible for Sylvia's current dilemma. Her aunt was hounding her to accept Lord Entshaw's suit and although Highslip had curbed his outrageous behavior, David had seen him watching the girl surreptitiously, like a starveling dog eyeing a bone.

So deep was David in his thoughts that Petrov's voice from behind caused him to whirl, his fists automatically at the ready.

"There is being another challenge, David!" the Russian declared, stepping back cautiously. "But is not being from me."

David shook his head apologetically. "Forgive me, Ivan. I am unaccountably distracted these days," he said, accepting the sealed missive from his friend.

Petrov nodded, his eyes sad with understanding, as David broke the wax and read the contents. A small group gathered around him.

"Who is it to be now?" Brummel asked, his boredom patent. The challenges had slowed, but the matches were more nuisance than sport since most of David's adversaries barely got past the opening moves.

"Lady Helena Balton? Do you know aught of her?" David asked.

"Well enough to look upon, though something of a bluestocking," was Brummel's evaluation. "The family has retired to the country, pockets to let, if I recall, so I suppose that is why she challenges you, David. Figures she has naught to lose but her reputation and lose it she shall. I doubt that she could beat you."

"Will you see to the arrangements, Petrov?" David asked, with a growing feeling of distaste as the knowing laughter erupted around him. He had eaten nothing since breaking his fast in the morning. But, even as he ordered his supper, David doubted that the queasy feeling in his stomach would be stilled by a meal.

Was this to be his destiny? To be forever challenged by pitiful chits and Friday-faced females at their last prayers? To be importuned constantly by women greedy for his wealth or his name?

"Why so glum, David," Brummel asked with a tight-lipped smile. "Surely you have no need to fear. You will defeat her as handily as you did all the others, I am certain."

David could not help but agree, yet the name Balton had a strange resonance. He had heard it before and connected to chess, he was sure, but where? Reluctant to make inquiries that might reveal his disquiet, David ate his meal as he searched his memory, scarcely tasting a morsel.

Around him, he could hear the quiet murmur of voices and the muffled thump of chess pieces being moved about the board. When recall yielded no clue, he decided that he had probed enough. Resolutely, he pushed the puzzle to the back of his mind, hoping that it would answer itself if left alone, as questions often did.

To distract himself, David wandered about the room, seeking comfort in the familiarity of the circle of chess aficionados whose company he had cultivated since his return to England. The "Pawn-pushers," as they were called by the other club members, had claimed this corner of White's, making it their own. Here, chess was paramount. As David passed, stopping to watch and comment, the gamesters looked up at him distractedly, favoring him with an occasional myopic smile as they listened to his opinions.

"But the game is not over, Petrov!" Freddy Dare's petulant protest elicited several demands for silence.

"We finish tomorrow." Petrov handed David a piece of foolscap. "Lord Donhill will be noting the position of the pieces for us. I am due at Harwell Ball."

"A bloody ball?" His partner proclaimed in disbelief. "But we are in the midst of a game of chess!"

"If you are not liking it, I concede," Petrov growled, tipping his king to the board before sweeping a farewell bow. "There are being more important things than chess, Freddy. An angel awaits. Goodnight."

The young man stared after the retreating Russian as if he had uttered a blasphemy. "Have you ever heard the like, Lord Donhill?" he asked. "What has come over Mr. Petrov, for I have never known him to leave when there is a game in progress? For a woman?"

"I believe it is a malady that strikes without rhyme or reason," David said morosely, knowing that Ivan was determined to woo Caroline. Little doubt that Sylvia would be at Harwell's as well.

As he waited for a servant to bring pen and ink, he had half a mind to follow his friend. Yet, what could he tell Sylvia? There was no news regarding her fortune. He reviewed the words of Sir Miles' puzzle yet again, but they sounded like a senseless litany in his mind.

He could not bring himself to face her, to see her eyes ask that silent question only to witness the death of her hopes yet again. He could not watch old Entshaw eyeing Sylvia with a possessive air as he bumbled with her across the floor. Mrs. Gabriel was gloating openly over the elderly lord's interest and David cursed himself roundly for his interference, ruing the day that he had agreed to Brummel's ill-conceived scheme. Because of their meddling, Sylvia might be forced to become an old man's Abishag. David listened with half an ear as young Freddy droned on about Petrov's foolishness.

"I hope I shall never be stricken by love," Freddy said devoutly. "Damme if I ever quit in the midst of a game for a petticoat."

"I shall take Ivan's place, if you like," David offered, hoping that the game would distract him from his melancholy thoughts. The young man nodded eager agreement and David slipped into the vacant seat. He moved mechanically, with only a fraction of his attention on the board, yet countering his opponent with ridiculous ease. The late Sir Miles' rhyme echoed in his head. "Yea, dance with a fool. . ." And play with a fool,

David thought glumly as Freddy moved his bishop into an obvious trap.

Lord Roberts headed for the door. "Leaving so soon, Roberts?" David asked. "I had hoped for a game later."

"Another night, perhaps," Lord Roberts said. "I promised my wife that I would look in on the Harwell Ball. Launching a daughter this Season, y'know," he added with a proud smile. "A fine gel. Does her mama proud."

"Shame how the fellow is in his wife's pocket. A quarter-century of servitude, if you can imagine! He's been married that long, y'know." Freddy grumbled as he watched the older man leave. "You're lucky indeed, milord, that you'll never be under petticoat government. I have half a mind to match your wager."

Freddy looked at David with an expression approaching reverence and David felt a trifle uneasy under the young man's worshipping gaze.

"Before you issue the challenge, Freddy, I suggest you improve your game or you will quickly find yourself wed," David declared, moving his bishop across the board to take Freddy's bishop and trap the king. "*Échec et mat*, I believe."

"My word, mate it is!" Freddy declared. "I had not seen that coming at all. Is that one of Philador's gambits? Can you explain it to me, sir?"

"Gabriel's," David said as he rose, suddenly eager to put as much distance as possible between himself and his young acolyte. "I shall show you the principles, but another time perhaps."

David scanned the tables, but there were few other pawn-pushers present. The more mature players, like Lord Roberts, had long ago taken their leave seeking the comforts of home and hearth or the demands of other interests. David felt a twinge of envy as he recalled the older man's obvious pride in his wife and daughter, his touching eagerness to be at their side.

The remnants in the room were of an age with Freddy, mere striplings, most with intellects as wooden as the chess pieces they played. Most came to this corner of White's because chess had suddenly become fashionable. With any luck, on the morrow they would more than likely flutter off elsewhere, hovering about the next newest, modish pursuit. Their immature faces were vapid, childishly eager. One or two callow youths even sported spectacles in imitation of himself, David realized in dismay and amusement.

"Ah, Brummel!" David latched on to his passing friend in relief. "Are you off now?"

"To Harwell's Ball," the Beau nodded.

"I shall join you," David declared, rolling his eyes in Freddy's direction.

"Of course," George agreed, understanding at once, staring significantly at Freddy to let David know that stripling worship was uncommonly tiresome.

"We shall stop at my apartments, if you do not mind," David said, looking down at his rumpled clothes. "I cannot attend in such a state, do you not agree?"

For once, the Beau was nonplussed.

...

"HE IS STARING AGAIN, CARO," Sylvia whispered between clenched teeth. She tried to fix a smile on her lips as she gazed out upon the sea of faces, conscious of her aunt's eyes upon her. Mrs. Gabriel hovered nearby, watching her niece's every expression and gesture, waiting for some gaffe that she might criticize. Sylvia attempted to change the direction of her thoughts, telling herself that she was being foolish. The Harwell Ball was a crush, with people so closely packed that there was barely room to raise an elbow. Yet, even though she could not see him, Sylvia felt as if an insect was creeping upon her skin and knew that somewhere, Hugo was watching.

"You imagine it, coz," Caroline said, shielding her face with the flutter of her fan. "Highslip has been all that is proper these days past, hoping to turn me up sweet. Besides, if staring was a crime, I suspect that half the men in the room would be bound for gaol. You look lovely, Syl."

Indeed, the mediocre modistes had outdone themselves. Sylvia's gown shimmered when she moved, as panels of silver cloth revealed themselves amidst folds of pure white samite. When the pattern had been planned, Sylvia had thought that the irregular gussets necessitated by the imperfections of the fabric would make her look like a tatterdemalion. Instead, the design gave the impression of continuous motion, as if the dress had a life of its own. By contrast, the burnished metallic gleam of the bodice made the halo of her golden hair seem like a flame alight amidst the glow of the tapers that lit the room.

There was no jealousy in Caroline's compliment, for she was looking across the floor as if the gate to Heaven itself had opened. Ivan Petrov had walked in the door. As the Russian crossed the room, Sylvia could see from the look in his eyes, that her cousin was the only woman he saw.

"Miss Gabriel," he said, bowing over Caroline's hand.

Although his voice was punctiliously formal, Sylvia heard the caress in its rich overtones, saw his reluctance as he relinquished her cousin's hand and felt a moment of envy.

"I do not see Lord Donhill," Sylvia attempted a teasing tone to cover her foolish disappointment. "I had thought the two of you came as a set."

"He was being engaged in a chess game, Miss Gabriel," Ivan said, exchanging a knowing glance with Caroline, who nodded ever so slightly. "I am sorry."

His look was one of abject sympathy and Sylvia realized that she was failing miserably at hiding her feelings. She took shelter in anger.

"Of course," Sylvia said, bile rising in her throat. "A chess game." She had no right to be annoyed. David had not promised his presence but somehow, she had expected it. Thus far, he had been at hand at nearly every entertainment that the Gabriels had attended, smoothing over the awkwardness that she felt, rescuing her from the hands of those whose intentions were insincere and attentions were too warm, distracting the boring Lord Entshaw or the ardent Mr. Colber.

"Where is dear Lord Entshaw?" Mrs. Gabriel asked Petrov, as if he had caused the elderly peer's absence.

Petrov shrugged. "I have not been seeing him since this afternoon at your parlor," he declared.

"You did promise him the first dance when he called this afternoon, Sylvia?" The matron's reminder was more of a threat than a question.

Sylvia nodded weakly. Her aunt had made her feelings on the matter explicitly known. Sylvia's subtle effort to discourage Entshaw's attentions had not gone unnoticed. She was to make every attempt to bring him up to scratch. Or else! The dire promise in Aunt Ruby's eyes had made Sylvia shiver.

"Are you talking of old Entshaw?"

The sound of Hugo's voice so close nearly caused Sylvia to jump.

"Poor old Entshaw," Lord Highslip drawled. "I am surprised you did not hear of it. A terrible accident, but then, the old fool was never known to have a skilled hand at the reins."

Mrs. Gabriel went pale at this talk of Sylvia's suitor in past tense. "Is he . . . d . . de," she stuttered unable to utter the final word.

"Thankfully, he was not killed," Highslip said, patting the matron's hand comfortingly. "Although, I doubt that he will be dancing for some time to come. Lord Entshaw's injuries were severe."

"That is grievous news," Brummel said, having caught Highslip's last few words. "I saw Entshaw only this afternoon at White's. An accident?"

Highslip nodded gravely. "That high perch phaeton he drove like a madman. A phaeton much like that owned by our Lord Donhill."

There was something in Hugo's tone that was disturbing and Sylvia would have brushed it off as another of her imaginings had she not caught the venomous look that Hugo directed toward the doorway. David's gaze swept the room, lighting upon her in an instant. His hand unconsciously strayed to his neckcloth, setting it askew in an effort to smooth the linen.

Sylvia could not help but smile at the boyish gesture. As he crossed the floor towards her, she could read a promise in his face, an assurance that was almost as real as a comforting hand upon the shoulder. There was nothing to fear now that he had come. Sylvia gave herself a mental shake. She was being unconscionably foolish, yet David's very presence bolstered her courage. Even Hugo was endurable, now that David was near.

Sylvia reminded David of a wild creature, trapped and afraid. Those wide green eyes spoke to him silently with a message that was part plea, part warning. The fingers that touched his in brief greeting were chill, but he did not allow his grasp to linger beyond propriety as he longed to, aware of Mrs. Gabriel's icy gaze.

"We were just talking of Lord Entshaw's terrible accident," Mrs. Gabriel said pointedly.

"Yes, I heard of it in the entry. 'Tis hard to credit. Entshaw was an excellent whip," David said.

"You own a phaeton," Mrs. Gabriel said reproachfully.

"I do," David acknowledged, feeling much as if he were being accused of some unspeakable crime. Mrs. Gabriel glared at him in annoyance as if he were somehow responsible for the fashion for phaetons and Lord Entshaw's wreck.

"Inherently unstable vehicles," Highslip pronounced. "I would not own one."

"Even could you afford one?" David asked, sotto voce to Sylvia, and was gratified to see a twitch of her lips, though she tried not to smile. Her pallor alarmed him. "How foolish of Lord Entshaw to involve himself in an accident," David declared aloud, "for now he must forgo his dance with you Miss Gabriel. If I might claim the privilege?"

Before her aunt could protest, he had whisked Sylvia off in the direction of the floor, but they skirted the dancers and went toward the open terrace doors beyond.

"I should not," Sylvia murmured, knowing that her aunt would not approve.

"You could use the air," David urged quietly. "It is far too close in here and you look pale as a ghost."

"Why thank you for the compliment, milord," Sylvia said, stepping gratefully out onto the terrace. She breathed deeply, trying to calm the frantic beat of her heart. "Poor Lord Entshaw." She spoke softly, moving away from the door and into the shadows. "'Tis reprehensible of me, I know, but all I can feel is blessed relief."

David said nothing, sensing her need for silence. Sylvia looked toward the night sky, her profile silhouetted against the darkness with the classic beauty of a Greek statue.

"What am I becoming, David?" she whispered. "How can I feel this way when a man has nearly met his death?"

She drooped like a wilting flower, her head bent in shame as she spoke in self-loathing. It surprised David that she should feel so, considering that Entshaw's suit had been nothing but a plague to her, but her fine sensibility touched him. Sylvia presented an adamantine aspect to the world, seeking protection behind the shield of cold indifference, much as he did himself. Yet, behind that marble exterior was a compassionate woman that she allowed but a privileged few to know. That core of vulnerability intrigued him, creating an emotional need to protect, to shelter her from further harm.

"Was your aunt pressing you that badly?" David asked. Her face was fully composed, only her lack of color and a slight quiver of her lower lip betrayed the extent of her agitation.

Sylvia leaned against the balustrade at the end of the terrace. "I used to think that I was strong enough to withstand anything, but Aunt Ruby is like water upon a stone, wearing me away bit by bit. I was beginning to fear that eventually I would agree to anything to be rid of that constant whine."

By the glow of moonlight, he was relieved to see that the color was returning to her cheeks. As she turned to him, he caught his breath. This was no statue, but a woman of flesh and blood.

David tried to halt the direction of his thoughts as

the desire to defend her turned into another type of passion. He knew that he had no right. No right to touch that soft skin, no right to yearn to hold her or for that matter, any other woman of gentle birth.

In assuring his freedom from entanglement, he had bound himself in the ropes of a despicable dilemma. There had never been any allowance in his life's strategy for a woman. His parents and his experiences with women had always posed a series of clear object lessons against the wedded state. It had seemed more than reasonable to make his position unassailable.

In doing so, he had put that possibility of marriage beyond his reach. Now that he realized that a husband was the only honorable defense for a female in Sylvia's exposed circumstance, he could not offer her that option, even if he wished. He had never reneged on a wager in his life.

A tear, limned in silver light, slid silently down her cheek and without thought, his hand reached out to brush it away.

"I am sorry," he whispered, the phrase seeming woefully inadequate. The feel of that warm skin melted his effort at control. He struggled, grasping desperately for his hold upon honor, but principle was a poor dam against an overwhelming tide of desire.

Sylvia felt the touch of his fingers, sliding gently on her cheek. She trembled within as she looked into his eyes, trying to read those pools of darkness. There was far more in his words than a mere apology. Was he sorry for her? Sorry for himself? She could not bring herself to ask, but closed her eyes, savored the sensation as he traced a line in her tears, prayed that he would forget himself for just a moment.

Does he feel more than friendship? She wondered. *Does he feel this strange awareness, as if something wonderful and frightening is about to happen?* Although she could not see him, she was conscious of his closeness. The sounds of the ballroom became distant echoes, mere background to the tempo of his breath as she felt it on her face.

"I am sorry," he murmured, as his lips touched hers. In a magical instant, the gentle kiss deepened as he gathered her to him, holding her against him as he buried his fingers in the silk of her hair.

She heard his heart beating, felt the steady pulse on his neck as her hands twined round him. His scent mingled with the smell of lilacs from the garden and the clean linen that pressed against her chin as he leaned down to kiss her once more. It was foolish to allow this, unconscionably foolish, but the move once made, could not be taken back. She had crossed over some invisible boundary into a realm of wonder.

Love, she put a name to her feelings at last, weeping with the joy of discovery. Her thoughts whirled giddily. If she told him that she had already trounced him on the chessboard, surely the terms of his wager would be satisfied. If he loved her, it would be so easy. If he loved her...

It was the salty taste of her tears that recalled him, requiring all his strength of will to step back. As he watched, her trembling hand reach up to touch her lips in a bewildered gesture, he wanted desperately to gather her in his arms once again, but his conscience would not allow it. "I am sorry," he whispered. "I did not mean to let it get out of hand. It will not happen again."

Opening her eyes once more, Sylvia felt the ache of disappointment. His demeanor was one of concern and guilt. From his words, it seemed likely that his kiss had been little more than an offer of comfort that had gone awry, not a token of love.

Sylvia had been kissed before. Yet, even when she

had been all but affianced to Highslip, she had never yielded herself so wholly. She turned away, leaning on the stone rail for support as she composed herself, an inner voice chiding for letting him slip past her defenses. Only a green girl would have been so swept away by a simple kiss. But, in truth, she knew that there had been nothing simple about that kiss, at least for her.

When she turned back to faced him, her expression was a smiling mask. Once again, Uncle Miles' training stood her in good stead. Not by so much as a quiver did she betray the depths of her disappointment and hurt, although her thoughts were gyring round like a child's whirligig top. There was little point in telling him now. As young Miles had often pointed out, David would likely feel honor-bound to marry her and she had no wish to bind him with honor if she could not win him with love. She moved away, making an effort at banter.

"I have ruined your neckcloth, David," Sylvia said, attempting a smile. "'Tis a shame, for it was nearly perfect."

"Brummel would be pleased to hear you say so," David attempted to match her light tone, but his voice was husky. "Sylvia . . . I," he began tentatively.

"Do not try to explain," she said, softly, hoping that she could salvage something from this awful moment. "It would be foolish to fuss over the gesture of a friend."

David's face betrayed no emotion although her casual dismissal cut him deeply. His senses were still reeling. The sound of his own heartbeat was pulsing in his ears, yet she seemed utterly calm as she reached up to check the state of her coiffure. *Had it meant so little to her?*

Yet, as he regained control, David told himself that what he felt was pique. She had not dissolved into a quivering lump of lovelorn adoration. Nor had she made any claims or demands upon him, despite the fact that he had made a move outside the rules of the courtship game.

His impulsive action had very nearly spoiled the first real friendship that he had ever shared with a female. That would have been a shame indeed. Luckily, Sylvia seemed to have far more sense than he. She deserved far better than furtive embraces in the garden. Unfortunately, hide-in-the-corner kisses were all he could offer. It would be foolish beyond permission to play with fire. He ought to be glad that her heart was not involved.

In silence, David offered Sylvia his arm and they returned to the ballroom. To his annoyance, Highslip was waiting by the door. The dark look upon the earl's face caused David to wonder just how much Highslip had seen. Sylvia's grip tightened upon David's arm. She too, was obviously concerned.

"Your aunt was seeking you, Sylvia," Highslip said, his voice deceptively silky. "I shall return you to her."

"No need, Highslip. I shall bring her back," David said.

"Best straighten out your neckcloth first," Highslip said, his poisonous stare saying far more than his seemingly casual words. "Or better still, go and size up the competition."

"Competition?" Sylvia asked, seizing on the opportunity to distract Hugo.

"'Tis no secret," Highslip declared maliciously. "The chess master has been challenged by Lord Balton's daughter. She is here tonight, with her drunkard papa."

"Lady Helena?" Sylvia asked.

"The same." Highslip's lip curled. "Horace Greenvale's girl."

"Greenvale?" David asked, in growing concern. In years past, Greenvale had been almost as much of a legend in the world of chess as the great Philador. Now David knew why the title had been vaguely familiar, although he had been unable to connect it to the family title. Although he was confident in his skills, if Lady Helena was Horace Greenvale's daughter, she might be a force to be reckoned with.

"Poor Helena," Sylvia said, shaking her head sadly.

"Do not pity her yet," Highslip sneered. "Perhaps our David will finally meet his feminine Goliath?"

"If you recall the story, Hugo, it was Goliath who came away the loser in that encounter," Sylvia said, annoyance creeping into her voice. "Yes, I pity her, as I feel for all the sacrifices in this little wager game of yours, milords."

"No one forces these women to challenge me, Sylvia," David said, seeking to defend himself.

"Helena's father gambled away the family fortune on the chessboard, milord. You represent a hope that she cannot resist - a future, a husband, a home of her own," Sylvia persisted, understanding Helena totally because that longing echoed within her. "And doubtless the same was true for many of the others who have challenged you."

"You are being unfair," David countered, feeling uneasy as he recalled the countenances of the females who had faced him across the chessboard. Although their motives might have differed, it was much as Sylvia said. The women had all shared a common air of desperation. It was foolish, he told himself, absurd to feel compassion for those pathetic creatures and yet, he felt a sudden pity for Lady Helena.

Sylvia had made the woman into more than an opponent. Suddenly, Lord Balton's daughter had become a human being and that was dangerous. "I am taking the risk here," he said, reminding himself as much as Sylvia. "What if I lose and I am suddenly obliged to marry an utter stranger who wants only my title and fortune? It is not beyond the bounds of possibility."

"You *chose* to take this risk, even though you truly believed in your hubris that you hazarded nothing. It would be an object lesson, David," Sylvia said, softening, the thought of losing him to Helena Greenvale beyond bearing. "Someday, you might find yourself facing your nemesis, but I doubt she will be named Helena. The Greenvales have always relied too heavily on strong offense, neglecting their pawns. At least," she added quickly. "Uncle Miles always claimed so."

"I shall remember," David said, gravely. "I shall mind my pawns, Sylvia, I promise."

"Do mind your pawns," Highslip broke in with a sneer. "You had best be on your mettle, Donhill, else you shall find your perpetual bachelorhood ended by that whey-faced bluestocking. A terrible fate indeed. And if not her, there shall be another and yet another."

Highslip's mocking snigger seemed to follow David as he returned Sylvia to her aunt's side.

"Mr. Colber has been waiting, Sylvia," Mrs. Gabriel scolded. "You had promised him the next dance." The matron all but pushed her niece into the pudgy young man's arms and out toward the floor.

She flicked open her fan as she turned to face David. "As for you, Lord Donhill," she said, her low tones conversational, but her tiny pupils like chips of grey ice. "It is ill-done of you to trifle with Sylvia under the pretense of finding her treasure. As Lord Highslip has pointed out, you can only further ruin her chances."

Highslip! David caught the earl's eye and Highslip raised his glass in mock salute, smiling derisively.

"After all," Mrs. Gabriel continued. "What can you honorably offer, milord?"

"Nothing," David said, achingly aware that although Mrs. Gabriel's motives were less than pure, she spoke no less than the truth. "I have nothing to offer." He watched helplessly as Colber swept Sylvia away into the crowd of dancers.

...

Sylvia sat down wearily in the dark library of the house on Berkeley Square, sighing as she eased her feet out of their satin slippers. She rubbed her big toe, wincing at the ache. If clumsiness was a measure of infatuation, Mr. Colber was obviously head over heels and Sylvia had felt those heels for much of the two dances that he had claimed. As for head, Sylvia thought ruefully, Mr. Colber did not have much to recommend him above the shirt-points and if his purse was not included, there was precious little below the neck as well. Yet, Aunt Ruby had obviously decided that Colber was to replace Entshaw as the suitor designate. If Sylvia wanted any peace, she would have to play the game by Aunt Ruby's ever-changing rules.

Uncle Miles' mahogany chess set cast dark shadows in the moonlight from the window and Sylvia lifted a wooden pawn, feeling the familiar shape of the polished wood as she tried to recall all she could about the Greenvale style of play. Lord Balton's daughter would be no match for David, or would she? Was Helena playing the same game as Sylvia, concealing her intellect behind a socially acceptable front? If David were defeated by a stranger, a woman who did not love him, it would be the ultimate irony.

Sylvia stared out into the night, remembering the feel of his arms around her and she sighed. There was no longer any doubt in her mind; she loved him, and it was equally clear that he did not share her feelings. How embarrassed he must have been! Sylvia felt her face growing hot at the memory; to be seized by a

MISS GABRIEL'S GAMBIT

lovesick female when all he had aimed to do was console. He had left immediately after delivering her to Aunt Ruby. Whatever did he think of her now? How could he know that her feelings for him had been growing long before she had ever met him?

Through his letters, she had come to respect and admire David Rutherford and now, that very regard was an insurmountable obstacle. She knew that she could win him, yet she could not bring herself to challenge him, to force him into marriage. Tonight had only confirmed her resolution.

David's feelings towards his mercenary challengers were obvious. She had no wish to earn his contempt, or if she were to lose, his pity. Besides, she told herself, she had no wish to suffer as her mother had, to be forever second to knights and bishops, kings and rooks. But the very thought of losing him made her wonder if she was being the worst of fools. She threw the pawn to the floor, watching it skitter off into the shadows.

"Miss Sylvia?" Boniface's silhouette loomed in the door

Sylvia was glad of the dark, hoping that servant could not see the tears on her cheeks. "Yes, 'tis I, Boniface. I am afraid my feet were too tired to carry me up the stairs."

"I thought it was you, Miss, for your aunt and cousins rarely use the library. A letter arrived for you after you had left for Lady Harwell's Ball. Do you wish me to light a taper?"

"No, Boniface," Sylvia said, ruefully. "I have no wish to set my aunt to stewing. You know her policy about unnecessary use of candles. I shall read it upstairs."

Taking the envelope, Sylvia dragged herself up to the nursery. Young Miles was snoring away, and she pulled the cover to his chin and kissed him gently. As she bent, she noticed the kite and reel standing at the ready by the boy's bed and groaned softly. Tomorrow was Friday; she had promised him that they would go kite-flying. Miles had been talking of nothing else for a week, reminding her of her word in a child's less-than-subtle way. Sylvia knew that, in all likelihood, the boy would be bustling about at dawn's first light, "accidentally" waking her.

At best, she would get a scant few hours of sleep, she thought as she went to her room, sorely tempted to fall into bed. Instead, Sylvia forced herself to undo the endless row of buttons, regretfully thinking, as she finally placed the gown in the wardrobe, of the days when her maid had done such trivial tasks. As she sat down upon the bed, a faint crackle beneath her reminded her of the envelope that Boniface had given her. It bore the seal of her late uncle's man of law.

She opened it, only to find that the requested copy of the Will had been forwarded to David Rutherford. She crumpled the note, wavering between disappointment and dread. Once again, the reins of her fate had been transferred to another's hands. Yet, she knew that despite the evening's events, David would keep his word and continue the search for the Rajah's treasure. She would see him again. Sylvia fell asleep clutching the letter in her hands and David in her dreams.

CHAPTER 7

The cold vapor was as damp as the fog that rises from the Thames. It wrapped itself around him like a macabre lover, touching David with icy fingers. The mist-filled room was much like the one at White's, but utterly empty except for the gilt table and chairs holding the huge chessboard, the white squares inlaid with silver coins, the black with golden guineas. David knew that he was dreaming, yet that knowledge was no comfort against the nameless terror that waited in the shadows. He struggled against sleep but he was powerless against the phantasms of the night.

He seated himself as the mists stirred with the murmur of high-pitched voices; vague shapes filled the darkness until, as before, a woman took form. She took the chair opposite, her face hidden by the shroud of vapors. However much he tried he could not discern her face. In the darkness behind her the amorphous shadows whispered, their laughter like the sound of wind through trees in winter. He knew that they were laughing at him.

"Your move," the woman said, her voice rasping and harsh.

"Your move. Your move!" The wraiths whispered like the chorus in a Greek play.

David examined the board carefully and took the obvious opening. "Check and mate," he declared triumphantly, attempting to move his queen, but the queen was stuck fast to the board.

"You cannot move the queen," the woman said, malice in her voice.

"That is unfair," David said.

"Unfair! Unfair!" The ghostly women echoed, but they chided him, not her.

"You lose, milord," the challenger sneered, her face taking shape at last. It was Mrs. Gabriel, her florid face reddening as she poked him with an iron finger. "You shall marry me."

"Marry me. Marry me. Marry me," repeated the voices.

"I shall not," David said, attempting to rise and leave as he had in previous dreams, but to his horror he found that he was chained to the board. "You have cheated."

"I concede," Mrs. Gabriel laughed. "But if you will not have me, then you shall play us all, milord."

"Play us all. Play us all. Play us all . . ." The faceless figures crowded towards him, reaching, laughing mockingly. "Play us all. Play us all."

The words reverberated in David's ears as he sat bolt upright in a tangle of sheets. The substance of the dream faded into a jumble of chessboards and ghosts, but the aura of fear remained as palpable as the clammy sheen of sweat upon his chest. He breathed slowly, deeply; fumbling for his glasses, praying that they would return the world to its proper perspective. With the spectacles in place, David focused on the reality of the morning sunlight that streamed through the gaps in the draperies until his heart stopped galloping.

"Ah, I thought that I heard you stirring," Harjit said, as he peered into the room, frowning at the sight of David's weary, pale countenance. "You slept poorly again."

"I have had more restful nights," David admitted, stretching his aching limbs as he rose to perform his morning ablutions. "This time, Mrs. Gabriel appeared, if you would believe it." He shuddered at the memory.

"That one is enough to terrify the most stalwart of men. It is no wonder that you cried out in your sleep," Harjit observed, shaking his head. "These dreams have plagued you every night this week past. Perhaps you should consult a soothsayer?"

David gave a short bark of laughter. "I need no soothsayer to tell me the source of my dreams, Harjit. What I need is coffee…dark, strong coffee." As the Sikh left to do David's bidding, the sense of foreboding returned, a piece of the night's horror creeping about in the daylight. The images had been clearer than those in any of his previous nightmares.

It was the Greenvale girl, of course, David decided as he poured water into the china basin upon a stand near the bed. For the first time, he was being faced by a female who might present something of a challenge. Even so, he had confronted far greater hurdles before and they had never disturbed his sleep. Some unknown danger lurked in those shadows, far stronger than any threat upon a chessboard, but the warnings were of no consequence until he could put a name to the threat.

By the time Harjit returned bearing a tray, David was wrapped in a robe and seated before the small table in the adjoining room.

"Ah, coffee, the brew of life's blood," David said, sniffing appreciatively. "I can almost feel my eyes opening."

Harjit poured the steaming liquid into the delicate

porcelain cup. "There was a messenger this morning." He picked up a silver salver with an envelope upon it. "You were waiting for papers."

David recognized the seal. "So, it would seem that even an ancient hand moves faster when greased by a few coins," he observed as he broke the wax.

"Even the gods themselves have been known to be propitiated by a judicious bribe," Harjit agreed. "I shall fetch your breakfast."

"The trick is knowing which god is playing with your fate," David mumbled to himself. "And whose palm is the proper one to grease." He skimmed through the document, jumping over the legal hedges with an ease born of long business experience until he reached the substance of the late Sir Miles' final bequests.

There were a myriad of small legacies to friends and retainers, even one to himself, "my teak-wood chessboard to my dear friend, David Rutherford of Bombay." Doubtless it had been sent to India and was even now, waiting in his home there.

As David read through the old man's last testament, he mourned the missed opportunity. David had fully intended to travel to Crown Beeches and meet Sir Miles once his business in London was completed. He had even carried the bundles of letters with him from India as material for mutual reminiscence.

His musings were disturbed by a knock at the door.

"Mr. Petrov," Harjit announced.

"Ivan? Before noon?" David asked incredulously, rising to greet his friend.

"I am to be needing your help, David," the Russian said, the increased mangling of his English pronunciation betraying his agitation. "I am to be meeting Caroline this morning and you must be coming alongside with mine self."

"Is this some strange Russian custom? To have a

friend accompany one upon an assignation with a lady?" David asked, teasing. "Here in England we usually conduct our *tête-à-têtes* by twos."

"Is why I am asking you," Petrov said. "Her cousin is being there with her. I am wishing you to protract Sylvia, so I can be talking with Caroline."

"Distract," David corrected. "You wish me to distract Sylvia."

"Is what I have been saying!" the Russian declared raising his voice in annoyance. "You detract Sylvia."

David chopped some sugar from the lump, staring into the cup as he stirred. The thought of facing Sylvia again so soon was almost unnerving. After he had left the Harwell Ball the previous evening, David had fully intended to follow Mrs. Gabriel's advice and keep his distance from her niece. Even in the cold logic of the light of day, the memory of last night's embrace still had the power to set his heart racing. Yet, despite the knowledge that he might be courting disaster, he wanted to see her. David slipped off his glasses, rubbing his eyes wearily.

"Maybe you could be talking to her about the treasure?" Petrov suggested, accepting Harjit's silent offer of coffee.

"And the damnable Will," David said, picking up the sheaf of papers. "I have it here and I fear, that there seems precious little new business to discuss."

"Nothing unusual?" Petrov asked.

"The baronet's bequests are all within the normal realm, the dispensation of trinkets and tokens mostly," he said, replacing his spectacles once again. "Gifts of money to old pensioners, a pianoforte to his niece Caroline..."

"She plays divinely," Petrov broke in.

"I am sure," David said acerbically, finding his place

in the document once again. "His chess library to . . . Sylvia? How odd. . ." David looked at his friend.

"Is being a clue, perhaps?" Petrov said, seizing eagerly on the excuse. "You must be asking."

"Very well, Ivan, I shall accompany you." David agreed, wondering if his friend had hit the mark. It certainly was an unusual legacy to bestow upon a female. "Harjit, has the new blue superfine jacket arrived from Weston?"

"No, it is expected this afternoon," the Sikh informed him.

David strode toward the wardrobe, pulling it open to stand before it.

"Where do we meet them, Ivan?" he asked, his head tilting in consideration as he eyed the array of clothing.

"Park," Ivan said. "They take the boy flying kite."

David recalled the scene in the nursery, Miles' towhead nestled on Sylvia's shoulder. " . . . you fly a kite better than any girl I know, don't cut up stiff at frogs neither," the boy had said. Well, David could only hope that she would not cut up stiff because of a moment of moonlit madness. Certainly, she had reacted well immediately after the previous night's kiss. So well, in fact, that it verged on the annoying.

"I shall wear the dove grey jacket," David decided, lifting the sleeve. "The trousers to match. Appropriate for an outing in the park. Don't you think?"

Petrov nearly dropped the cup of coffee that he carried, shaking his head in disbelief. "Highslip is making convert of you," he declared.

"I am merely following the terms of the wager," David declared loftily. "Highslip has nothing to do with it."

Petrov opened his mouth, started to reply, then sat down and turned his attention to the plate of pastries upon the table.

"What were you about to say?" David asked.

"Nothing that might be of helping to you," Petrov said. "Better not to touch a piece on the board if you are not having intent to move it."

. . .

Above Green Park, a puff of clouds scudded across a field of clear blue. The hour was still too early for the invasion of nannies, maids and children that was sure to come on such a fine spring day. Sylvia, Caroline and Miles had the field to themselves while a maid hovered discreetly in the background. The boy licked his finger and held it up to the wind to ascertain its direction as the tail of the kite lashed about, almost like that of a living creature.

"You see, Syl," Miles called exulting. "Look! Like a bird, I almost have to keep it from flying. It's the best kite we ever made."

"It surely is," Sylvia said, stifling a yawn as she watched the painted diamond shape dance against the boy's hold.

"Why don't you hold the kite up, Caro," Miles suggested, noticing his cousin's weariness "I'll run into the wind with it."

"I think not," Caroline said, seating herself beneath a tree. "It might disarrange my hair."

Miles threw his sister an exasperated look. "Why did you come anyway?" he asked.

"Give it here, Miles," Sylvia intervened, although she would have liked to hear the answer to the question. Caro's sudden taste for fresh air was not the least bit believable. "She would just tree it anyway," she whispered, taking the kite from the boy.

Miles grinned in agreement as he let out line and waited for the breeze.

"Now!" he shouted.

His pudgy legs pumped as he ran into the breeze, pulling the string while he looked over his shoulder at the kite. Sylvia watched as he raced across the field, the kite weaving and dipping behind him. It was lifting but not high enough. All at once, it crashed to the ground.

"Bother!" he declared, winding in his reel as he went to examine the kite. Luckily, it was undamaged. "Can't get enough of a lift to it," he complained, panting with effort as Sylvia came up beside him. Caro's laughter came floating across the field. "Like to see her get it flying!"

Sylvia looked at the boy in sympathy. Miles looked spent and bereft. "Shall I give it a try?" she asked.

"You didn't get much sleep last night," Miles observed guiltily.

"I could use the run," Sylvia said, realizing that it was true. The restless energy within her needed some release. She was tired of keeping herself constantly under tight rein. In the small world of the Ton, it was as if she were forever on exhibition, every move watched, every expression analyzed, every utterance assessed. Now that she knew herself to be in love with David, she needed to be especially wary of her words. She could not let him know the true depth of her feelings.

"You are a prime goer, Syl!" Miles declared, picking up the kite and holding it aloft.

Sylvia gathered up her skirt, holding the reel in her other hand as she ran into the wind.

"Faster, Syl!" Miles called. "The wind's catching it. Let out some rope!"

She tugged against the resistance, paying out more line as the diamond of wood and paper began to sail aloft. Miles shouted behind her and she looked over her shoulder to see the boy jumping up and down, pointing excitedly. Even though the kite was well over the trees, she did not want to stop running, savoring the sheer joy of unfettered motion, the feel of her blood pounding in her ears, the warmth of the sun upon her cheeks. Sylvia flew across the open space, heedless of any would-be watchers.

...

DAVID STOOD at the edge of the field, thinking that he had never seen Sylvia more beautiful. Her hair came loose from its mooring pins, streaming out behind her like a cloud of golden gossamer, shimmering in the spring sunlight. Upon her face was an expression of wonder, a smile of elation that had little resemblance to the social barricade of polite nonchalance she wore of late. The cold wall of unapproachability had utterly crumbled.

The kite sailed above her, miming her motion. Sylvia skipped, jumped and cavorted across the field, her joyous dance much like the prancing of a long-stabled filly let out into pasture after a hard, cold winter.

"Look, Lord Donhill! Look how high we got it!" Miles called.

Sylvia whirled in her tracks. Lord Donhill? What in the world? She saw Mr. Petrov standing near the tree where her cousin sat and knew at once why Caroline had risen at an unheard of hour to come kite-flying. Her aunt would be furious if she found out about this assignation and Sylvia had little doubt upon whose head the blame would fall.

David was smiling at her, probably holding back his amusement at her appearance. Sylvia suddenly blushed to realize the picture that she must present. Her hair had come all unpinned and was falling about her shoulders in a mane. The faded blue dress that she wore was one of her oldest garments, not even fit to give the servants but hitherto perfectly suitable for the rigors of kite-flying. She must look a veritable Gypsy, she thought as she handed the line to Miles. The prospect of wringing her cousin's neck was at the fore of her mind as she walked toward them.

Her murderous expression must have been obvious. "Sylvia," Caroline said, flushing with poorly acted innocence, "who would believe that Mr. Petrov would find us here?"

"Only an utter flat," Sylvia said, refusing to play the game of pretense. "Oh, Caro, whatever will your mama say should she find out about this?"

"Daisy will not tell," said Caroline, gesturing toward the maid. "Neither will Miles. For all his fits and starts, my brother is no tell-tale. That leaves only you, Syl."

"I am not being fond of deceiving either," Mr. Petrov said solemnly. "But your aunt is meaning to force Lord Highslip on your cousin. Do you wish this?"

Sylvia's countenance had become closed once more. "No," she said, softly. "I would not want you to marry Hugo, Caro."

The expression in her eyes betrayed something of her inner turmoil and David wondered if it was entirely for her cousin's sake that Sylvia agreed to assist in foiling her aunt's plans. There was an adamant quality to her words, as if she would move the very earth to prevent Hugo's proposal.

"Oh thank you, Syl," Caroline said, hugging her cousin close. "I knew that I might depend on you."

"You have mine thanks, as well, Sylvia," Petrov said, bowing in acknowledgement. "And now, we must talk, Caroline and I."

"I think we are being dismissed," David said. "Shall we go help Miles with the kite?"

As she fell into step beside David, Sylvia tried to calm the tempest of emotion within. His very proximity was enough to send her soaring like Miles' kite, to rise and fall with the currents of his looks, his words. It was unforgivably dangerous, to allow herself to be swept away like this, to fly upon the memory of last night's moment, stolen in the darkness. But it was like trying to quell the wind. She watched Caroline and her beau enviously, vowing that she would not allow Hugo to destroy her cousin's happiness. "I will not let Hugo have her," she said, half to herself.

Sylvia's words were quiet, but they had the force of an oath, throwing David into confusion. Was it was possible that Sylvia still desired the earl for herself? Certainly, it was no business of his if she wished to wear the willow for that conceited fop! Yet, the thought that she might be unable to see beyond Highslip's handsome, stylish veneer was curiously irksome.

Over the years, David had come to consider himself something of a shrewd judge of character and he knew that there was an undercurrent of malice in the earl. Highslip exhibited a true malevolence that manifested itself in that wicked tongue of his. He would never marry Sylvia, not without her fortune to line his pockets. Fortune . . . David's attention focused back upon that blasted Will. What if the chess library held the key? It would certainly give her the means to marry Highslip.

"I am told you received a copy of the Will?" Sylvia ventured. "Did you get a chance to study it?"

It was almost as if she could read his mind. David nodded. "I read it through briefly," he admitted, his native integrity warring with his desire to spare her from Highslip.

"Anything that struck you as unusual?" she asked, hope in her eyes.

David's sense of honesty won. "The bequest of the chess library," he said, reluctantly. "That seemed most peculiar to me. Do you think it might be a clue, Sylvia? Why else leave a chess library to a female?"

Why, indeed? Sylvia thought, scrambling for a logical explanation for her uncle's disposition of his most treasured possession. "My brother William is terribly careless with books," she lied. "And some of Uncle's volumes were quite valuable. I suppose that he trusted me to take care of them properly." She prayed that he would accept her ploy.

"I admit that I, too, had thought the books might contain a clue when I initially heard the bequest. I went through every one of the volumes thoroughly at Crown Beeches and in the small part of the collection that is here when we arrived in Town. I found nothing then."

"Then it seems we are back to *point non plus*," David said glumly.

"However," Sylvia added, "I did remember something that I found in my search that might be of some use to you. Uncle wrote down the details of almost every game that he ever played. In his youth, I believe, he played Horace Greenvale most frequently. If Lady Helena's manner of play is in any way like her father's, Uncle's playbook could be of help to you. I shall loan it, if you would wish."

Sylvia avoided his eyes, afraid that he would discern the truth. It was utter selfishness that had prompted the offer of the book; the fear of losing him to Helena Greenvale. She wanted him to win, as much for her sake as for his. It was a foolish hope, she knew, but if given time he might come to care for her. At that point, she would reveal her chess-playing skill so that she might release him from his wager. But, until that unlikely time, she did not dare reveal her feelings else the fragile friendship between them might be broken. That was to be avoided at all cost, for it would be more than she could bear to lose him completely.

David berated himself. She was offering him her help in retaining his freedom, yet all he could feel was a profound sense of relief that her fortune remained lost. As long as she was poor, she was safe from Highslip. "Thank you, Sylvia, I would appreciate the book," David said, sensing her discomfort. "That is extremely thoughtful of you." He hesitated, but moved forward, determined to dispel the growing uneasiness.

"Sylvia, about what occurred . . ." he began.

"There is no need," she murmured.

"Oh yes, there is," David asserted. "I would not have it hanging here between us. We were friends, I would have us remain so."

"We still are friends, David," she said focusing upon Miles' kite. She would not cry. She would not let him know that kiss had completely undone her. Before he had held her in his arms, she had been able to lie to herself, to half-convince herself that she was not in love with him. Now, there was no denial, only profound pain.

"I am sorry," David said. "Doubtless, I am not the first man who has ever made a fool of himself because of your beauty."

Fool. The word made itself heard above the others. He counted the kiss an act of foolishness, prompted entirely by her looks. She was glad that he found her attractive and yet, perversely, she cursed her own beauty. In a strange way, he had not really kissed Sylvia Gabriel at all, just her shell, the chimera of her appearance. He thought of her in the same way that one would a lovely painting or an excellent sculpture. One might admire a work of art but it was foolish to kiss it.

"Oh no, milord," Sylvia said taking refuge in ridicule. "You are certainly not the only one who has made a cake of himself over me, by no means. I would not stoop to compare your kiss with the myriads of others that I received."

In some contrary way, her assertion was in no manner comforting to David. He removed his glasses taking comfort in the familiar motions of cleaning the lenses. The thought that he was but one among many who had tasted her lips was almost a shock. There had seemed to be an inherent innocence to her kiss, a delight that sprang from new experience.

"Although I lived in the country, milord, I was no hermit. Uncle saw to it that I attended the usual run of balls and dinners," Sylvia asserted, running on when she noticed that David had so forgotten himself that he was, once again, using his neckcloth as a wipe for his spectacles. "I have had odes written to my eyelashes, sonnets to my earlobes and rhymed couplets, if you would believe, to my nostrils. Why, one young man even composed an epic to my entire anatomy. Mere speculation, of course."

"Of course," David agreed weakly.

His countenance became a pattern-card of consternation and her sense of the ridiculous took control. "The recital took an entire afternoon. It began *'Oh, divine left toe were I thee,'*" she intoned. All of a sudden it all became too much and she began to sputter, trying to hold the laughter at bay.

A choking noise disrupted the morose direction of David's thoughts. He returned his glasses to his nose and realized that Sylvia was nearly overcome, trying to stifle her amusement.

"Myriad's, eh?" he shook his head at himself, wondering why he was behaving with such total irrationality. What did it matter to him how many men might have kissed her? "Epics?"

"If you could but have seen your face, David!" Sylvia let go in a gale of mirth, allowing her tears to masquerade under the cover of amusement.

David too, began to chuckle, trying to cover his own confusion, wondering at his own pain as she dismissed the entire episode, made light of it. Surely, that was what he had desired, wasn't it? He nearly jumped when a voice asked from nearby.

"What's so funny?" Miles queried, playing the kite on the breeze.

Neither of them had noticed that the boy had moved closer.

"Nothing youngling," Sylvia giggled.

"Awful lot of fuss for nothing, if you ask me," Miles grumbled, moving across the open field to guide the kite away from the treetops.

"He is right, you know," David said. "It is a lot of fuss about nothing. Pax?" he asked, offering his hand.

"Pax," Sylvia agreed, putting her palm in his, enjoying the grasp of his strong fingers as they shook hands with the mock solemnity of two children. She squinted up at the kite and allowed the tears caused by David's new avowal to mingle with the old. Nothing. He accounted that kiss as nothing. The flame of hope was flickering low indeed.

"Did you find anything else of interest in the copy you received?" she asked, moving the conversation from the dangerous topic of the previous evening.

"I had not known that your Uncle had left me a chess set," David said.

"Unfortunately, due to the sorry state of affairs after Uncle's death, I was unable to have it sent off until several months had passed," Sylvia said, bending down to pull a blade of grass and twisting it distractedly in her fingers. "There was much debate over the clause in Uncle's last instructions forbidding mourning."

"I would imagine so," David said. "Apparently, your aunt was willing to sustain a serious financial loss rather than defy the proprieties and forgo the usual period of bereavement. Your uncle left a substantial amount of money to finance your debut with Caroline's."

"But that money was hers only if Aunt Ruby repaired to London immediately after Uncle's death," Sylvia said. "She had no desire to eschew proper decorum for my benefit and risk Caroline's chances. It didn't matter to me really, because at that point I did not give a fig for a London Season. The money went to charity instead."

"Obviously, Sir Miles wished you to go to town right away," David said. "He offered considerable incentive, but why?"

Sylvia was unable to keep the bitterness from her voice. "Why, indeed! 'Tis a question that I ask quite often. Uncle Miles disliked Hugo from the start. 'Twas the only thing we ever quarreled over. Uncle knew that I would have control over my father's fortune within the year. I am sure he feared that the state of his health would not give him time to attempt to change my mind. His testament dates just before he fell into his final illness. Hugo urged me to marry him when Uncle was too much out of his mind to naysay us, but I would not leave Uncle Miles."

She stared up at the kite, trying to find the right words.

"Hugo was the one man who did not seem intimidated by my looks, you see," Sylvia added, feeling a need to explain her attraction to the earl. "He was so handsome himself. He was utterly devoted to me, polite, considerate, seemingly all that one would wish in a husband. He listened to me, David. Hugo was the first man who actually accounted that I might have more wit than a child's wax doll."

Yet, she realized, she had never trusted him with her innermost thoughts. Hugo had not even known that she played chess, for she had felt that he might disapprove. There was always some part of her that had held back, waiting, until David had kissed her.

"Lord Donhill, Syl, look!" Miles called

The two watched as the boy played the line expertly, causing the kite to swoop and sway like a gaudy bird. Higher and higher it flew, pulling the length of string to the limit. Then, suddenly a gust of wind came, bending the crowns of the trees with its force, almost tugging the reel from Miles' hand. The boy held fast, desperately trying to pull back against the force of the billowing breeze until the taut line snapped and the kite sailed away free, carried aloft over the park and out of sight. The child watched with a bereft expression as it disappeared; the now-empty looping line fell from above.

Sylvia and David hurried to the boy's side. Caroline and Ivan too, saw the mishap and abandoned their conversation.

"Oh Miles, I am so sorry," Sylvia said, taking the reel from Miles' fingers and winding in the string. She put her hand on the boy's shoulder as he manfully struggled against tears. "We shall build a new kite," Sylvia promised, touching the boy's shoulder.

"No, we won't," Miles said, his lower lip trembling. "You don't have time for nothing no more, not even lessons. Mama says that you are going to marry that snuffy old Lord Entshaw or that other dumpling of a fellow and go far away to live and I won't see you hardly ever."

"That is not true, Miles," Sylvia said. "I shall marry

neither Lord Entshaw nor that other dumpling of a fellow. Remember, I am pledged to you."

"Truly?" Miles asked, brightening.

"Truly," Sylvia declared, solemnly. "As for the kite, youngling, I shall find the time."

"Miles, can you not see how tired Sylvia is?" Caroline declared, glaring at her brother. "Mama is running her ragged planning my ball and you wish her to exhaust herself over your silly kite?"

"I'm sorry, Syl," Miles said contritely. "We ain't been flying much anyway. Don't trouble yourself about it."

"We shall start on it immediately once we get home, never you fear," Sylvia said, looking significantly at Caroline.

"Perhaps we should be getting back," Caroline said reluctantly. "Mr. Colber is due to call upon Sylvia this afternoon and Mama wished us to return early."

"Your mother is truly entertaining that mushroom's suit?" David said, incredulously.

"Aunt Ruby would serve tea to the devil himself, were she convinced that he was sufficiently warm in the pocket," Sylvia said.

"Is not the title she is being concerned with?" Petrov questioned anxiously. "Entshaw is lord, a peer."

"No," Sylvia said. "Although rank is certainly a consideration, I believe that lucre is her primary love."

A smile stretching across Petrov's lean face. "Is most wonderful news, Miss Gabriel," he declared. "Wonderful!"

"Whatever do you mean, Ivan?" Caroline asked. "I had thought that you were poor as a church-mouse."

"And still you love me, my sweet." There was worship in Petrov's eyes. "But poor, I am not."

David began to laugh. "Something of an understatement, would you not say, Ivan?"

The Russian reddened, tugging at his collar as if it

had suddenly become too tight. "I do not know how to be saying this, Caro."

"Shall I?" David asked. Petrov nodded.

"Ivan is a partner in my business, Miss Gabriel," David said. "He just did not wish anyone to know that he had soiled his hands in trade. I believe his assets more than equal my own and I am considered something of a nabob."

Caroline looked at Ivan, her eyes wide with questions.

"Is true," Petrov said, his head bent in shame. "I do business. I roll in filthy money. Are you still loving me, Caro?"

"You Russian idiot!" she exploded. "Of course, I love you, even though you are rich."

Miles looked from his sister to Petrov, utterly baffled. "You are angry because he told you that he has money? Why?" he asked Caroline.

"Because Mr. Petrov concealed something of great importance," Caroline declared sniffing in high dudgeon.

"But you liked him without the money anyway," Miles said. "So why are you acting barmy?"

"Why, indeed?" David asked. "You are a lucky man, Ivan, to know that Miss Gabriel values you for yourself and not your fortune."

"Yes," Petrov said proudly. "The luckiest of men and now, there is to be no more meeting behind your mama's back, Caroline."

"Well, you should have trusted me," Caroline said, softening, unable to maintain her anger in the face of Petrov's happiness.

"In everything, my sweet," he murmured, taking her hand. "From now until forever."

David felt a stab of envy, watching the two exchanged whispered confidences as they walked together.

"I am so happy for them," Sylvia said. "I am sure that my aunt shall not oppose the match now."

Happy for them, or for yourself? David wondered. *Highslip is available once more.*

"Do people always act stupid when they're grown-up?" Miles asked, tugging at David's sleeve. He was panting, half-running to keep up with the stride of the adults.

"Sometimes," David said, slowing his pace, glad for the interruption of his direction of thought.

"I don't know if I want to grow up," Miles said.

"I am afraid you have no choice, m'boy," David said, hoisting the child onto his shoulders. "Unfortunately, some of us grow up later than others," he murmured to himself.

Miles squealed with delight. "Thank you, sir. This is famous! Almost as good as being up in a tree."

"David, your jacket!" Sylvia exclaimed. "'Tis all muddy now from Miles' boots."

"Why, so it is," David agreed, ruefully, "but my young friend here seemed a trifle worn from his tangle with the wind."

She looked at him, his hair tousled, the glasses sliding to the tip of his nose and the perfection of his cravat spattered with mud; and she laughed. "I almost believe I prefer you this way, David. Disorder suits you."

"As perfection suits Highslip?" David retorted, regretting his mention of Highslip almost at once. Sylvia's face became shuttered and she fell into a silence that lasted until he set Miles down and they parted at the park gate. David silently applauded his late chess partner for his bold final move. Although Sylvia seemed not to fully realize it, her uncle had shielded her from a fate far worse than poverty.

...

THAT AFTERNOON, in the parlor, Sylvia could scarcely keep her eyes open as the gilt clock ticked away the time. Her aunt refused to excuse her until Colber paid his promised call. Even the knowledge that Hugo was watching her in his usual surreptitious manner could not keep her from drowsing. The endless drone of gossip was surprisingly soporific. More than once, a jab of reminder from Caroline's elbow jerked Sylvia awake.

"Ah, Mr. Brummel," Mrs. Gabriel greeted the dandy with pleasure as he entered the room.

Sylvia roused herself to note that David and Mr. Petrov were both absent. Earlier, her Aunt had bluntly told Sylvia and her daughter that she would tolerate no deviation from the path down the aisle that she had determined for them both. Aunt Ruby had even outlined her conversation with David. Even though Sylvia was mortified, she tried to believe it might be for the best.

Brummel seated himself beside his hostess and began to converse in tones that were more confidential than customary.

"You do not say!" Mrs. Gabriel exclaimed. "A vast fortune?"

Sylvia sat upright with a start, jarred by her aunt's loud surprise.

"Rich as Croesus," Brummel assured the matron solemnly. "An inheritance is what I heard."

"Why Mr. Petrov is so modest," Mrs. Gabriel said, her timbre conveying more annoyance than approval. "And he is a nephew to a Grand Duke, you say?"

Sylvia smiled to herself, knowing that her Aunt was no doubt horrified that she had almost let that bird slip from her hands. In Aunt Ruby's social ledger a rich Russian who was socially well-connected was worth far more than an out-of-pocket earl.

"He does not noise about his connections or flash his blunt like some; Colber, for instance, poor devil was always waving his purse about. 'Tis that what got him into trouble I suppose," Brummel said.

"What trouble, Mr. Brummel?" Caroline asked.

"Surely, you have heard, Miss Gabriel," Brummel said. "Mr. Colber was set upon by thieves as he was leaving his club last night. They beat him severely, left him for dead. It is unknown if he will recover."

The room began to whirl as Sylvia looked into Hugo's eyes. There was a disturbing look of triumph in that hard blue gaze. It was absurd and yet, as she thought of Colber and Lord Entshaw's mysterious accident, a dreadful certainty rose within her. She remembered the horse that her uncle had purchased from Hugo's father so long ago.

Mrs. Gabriel gave a cry of dismay as Sylvia rose abruptly and excused herself. "The poor dear, she is quite overset, for Mr. Colber was most attentive to her," Mrs. Gabriel said.

Only Sylvia saw Hugo's smirk as she left the room.

CHAPTER 8

Lord Highslip sat before the bow window at White's staring out into the darkness of St. James Street. Brummel, Alvaney and their crowd were at Carlton House disporting themselves with Prinny, so Highslip could trespass upon the sacred spot with impunity. Those members of the club who considered rebuking him immediately thought it better to leave the earl be, especially when they saw the formidable expression upon his face.

Indeed, Highslip had ample reason to brood. He was out of pocket three-hundred pounds, money he could ill afford. Worse still, the blunt had been an utter waste. Helena Greenvale had failed.

It had seemed an excellent plan at the time. Highslip had approached Lord Balton's daughter, dangling David Rutherford before her like a carrot before a mare, but the chess-playing chit had proven far cannier than he had anticipated. Although Helena had considerable confidence in her skills, she had hesitated to challenge Lord Donhill, demanding some surety for the risk to her reputation should she fail to win. Helena had deemed the possible damage to her character worth five hundred guineas, but Highslip had managed to discount the price of her good name to three hundred. The shrew had demanded her payment in advance, win or lose.

For a short time this afternoon, it had seemed that Highslip had invested wisely. Helena had played her match boldly, striking blow after blow until it seemed that Donhill would be subject to an utter rout, but the man had only been biding his time. Bit by bit, the chess master had beaten back her assault into abject defeat.

Three hundred pounds, thrown away, Highslip thought, clenching his fists as he contemplated the pack of creditors that had begun to haunt his footsteps and deny him merchandise until debts were paid. It was little consolation that Helena's payment had come from Colber's stolen purse.

The only thing that was keeping the duns at bay was the possibility of his marriage to Caroline Gabriel. Yet, even that hope of financial salvation seemed more remote. Now that Petrov's fortune had become widely known, her mother, the greedy bitch, was chasing the scent of both social credit and money.

At Almack's Mrs. Gabriel had allowed the Russian to dance with her daughter twice, while restricting the earl to only one country dance. Petrov would have to be taken care of, Highslip decided, but it was far too soon. Three accidents to Gabriel suitors in so short a time would certainly be remarked.

Highslip glared at the carriage lamps passing in the street below as he considered his options. He would have to bring Caroline to heel before they put him in the Fleet. Luckily, the chit seemed biddable enough, passing pretty too, except for that unfortunate nose, but when compared to her Incomparable cousin, Caroline came out the complete loser.

Sylvia. . . that marvel of female flawlessness . . . Highslip's blood boiled at the thought of the woman that had nearly been his; a face as perfect as his own, a form that would make the gods envious; snatched from him at the lip of the grave by that querulous old fool of an uncle. Breaking his attachment to Sylvia was by far the hardest thing that Highslip had ever done, but there had been no choice. Love alone would not support.

Poor girl, she had been overcome with relief the other day not to be put upon any longer by that purse-proud cit. The way that she had looked at him just before she had left the room had made him long to tell her of his secret gallantry on her behalf, but he could not. She loved him still, he knew, although her heart was broken and she proudly pretended otherwise.

Yet, Highslip's brow furrowed as he wondered if her heart might be growing somewhat fickle. The blood rushed to the earl's face infusing his countenance with a devilish cast as he recalled the picture of Sylvia in Donhill's arms. It was the chess player's profound luck that unlike Colber and Entshaw, David Rutherford presented no true threat. His notorious wager had made the baron wholly ineligible and not worth the blunt and suspicion it would cost to remove him from the game.

Highslip had hoped that Helena would rid him of Donhill and the odious wager altogether. Now, he would have to make other plans. First though, he would have to find some sop to throw the creditors until he plighted his troth.

Highslip rose, turning from the window. The hour was late and he had little doubt that a likely flat could be found deep enough in the bottle and warm enough in the pockets for fleecing. Like the answer to a prayer, Highslip spotted a group of three young sprigs, green as April and half-foxed by the looks of them.

"Sir," one of them began. "Would you know where I might locate Lord Donhill?"

"In hell, I ..." Highslip began, cutting himself off as he recognized the boy. Sylvia's eyes stared out from a young man's countenance, her delicate features hardened in a masculine visage. He cast about in his mind for the youth's name. "Why, 'tis young William," the earl declared, putting on a mask of joviality. "What brings you to London, lad?"

The young man's face flushed with embarrassment as he recognized Lord Highslip. Although he was unfamiliar with the complete details of his sister's broken betrothal, he knew that the earl had caused her a good deal of grief. "I have come at Lord Donhill's request, milord. He wishes to speak to me regarding my late uncle."

"Dear Sir Miles," Highslip said, wearing a suitably grieved expression. "We all miss him so." Unlike his sister, William's face was ridiculously simple to read. Even as the earl did his utmost to lull the lad's uneasiness, a scheme began to take shape. "Unfortunately, I left Lord Donhill at a ball; I doubt that he will be here at all tonight. Surely you will find him at his residence tomorrow morning."

The young man nodded and made ready to take his leave. "Thank you, Lord Highslip. I shall see him then."

His companions looked up in awe.

"Lord Highslip, the noted Corinthian," one of them said in whispered awe.

It could not have gone better had Highslip planned it so. "I find myself alone this evening," he said. "Perhaps you and your friends might care to accompany me about town for a bit."

The reluctant William did not have a chance. His friends clearly would not have forgiven him had he refused this golden bit of good fortune, an opportunity for them to see London in the company of the famous Lord Highslip.

"Thank you, milord," William answered. "It would be an honor."

...

"Hsssst, Syl!"

At first, Sylvia thought she was still dreaming. She sat upright in her bed wondering where David had gone. Once again, he had visited her sleep, holding her in his arms, whispering words of endearment.

"Syl!"

The hissing syllable came again through the open window punctuated by a spatter of pebbles against the pane. Sylvia drew on her robe and peered out her window to the garden below. "William?" she whispered. "Whatever are you doing here?" Luckily, the nursery stairs connected with the garden door and she was able to go directly down to let her brother in.

"Syl, oh Syl." William broke into a sob as Sylvia hugged him to her. "I have been such a fool . . . an utter fool."

She smelled the liquor upon his breath. "It will look better in the morning," she said comfortingly. "Although you will have the devil of a head. I shall get you past Aunt Ruby."

"No, Syl," he moaned, disengaging himself from her arms. "'Tis far worse than being cast away I fear."

The expression of utter despair on his face was frightening. "Did you get sent down, William?" Sylvia whispered in growing dread.

"Would that it were that simple," her brother groaned, sitting on a nearby bench, his head in his hands. "I have lost five hundred and fifty pounds tonight, Syl."

Five hundred and fifty pounds. Aunt Ruby would never agree to pay that enormous sum to tow her nephew from the River Tick. As it was she begrudged every groat she spent on the lad above what Uncle Miles had provided.

"How?" she asked, sitting down beside him.

"Cards," William said. "I won't tell you who holds the debt, so do not ask."

"You must beg for some time," Sylvia said, her mind racing frantically for a solution. "In the meanwhile, Aunt Ruby must not find you like this. Your old room is still unoccupied, doss yourself there tonight and I will have a talk with Boniface."

"What shall I do?" William groaned.

A number of bitter retorts flew through Sylvia's head, but she held her peace. Recriminations would do little good now. "Get some sleep," she advised. "It will look better in the morning," she repeated, trying to convince herself as much as her brother.

"I doubt it," William said.

So do I, Sylvia thought as she mounted the stairs.

...

Luckily, the house on Berkeley Square was all a-dither with preparations for Caroline's ball. William's sudden presence was scarcely remarked as Mrs. Gabriel bustled about in a frenzy, bringing half the staff to the brink of resignation. It was left to Sylvia to console the cook and mollify the maids as well as organize the bulk of the arrangements. Mrs. Gabriel's constant carping was almost welcome, although it could not fully take Sylvia's mind off William's revelation.

Unfortunately, any distractions were temporary at best. William moved about the house like a shadow, offering his help with the backbreaking task of removing the furnishings that cluttered the room off the garden. Aunt Ruby had decided that it would do well for those who wished to play cards rather than dance.

They had loaded most of the pieces into a cart to be transported for sale and were starting to roll up the rug protecting the floor beneath when Mrs. Gabriel came to the door to survey their progress. "No!" she proclaimed, at last, "it shall not do. It is far too old-fashioned."

"But Aunt Ruby," William protested weakly. "Uncle Miles completely refurbished this room just before we came to London to launch Sylvia. Hired a gang of Italians to do the stonework. I recall him saying that it cost him a fortune."

"Wasted!" Mrs. Gabriel pronounced. "This room is certainly not the mode. The room near the terrace will do. We must clear it immediately. Come along!"

William eyed his sister with a martyred expression as he trudged off behind his aunt to labor yet again.

Poor William! It was unlikely that his acts of contrition would do any good, once Aunt Ruby found the true extent of his sins. Undoubtedly, she would demand that the boy pay his debt from the funds Uncle Miles had set aside for his education and that would mean no less than the destruction of her brother's future.

Sylvia leaned against the jamb, trying to find some way out of the predicament, but there was no clear move that would provide any solution. Damn Uncle Miles. She could forgive him for hiding her father's fortune in hoping to protect her from Hugo, but it was unfair that William should suffer.

"Sylvia."

It was as if he had been conjured up by a thought. Sylvia turned in surprise to find Hugo standing behind her, regarding her with a look that made her feel decidedly strange. "It is rather early for callers," she said, her discomfort growing as he continued to stare.

"The door was open," Highslip said at last. "I have come to talk to you, Sylvia."

"I cannot think what we have to say to each other, milord," Sylvia said, attempting to sweep past him, but he grabbed hold of her arm.

"Do not be foolish, my girl," Highslip said, enjoying her struggle. "You would not wish your aunt to find out about your brother."

There was a soft menace in his tone that caused her to cease her effort to get away. "What do you know of William's situation?" she asked warily.

"Shall we discuss this matter privately?" Highslip asked gesturing toward the garden door.

...

DAVID ARRIVED at the house on Berkeley Square to find things in chaos. No one was attending the front entry, yet servants were everywhere, polishing and cleaning. David clutched the dragon kite in his hand, wondering if he ought to return at another time when young Miles charged down the stairs.

"I saw you from the window in the nursery," he said breathlessly. "What a wonderful kite! Will you fly it? Can I come?"

"Actually," David said, holding out the fantastic construction of wood and paper, "this is for you. The children of the Orient fly kites like these and I had this made." The delight on the boy's face was well worth the price, David decided.

Miles took the red and gold dragon reverently in

MISS GABRIEL'S GAMBIT

hand. "Wait till I show Cousin William this!" he declared.

"Your cousin is here?" David asked, glad that the lad had responded to his letter at last. "When did he arrive?"

"Oh t'other night," Miles said. "If you are seeking him out, Mama has him moving furniture in the room near the garden, I think." He gestured the way as a servant brushed by, nearly causing a rip in the paper. "I shall put this in the nursery now, 'fore it gets broke. Thank you, Lord Donhill." He flashed a smile before running upstairs with the kite flying behind him.

David decided to seek William Gabriel out. Surely two men of outstanding chess skills could solve Sir Miles' puzzle.

. . .

"THE GARDEN IS SO LOVELY this time of year," Hugo said, brushing off a bench with his handkerchief. "Shall we sit outside here, in the sunshine? You are looking a bit peaked. That harridan aunt of yours is running you to rags."

"You obviously did not come here to discuss my health, milord," Sylvia said, watching his face with growing uneasiness. There was a cat in the cream pot expression there that she could not like.

"Oh, but I did, my love, I did and you ought not to call me 'milord,'" Highslip said.

"And you ought not to call me 'my love,'" she retorted. "You gave up any right to that more than a year ago."

Highslip plucked a lilac from a nearby bush, crushing

the delicate blossoms in his fingers. "You always wore lilacs, Sylvia," he said. "Every time I smell that scent it haunts me, as you do. I have never forgotten you. Never. I knew that someday you would be mine."

Sylvia looked around in growing dismay. It had been unwise to come out here with him alone. "What do you wish to tell me about William?" Sylvia asked, rising to put the chair between herself and Hugo.

"You still love me, Sylvia. I know you do," Highslip whispered, almost to himself.

In her childhood in India, Sylvia had seen a mongoose confront a cobra, its rising hooded head glaring at the furry creature with a mesmerizing threat. Now she understood the paralyzing terror of a cobra's glare.

"You see, I hold your brother's notes, my love. Five hundred and fifty pounds of his vowels and I know exactly what your dear aunt would do were she to find out about his little peccadillo."

He spoke conversationally, as if he were talking about the weather. "You are a true friend, Hugo," Sylvia said, holding her voice steady. "How like you to protect dear William."

"Oh, I shall protect him, Sylvia," Highslip said. "As long as it is in my interest to do so. I want only one thing in return. I want to protect you."

"I cannot marry you, Hugo," Sylvia said, the scent of crushed lilacs rose in her nostrils as he drew closer. She willed herself not to flinch as his hand touched her shoulder.

"Marriage? I had not mentioned marriage," Highslip said, throwing back his head in laughter. "Stupid! You would be my mistress."

The sibilant hiss of the word caused Sylvia to shiver despite the sunlight's warmth.

"Dreadful things might happen to those who do not pay their debts of honor. Thanks to your damned uncle, you have nothing," Highslip said. "Nonetheless, I want you Sylvia. I will forgive your brother's debt if you will give yourself to me."

"You are offering me *carte blanche*," Sylvia said, trying to contain her revulsion. Beyond the fact of William's debt, she had little doubt that Hugo would do her brother harm, if she tried to thwart him. The earl was mad.

SAVE for a few sticks of furniture swathed in holland covers, the room Miles had indicated was empty, but the sound of voices guided David to the open door.

"I love you, Sylvia. I own a delightful house on Marybone Lane which shall be yours and once I marry, you shall have jewels, clothes, everything that you would ever need to adorn your beauty."

David stopped in his tracks. It was Highslip's voice.

"Tell me that you love me, Sylvia," Highslip demanded. "Tell me that you will come away with me. Be my mistress."

David knew that he ought to leave, but he stayed beside the drapery, listening.

"I need time to consider, Hugo," Sylvia's voice came drifting through the door. "This is a serious move."

"Do you wish to be your aunt's dogsbody for the rest of your days?" Highslip asked, his voice petulant. "Fetching and carrying like a servant? You could have everything for the asking Sylvia...everything, if you would just be mine. You loved me. Tell me how you loved me."

"I loved you, Hugo." The soft words seemed to be wrung from her, but David heard them clearly, his heart sinking. The little fool was actually considering Highslip's offer. It was all David could do to keep from bursting upon them and venting his disgust.

"I knew it," Highslip declared his voice triumphant.

It needed little imagination for David to envision what happened in the long silence that followed. Highslip was holding Sylvia in his arms, kissing her. David waited in agony for the quiet to end.

"I shall await your answer, my love. Meet me here the night of Caroline's ball," Highslip said. "I shall let myself out the garden gate."

David waited until the sound of Highslip's footsteps faded and the sound of the garden door echoed as it shut.

...

SYLVIA HELD HER BREATH, waiting until she could be sure that Hugo was gone. His embrace had left her feeling soiled, as if she had been touched by something unspeakably filthy. She wiped her mouth upon her sleeve. Her legs began to buckle as she collapsed upon the stone bench. She wanted to scream, but a wave of nausea rose in her throat, nearly overcoming her. *A madman's mistress* she thought, *with five hundred fifty pounds as the price for my soul.*

The sound of approaching footsteps at her back set her to trembling. Someone was coming. William might be returning and she could not let her brother see her fear and agitation. She had to think this through.

It is a game of chess, she told herself; *do not let the opponent see your weakness.* Thus, Sylvia was able to rise steadily, turn with a semblance of a smile, but the false expression vanished when she saw David. His face was like a thunderstorm, ready to break.

"A delightful garden," he said, coming to stand beside her, "perfect for a private talk."

"You heard," Sylvia stated flatly, searching his eyes, flinching inwardly at the contempt she saw there. "You do not understand."

"I heard enough," David said. "Enough to know that Highslip has offered to make you his paramour and that you are a fair way to accepting. Do you seriously think that he would marry you once your cousin Caroline refuses him? For you know that she intends to have Petrov. You would be a fool to think that Highslip wants you out of love." He made the last word into a sneer. "However, if you are seriously considering entering the ranks of the demimonde I think you would be foolish to consider the post until you have entertained all bidders."

"All bidders?" Sylvia repeated, keeping her voice steady.

"Myself, for instance," David declared. "You would do far better for yourself under my protection. I would double Highslip's offer, a house in St. John's Wood with the title in your name, a pair and carriage and of course the usual clothing and jewelry."

"I see," Sylvia said, the anger rising through her like a ramrod. The moment of weakness had passed. How dare he? How could he consider that she would act in such an infamous manner? "But we are speaking of twice the usual, are we not?" she said stiffly. "What would that be in pounds and pence, milord, for being new to this game, I would know the stakes."

He named a sum that made her gasp involuntarily.

"I can well afford it, Sylvia. Consider that Highslip has pockets to let and will likely leave you high and dry," he said.

Sylvia's face had become a block of marble set with glittering emeralds that pierced him to the marrow. She would be, by far, the most expensive mistress that he had ever mounted. Yet, he felt that it was well worth the price to save her from Highslip. There was something in her calm, steady gaze that made him uneasy. It was as if she had retreated to some distant place within herself and when she spoke, he felt that he was hearing her voice from afar.

"Indeed, one cannot be too careful. Used goods are cheap," she said, looking him straight in the eye.

It was as if she was discussing the price of tea or rubber or some other commodity, not herself. David squirmed uncomfortably as the silence lengthened.

"I care for you, Sylvia," David said. "I think we would deal well together."

"How interesting," Sylvia observed, her head cocking to one side as she spoke. "You claim to care for me, yet you would make me your whore."

"You cannot be such a fool as to think Highslip loves you?" David asked. "Highslip loves only himself. You have no hope of an honorable offer from him."

"I know," Sylvia said her lips rising wryly. "I know Hugo far better than you think, milord. As for love, do they not say 'far better the devil you do know than the devil you don't?' I have suddenly found that I do not know you at all."

"I think that this would be the better move."

"Do you?" she asked, rising to her feet. "Damn you, I am tired of being forced into moves by men who think to manipulate me like a pawn. I must needs pay for every one of their stupid plays, my uncle, my brother, Hugo, and now you, milord. I have no hope of an honorable offer, so you make me a dishonorable one."

"Indeed, I am not the first," David pointed out.

"Truly, I am in alt," Sylvia said, her voice resonant with sarcasm "I am transported! Two slips on the shoulder in less than ten minutes. I am quite certain that even the would-be beaus of White's would hesitate to wager that such would occur. Now, which should I select, milord the nabob, or milord the earl? I shall have to consider most carefully whose bed I choose to warm."

Somehow the thought of her in Highslip's bed acted as a goad. "You might add this to your calculations," David said. He pulled her into his arms, covering her lips with his. His tongue parted her teeth, probing the depths of her mouth as his fingers gathered the silk of her hair, twining its strands into a shimmering rope that held her in thrall

Sylvia moaned softly as she felt his questing hands, her eyes stinging behind closed lids. All restraint was gone, replaced by a burning desire that seared her very soul. He frightened her, but not as Hugo had. What she feared was her own flaring passion. How was it possible to be divided into two separate people? One half of herself stood apart, an observer that commented coldly in her mind as the other half yielded to be swept away on a tide of sensation.

But the knowledge that she loved him gave rise to a growing bitterness. She was not even to be left with an illusion, a memory of a sweet moment in a moonlit garden. Instead, there would be only harsh sunlight and the smell of dying lilacs. The cold observer within commented on the betrayal of her body as her arms went around his neck of their own volition drawing him closer to her. Her dearest dream had become a nightmare.

She could not allow this. Would not. Using anger as a tool to gather the shattered remnants of her will, Sylvia pulled herself together. Her fingers meshed in the tangle of his hair grasped and pulled back with a force that made him cry out, knocking his spectacles from his nose. Disoriented, he loosed his hold upon her and she took the opportunity to move away.

"Sylvia," he sputtered, "what the devil are you about?"

"I had decided that I had enough of a sample upon which to base my decision, milord. You, sir, are likely the superior lover. Having determined that, I have decided that I have given enough of my wares for free."

David could see her, but her features were unclear. For a moment he felt as if he had been transported to the world of his recurring nightmare, where all was blurred with distortion. He sought to reason with her. "I had thought that we were friends, Sylvia. Surely, that would be a good beginning."

"I too, had thought that there was friendship between us, David," she said, her timbre suddenly sad. "But now I see that I was wrong. Friends do not believe the worst of each other. I am sorry, but I am afraid I cannot oblige you, milord."

"And you will go to Highslip?" he asked, bending to search the ground for his glasses.

"I will consider all my options carefully," Sylvia said. "Regardless, I shall find a way to contrive. I owe you and Lord Highslip my thanks, in a way. For I am now aware of the value of the only commodity I truly own - myself. And I begin to think that you cannot afford me."

David felt at a total disadvantage. There was something in her voice that mocked him, yet he could not discern her expression. He felt the ground around him seeking the gleam of glass.

Somehow, Sylvia could not bear to see him scrabbling about so. "I fear your trousers will be quite ruined, milord," she said, picking up the lenses. "Here are your spectacles."

He got up and reached out. The frames were slightly bent, but intact. "It is a lucky thing that the glass is not broken," he said, a trifle petulantly. He slid them back on his nose bringing the world back into focus. "I cannot see a thing without them." He looked at Sylvia and saw the trail of tears streaming down her face.

"It seems to me, milord, that you do not see a great deal...even with their aid," Sylvia commented softly.

He took a step forward.

"No," she said. "Do not touch me again."

"I only wish to help you," he said.

"Help yourself, you mean," Sylvia said her words rife with the bitterness. "Is that what you wanted all along, milord? Was all this nonsense about solving my uncle's riddle a pretense, so that you might insinuate yourself into my family? My father used that strategy often, infiltrating his opponent's ranks gradually, and then wreaking havoc. 'Help' you say? You have brought nothing but chaos to my life. 'Tis your interference that has led me to this pass and now you have the gall to present yourself as the solution to my difficulties? A rather neat gambit, I would say, but I refuse your offer David Rutherford. I do not want your help."

Her voice was calm, but the flow of tears continued unabated. "Because my uncle was your friend, I shall give you a piece of advice. Stay away from me, else you might find yourself in a dangerous position," she said. If Hugo were to somehow get wind of David's less than casual interest in her, he could be in serious jeopardy.

"And as a friend," David said quietly, "I would warn you against Highslip."

"You are not my friend, milord. I begin to believe you never truly were. As for Hugo, that is my affair."

Sylvia turned, fleeing from the garden to the nursery stairs.

David took off his glasses, polishing them absently as he tried to control the sudden turmoil within. As he reviewed his words, they seemed totally clear, his proposal to Sylvia perfectly logical. Yet, he was growing increasingly certain that he had missed some critical move, that rationality notwithstanding, there was some hidden flaw that he had overlooked. He left the garden feeling a sense of absolute loss.

As he departed the Gabriel household, David suddenly knew the critical piece that he had ignored. He loved her. Re-examining the course of events, he realized that Sylvia had spoken no less than the truth. He had wanted her, almost from the start, but had ignored his feelings because there had been no honorable course to pursue.

The overheard conversation in the garden had presented him with a seeming solution to his problem.

He desired Sylvia.

There was no reasonable route to her affections.

A dishonorable route had presented itself.

He had taken the move like a green player, not pausing to think of all the possible consequences. Now, he had lost her. As with most foolish moves, the consequences might be impossible to correct. But the game was not yet over. David knew that somehow, he had to redeem himself.

...

Sylvia threw herself into the preparations for Caroline's ball, running about the house in a veritable turmoil of activity, trying to keep her thoughts at bay. Yet, at odd moments, the memory of David's face haunted her, his look of utter disgust, the insult of his kiss. Hardest of all to bear was the absolute betrayal of her own emotions. The morning's events ought to have utterly cured her of any feelings for that wretched man, but she knew that she loved him and likely always would. His offer had been the worst of affronts, yet a part of her was tempted to accept...told her it would be preferable to be David's lover, even temporarily, than Highslip's slave forever.

"Sylvia," William called, meeting her later in the afternoon upon the backstairs.

The smile upon his face made her hope that he had come up with some solution to his dilemma.

"I have spoken with the gentleman who holds my vowels," William declared enthusiastically. "He has promised to give me all the time I need, says he is sure that we might work something out. A capital fellow. I am sorry to have troubled you Syl. I ought not to have dumped this in your skirts."

It was all Sylvia could do to keep from screaming at her brother's beaming face. *He wants me to work it out on my back, you imbecile! A capital fellow indeed!* But, with a speed borne of habit she calculated the possible consequences of such a move. William would undoubtedly feel constrained to challenge Hugo to a duel. Hugo would, without any question, kill or wound the boy. So, the alternatives were either, William's ruin or William's death or, she added reluctantly, her ruin.

Sylvia patted her brother on the hand. "That is splendid, William," she lied. "But you must realize that the debt must be paid."

"I have reckoned that if I set aside a portion of my quarterly allowance at a rate of..." William began to explain his reckoning.

Sylvia realized that she would indeed scream if she had to stand through her brother's careful calculations and she cut him off abruptly. "Another time, please. I am terribly busy."

"You look utterly fagged," the young man said with a brother's brutal honesty.

"Thank you, William," Sylvia said with a sigh as she

continued the climb to the nursery. She found Miles in the schoolroom, racing to and fro with an enormous kite trailing behind him.

"Lord Donhill brought it for me," the boy volunteered. "Ain't it the most wonderful kite ever? Do you see how the gilt eyes flash in the light? You think we could go flying it with Lord Donhill soon?"

"I think not," Sylvia said, collapsing into a chair before the barrage of questions. "Lord Donhill is a very busy man and right now, I am afraid your mama cannot spare me."

"Pooh!" Miles exclaimed. "You are always too busy to have any fun these days. How long is it till Caro's stupid ball is over? Can we go after?"

"One week," Sylvia said, bowing her head. One week before she must give Hugo her answer. Once more, she weighed all the alternatives, considered all the consequences, but there was no solution. She was trapped. Any way that she looked at it, it was check and mate.

"One week?" Miles spoke as if it was an eternity. "Do you think Lord Donhill could come then?"

"I do not know, Miles," Sylvia said, wearily. "Somehow, I doubt it."

"If you were married to him, we could see Lord Donhill all the time," Miles said archly, swishing the kite round his head.

Sylvia looked up, startled.

Miles saw her strange expression and continued on the same tack, driving his point home. "You could beat him at chess n' marry him and then he could come kite-flying."

"But you wished to marry me, dear boy," Sylvia said, her eyes shining. *Out of the mouths of babes*, they said.

"Well, if you married Lord Donhill, he might get me more kites," Miles said.

"Wretch!" But contrarily, Sylvia ran to the boy and hugged him, disregarding his squeal of dismay.

"Be careful," he cried. "You shall wreck my kite!"

She let Miles go and beamed. "We shall go kite-flying after Caro's ball," she promised. "And to Gunther's for an ice."

"Really?" Miles asked. "Gunther's?"

Sylvia nodded.

"And what about Lord Donhill?" Miles asked, refusing to let the matter die. "Will he come?"

"I am of the opinion," Sylvia said, a slow smile dawning, "that it might take Lord Donhill some time to recover."

"Is he ill?" Miles asked, worried. "He seemed quite fine to me this morning."

"No, he is not ill, but I believe he may soon be suffering a small *crise de nerfs*," Sylvia said. "He will take his medicine and it may be rather hard to swallow."

Miles looked at his cousin in puzzlement, opened his mouth, but obviously decided to keep his peace.

CHAPTER 9

White's was unnaturally well populated for early upon a rainy morning. Flocks of fashionable sprigs pestered Ivan Petrov, trying to discern the truth of the rumors regarding Lord Donhill's anticipated chess match. Brummel's expression equaled the grey mizzle that prevailed out of doors as he dispersed the hangers-on with an icy stare and gestured the Russian to a seat in the bow window overlooking St. James Street. Neither of the men noticed Lord Highslip lounging at the corner, hoping to overhear their conversation.

"I cannot like it, Petrov," Brummel said, shaking his head. "David has agreed to all of this Madame Echec's conditions without question."

"Everything she asks," Petrov agreed miserably. "This woman is clever without doubt. No other challenger has been thinking to disguise self to protect reputation, but is not that demand gives me worry, Brummel. Is almost seeming to me David is wishing to lose."

"He would not lose deliberately!" Brummel exclaimed, drawing himself up in indignation at the very thought.

"*Nyet, nyet,*" Petrov corrected himself hastily. "Never would he be doing so. Is just that these past days, he cares for nothing."

"He has agreed for the game to be timed by some sort of hourglass contraption. How does that work precisely?" Brummel asked.

"Is simple device," Petrov explained. "Two hourglasses, one for each. His hourglass running, David makes move. He stops his hourglass, sets challenger's running. Is finished her move she is starting David's glass going again. Game is continuing on till one says 'check and mate' to win or sand is running out."

"And if the sand runs out, it is forfeit?" Brummel asked.

"Is correct," Petrov said, his expression grim. "I am never seeing David play this way before."

Highslip quietly withdrew from his listening post, smiling in satisfaction. Perhaps this mysterious female would succeed where Helena Greenvale had failed. While the odds were still decidedly in Lord Donhill's favor, Highslip decided to risk a wager upon Madame Echec. He was still somewhat flush after his fleecing of William Gabriel and his friends. Even a small bet could pay off handsomely.

Just before the appointed hour, 37 St. James all but emptied as a parade of umbrellas proceeded from White's down the street to the Cocoa Tree chocolate house, the chosen meeting place. Even for so sacred a cause as a wager, no female could be allowed to trespass in the male sanctum sanctorum.

"Are you not going, Byron?" Brummel asked, noticing the poetic lord still reading by the fireside.

"Life is too short for chess," Byron said, returning his attention to his volume. "Perhaps, I shall stop by later."

AT THE CHOCOLATE HOUSE, David sat before the table setting up the board. A young man hesitantly came up to the chess master, his boyish looks oddly familiar.

"Good luck, Lord Donhill," the youth said, extending his hand shyly, "I am sorry that we have had no chance to meet before. I am William Gabriel."

"Ah, Gabriel," David said, his confusion clearing. The lad resembled his sister. It was a pity that the young man had not come up sooner, his aid might have been of use.

Unfortunately, there had been a bitter finality in Sylvia's words. "I do not want your help," she had declared, her feelings upon the matter painfully clear. Nonetheless, David decided, it was not her fortune alone, it was her brother's as well. "I have been longing to meet you over the chessboard. There are some matters that we must needs discuss."

"Chess? Me, sir?" The young man gave a bark of laughter. "Surely you jest? Father was hard pressed to teach me the rudiments."

"There is no need for false modesty," David said with a smile. "I know what manner of player you are."

"David, here is second sandglass," Petrov said, grunting as he set the other hourglass with its base of heavy mahogany into place. "You are giving Madame Echec white pieces?"

"As a matter of courtesy, since it was I who issued this damned challenge," David confirmed, then turned to William once more. "I would like to speak to you later, Gabriel."

The youth nodded and withdrew to join the crowd

as David frowned after him, thoughts of Sylvia rising in her brother's wake. But banishing Sylvia's image only gave sway to other worries. The simple task of arranging the board usually settled him, but now it caused him to become uneasy. Even as he put the last pawn into place, he began to wonder if he was being foolish to allow Madame Echec to set the pace of the game.

He pushed idly at the chess hourglass, watching the sand run down in a steady stream, one hour's worth of time in each glass for a total of two hours. Two hours to decide the rest of his days. Unbidden, Sylvia's words came to mind. "People's lives are not pieces to be lost and won by skill or luck."

No matter of luck there. He had well and truly lost her by his own stupidity. Now, it seemed to matter little if he lost himself.

David heard a high-pitched snigger, the sound as familiar as a filthy song that cannot be erased from memory however much one tries. It was Highslip's laugh.

"I am wagering against you," the earl called when he noticed that he had caught Donhill's attention.

"'Tis your money to lose," David replied, his casual shrug belying the smoldering anger within. If Sylvia was foolish enough to accept Highslip's blandishments it was none of his concern, but David would be damned if he would bankroll her seducer. His apathy diminishing, David tipped the hourglass back, emptying it once again to set it in readiness. Would that time itself could be recalled so easily.

There was a stir at the door and the wagers and speculation ceased momentarily as the crowd gave way for a dark figure. She was swathed from head to toe in swirling robes. The voluminous black fabric yielded no clues as to age or form. The heavy layers of veiling shielded her face from even the most penetrating of eyes. She moved toward the board with a silent grace that suggested youth.

"*Je suis* Madame Echec. My conditions, zey have been met?" she asked.

Her voice was low and throaty with age or guile. The accent could have been truly French or a mere disguise. It was impossible to determine. David gestured toward the hourglasses, about to speak when Petrov stepped forward.

"To the letter, Madame, we have been obeying your requests. However, before we are beginning, is one requirement I am proposing," the Russian said.

The black cloaked head inclined, listening.

"Lord Donhill risks everything, you... nothing. If you are losing, you must unmask yourself," Petrov demanded. "Or else you may be retiring now, your identity safe."

There was a general murmur of approval, for the dandies of St. James had been less than pleased to be deprived of their sport. The woman stood for a moment, her posture one of indecision.

"Very well," her muffled voice replied, slowly. "I shall hazard it."

Petrov stepped back, glad that he had secured his friend at least this small advantage. Madame Echec would have some cause to be nervous now, and that anxiety would likely make her vulnerable. Although none but a close comrade could have discerned it, David seemed less than his usual imperturbable self.

The Russian began to fear for his friend. It did not auger well that Madame Echec was confident enough to risk the revelation of that which she had taken great pains to conceal. Indeed, many others seemed to be thinking upon those same lines. The whispered odds against Madame Echec were decreasing.

Her gloved hands touched the mahogany base of the hourglass as she tilted first one, then the other, to and fro.

"It is well," she whispered. "Shall we begin? Let us choose white or black?"

David gestured to the seat before the white pieces. "The Lady first."

"Ah, *un gentleman*." Madame Echec shook her head. "*Mais non*, Madame Echec would not have it said that she took advantage. We choose now."

There was a wave of murmurs in the room as the odds changed once again.

She took up a pawn from each side of the board and concealed them behind her back, then stretched her clenched gloved hands before her opponent.

David gestured to her right.

Black. He moved to his place as Madame Echec seated herself on white's side. Eschewing the offered advantage of first move was just another means of trying to rattle him, to put him at a disadvantage, he told himself. Many had tried those tactics and failed.

She set her sand in motion.

It was like being within the realms of his nightmares, David decided as he automatically responded to her opening sally with king's pawn and flipped Madame Echec's sand to running.

The faceless figure reached out with confidence, advancing her pieces in mere seconds, setting his sandglass sifting with swift moves obviously borne of long practice. David forgot to set her hourglass running after one of his moves. Only a shouted remark from the audience prompted him to correct his error and the hourglasses were stopped momentarily while the matter was debated. Madame Echec graciously declined to exact a penalty, while David chided himself for stupidity, knowing that his hesitation could very well cost him the game.

The sands were set to their rotations again. The world narrowed to the space of sixty-four squares of black and white and the click of pieces against the board.

Sylvia had barely slept contemplating her strategy. Knowing her opponent's penchant for careful defense, she moved with rapid precision countering him as his own intent unfolded. As she stopped her time and set his running out, she studied what little she could see of his face. Although the veiling obscured her vision, she could detect the small signs of growing nervousness, the tightness of his jaw, and the lines around his eyes.

"Your move, Madame," David said, tipping her glass with a pleased smile.

Sylvia could hear the whisper of hushed approval. He had her trapped in a fork, his knight poised to take either rook or bishop. She was glad of the curtain concealing her face as she moved the rook aside to sacrifice the bishop. Would he discern what she was planning? She swiftly set his glass flowing again.

The inexorably shifting sand was almost a palpable force. David knew protracted consideration was a sure path to loss. The pieces retired to the side of the board showed that they were nearly even in power. He led by a single pawn, but Madame Echec seemed to have more grains of sand in the glass. It might represent only a few minutes, yet those few granules of time might make a crucial difference if she chose to draw the game out. He took the bishop.

Beneath the veil, Sylvia suppressed a delighted grin, even though she knew he could not see her. He could still recoup, withdraw himself from the brink of disaster, but it seemed that he was taking the bait. Deliberately, she drew his attention to the other side of the board, feinting an attack with her knight. She leaned back to watch, feeling the sweat run down her neck. Between the veiling, the heavy chador and the press of bodies, the heat was almost beyond endurance, but she would endure. She had to.

David saw the opening immediately and took advantage of the seeming carelessness. "*Échec*," he said, bringing his queen across the board. He tilted her hourglass with a triumphant flair, then leaned back to polish his glasses in a show of nonchalance.

"Blast," David heard Highslip curse softly. "He is winning, damn him."

David set his spectacles on the table momentarily as he massaged his eyes. There was a clattering sound from the street outside and the shouted imprecations of draymen. Obviously, an accident had occurred.

Madame Echec's head was turned for a moment and Highslip took a step forward. While everyone's attention was temporarily directed elsewhere, he reached out to sweep Rutherford's glasses to the floor.

Madame Echec returned her regard to the board, moving her rook forward to protect her king. "Your move, milord," she growled.

As she leaned to set his sand running, David's fingers reached for his glasses, but encountered only empty space.

"Halt the clock!" he demanded. "My spectacles are gone."

Madame Echec left his hourglass in the neutral position.

"No one move!" David warned "No one..." There was a heart-sickening crunch and Petrov bent down to pick up the lenses.

Sylvia chanced to notice Lord Highslip as he

stepped back to stand near the Russian. His visage was a mask of polite regret, but she could discern the glow of triumph as Petrov handed David the shattered glasses, one lens completely broken. She was about to speak when her opponent pointed an accusing finger across the board.

"You!" he roared. "You deliberately caused my spectacles to be destroyed. Did you think that I would concede to such tactics?"

Her words although muffled were filled with cold hauteur. "Indeed, I did not, milor'," she rasped, her fury rising. "*C'est répréhensible!* I deny your accusation. How is it *possible* I have touched your spectacles?"

To demonstrate, she leaned across the board, the sweep of her gown threatening to knock over the pieces as she reached toward where his glasses had rested.

"Then there is being no choice but postponement," Petrov declared. "Until we retrieve his other pair of spectacles. Tomorrow we will return."

"*Non!*" Sylvia declared with quiet vehemence. She would not go through with this again. There was no time. "We shall continue the game, *oui*? Were I *un homme*, I would duel you milor', for falsely naming me ze cheat. Instead, I shall take great pleasure in trouncing you."

"You have my apologies, Madame," David said, realizing that she had spoken the truth. She could not possibly have tampered with his glasses. "But I am now a one-eyed man and a blurry-eyed fellow at that. How do you propose to play on?"

"Are you wishing to be making ze forfeit?" she asked, amusement in her muffled tones.

Petrov hushed the rising murmurs of indignation with a declaration of his own. "The conditions of wager are implying fair match, Madame! For David not to be seeing is unfair!"

"I agree! If you are to be playing blind, I too, shall be blind, milor'," she said, turning her back to the board. "I will play from memory, if you shall do ze same. You have played blindfolded before, *non?*"

David blinked, but the hazy world would not come into focus. He knew that there would be no awakening from this bizarre reality. Fleetingly, he thought to argue for postponement, but knew that after his false charge of cheating and her gallant offer to play blindly herself, it would be an act of unpardonable cowardice to refuse her. Resolutely, he quashed the sinking feeling in the pit of his stomach.

The air of mystery was a deliberate distraction, an effort on her part to seek an advantage by putting him on the defensive. The inability to read his opponent's face had been a distinct drawback. Now, he realized with satisfaction, she would be unable to study him.

"I must trust someone to turn to make my moves and turn ze sandglasses for me," Sylvia murmured as she wondered who to appoint? Her gaze fell upon a familiar figure. "Will you do ze honors, Lord Byron?"

"I thought life was too short for chess, Byron?" Brummel asked, repeating the poet's words sardonically.

"Ah, but this seems more than a mere game of chess," Byron replied, as he limped to the front of the room. "There was a loud noise from St. James Street and I looked up from my book to find White's utterly deserted. So, I decided to come and see for myself and lucky that I did, else I would have missed this cataclysmic event. I applaud your bravery, Madame Echec, and account it a privilege to be the keeper of time in this battle between the sexes."

"Petrov, will you act on my behalf?" David asked.

Petrov took his place by the hourglass as David turned his chair around. Visualizing the board in his mind, he waited until he saw every piece clearly, standing as they had just before the world had gone to a blur.

"Your last move, Madame, was rook to thwart check?" he asked, once the picture was fixed in his head.

"Oui." The answer drifted from behind him.

"Then we begin. Set the sand in motion, Mr. Petrov," David said, sending his bishop sailing across the board in his mind. "Bishop to my queen's third rank."

Madame Echec countered with her knight. David shut his mind to everything but the sound of her voice and his vision of their pieces and positions.

The pace of the game increased. David called out his moves rapidly, but there was scarcely enough time to shift the piece and turn the glasses before Madame Echec called out her move. The rapid susurration of sifting sand, first at his left, then at his right indicated that both timekeepers were concentrating diligently on their tasks. The crowd whispered softly at the ever-shifting balance of power.

David knew that he had never played so well, but the shrouded woman was his equal. Perhaps, he realized with growing dismay, more than his equal; Madame Echec moved with a calculated ruthless speed that kept him scrambling to keep pace.

"Knight takes pawn - *échec*," Madame Echec called. David smiled inwardly. She was good, but not good enough.

Sylvia ignored the titters of laughter that erupted. *Fools! They could not see beyond four moves upon the board.* She would not oblige them by failing. Too much was at stake. *Take the knight;* the thought became a prayer. *Take the knight and be damned.*

"Queen takes knight."

When she heard the smug, condescending tone in his voice, it was all that she could do to keep from jumping up and shouting with glee. Although David did not yet know it, he had just sealed his fate. "Castle, queen's side," she said, barely keeping the triumph from her tone.

There was a gasp from the chess aficionados at this seemingly risky move, but David, with dawning dismay, visualized what the woman was about. In one swoop, she had shifted the entire balance of the board, weakening his ability to mount a focused attack. He responded, desperately trying to marshal his forces once more, but it was a futile effort. Madame Echec attacked with ruthless efficiency, bringing her reserve into play with swift skill, hammering at him until his king was completely cut off, cornered.

"I believe that is *échec et mat*," she crowed. "You agree, *non?*"

"David! Your time!" Petrov urged. "Is nearly being up. You must move."

"My time is up, my friend," David said wearily, rising to turn and look at the dark figure. "It is checkmate, Madame. You have beaten me." He toppled his king in a gesture of defeat.

Madame Echec rose and once more, faced her opponent. David eyed his nightmare, knowing full well what was expected of him, yet the words stuck like a bone in his craw. He cleared his throat. "I suppose this means you shall marry me," he said, rebelling with every fiber of his being as he choked out the words.

"Hardly a gracious proposal, eh, Donhill?" Highslip remarked as he gleefully raked in the results of his wagers.

David glared in Highslip's direction. "Do you expect me to get on my knees to the woman?" he asked.

There was a cheer from the crowd. "Do it up proper, Donhill," Highslip called. "Act the gentleman."

"*Oui*," declared the muffled voice, Madame Echec slipped off a dark glove and extended her hand. "I believe zat you must do it so."

David stepped slowly toward the black shrouded figure, then bent in stiff obeisance until his buff-trousered knee was flush with the floor. He captured the proffered hand that peeked from the voluminous black sleeves, clasping her fingers so tightly that he could hear her wince as the fragile bones ground together.

Through her veil, Sylvia saw that his eyes were dull and glassy, like a man walking in the midst of sleep. He bent before her and she felt a thrill of pleasure. All of his remarks about females and chess were being disproved. She had brought him to his knees, truly.

Yet, when those hazel eyes glared up at her, the expression in them reminded her of an animal caught in a trap before the hunter. She, of all people, knew what it was to be ensnared without hope of escape and regretted the evil impulse that had led her to heed Hugo's malicious suggestion. "Milor'," she began, "you do not . . "

"Will you marry me?" he asked. The words grating past clenched teeth as the crowd around him guffawed. Except for Petrov and Brummel, all were laughing, enjoying the spectacle of his humiliation. There was no appeal for mercy, only rage sparking in those earth-toned depths. He was a man bending his head at the chopping block, awaiting the stroke of the executioner's axe. Despite the calm delivery, the words were wrenched from him.

Sylvia could only guess at the agony they caused.

Her feeling of triumph dissolved rapidly into a maelstrom of mixed emotions. *Will you marry me?* The phrase that she had longed for echoed in her mind, the culmination of all her plans, yet now she wavered.

As she had contemplated it before, it had seemed the most delicious of ironies to eschew a slip on the shoulder for a wedding ring. Although Sylvia had every right to say "yes," as she had intended, she could not. David had wanted her, but he did not love her. It would be hell to endure that inequity of feeling for the rest of her days. He would despise her for forcing him into marriage. Despite what he had done she still loved him with all her being.

David waited in an agony of anticipation. The silence stretched as they all hung upon her undoubted answer. Looking away from that hazy veiled face, he felt an utter fool, knowing that he would be obliged to spend the rest of his days with this unknown, all for a drunken wager.

Sylvia had been correct. He had foolishly hazarded everything in his life that was worthwhile. David gazed at the woman's hand, the only part of her that he could see closely enough to be in focus. It was smooth and slender, a young hand with delicate nails, marred only by a jagged scar. A familiar scar. He blinked, moving closer to peer at the healing skin. Once jogged, his memory went rapidly to that morning in Green Park, a ragged wound caused by a vicious dog.

Sylvia? As he looked at the healing wound, all began to make sense. William Gabriel's protestations of ignorance regarding the Game of Kings. Her inadvertent slips of chess knowledge. Had she planned this all along? No wonder she had refused his *carte blanche*. Why choose the post of mistress when one could be a wife? She had deliberately concealed her expertise in the hopes of trapping him.

She had brought him to his knees and now, she would claim his name and title in the manner of all greedy females. However, she might find that Lady Donhill was not so easy a position. The thought brought a smile to his face. She would be taught a lesson. Surprisingly, David found himself relaxing, even enjoying the prospect. It was something of a relief to know that his wife-to-be was neither a chatterbox chit nor an ape leader. Certainly, he would never lack for a chess partner.

"Milor'," she spoke again.

The sound of her voice directed his attention upward once more and he tried to pierce the layer of veils. He identified the smell below the camphor. It was lilac, the sweet lilac she always wore. Dimly, David recalled Sylvia's tale of her father's escaping the pasha's wrath garbed in women's clothing.

"You do me no honor at all if you marry me out of foolish obligation," she declared, her voice low as she pulled her hand from his. "I say you *non*, milor'. For I have now just determined to marry only a man who can best me at chess."

The crowd gasped. Highslip went as white as his necklinen.

David rose dizzily. She had rejected him. The prize in her grasp, she had thrown it back in his face. His feeling of temporary relief gave way to a realization that he had just been heartily insulted. Why?

"I shall take a thousand pounds as my forfeit. You may dispose of your person as you please," Madame Echec declared, laughter in her throaty voice.

She swept David a mocking curtsy whose grace erased any lingering doubts about the female chess mistress's femininity in all minds but one.

"She is no woman!" Highslip growled. "No female

can play with such skill! I demand proof that the terms of the wager have been discharged."

David looked to Sylvia in growing amusement wondering how she would handle this problem.

But she had come prepared. "I have no intention of disclosing my identity, *monsieur*. However, if you shall summon ze maid, I shall prove I am *une femme*."

A scullery maid was brought from the Cocoa Tree's kitchens and the two were closeted for a short time, while the members of White's congratulated David on his narrow escape. He wondered just how lucky he was.

"She be a mort awright," the girl declared, gesturing broadly with her hands to her chest. "Ain't no man got a pair like 'ers."

The gathering of gentleman laughed heartily. "Well, Highslip," Brummel urged with a wicked grin. "Time to pay up."

Highslip reached into his pocket, pulling out a wad of bills so lately collected from the losers. He counted painstakingly until the full sum that he had just won was exhausted. Digging into his purse once more, he added a few bills.

"Here!" the earl said, throwing the money to the table with such force that some notes scattered to the floor.

"How gracious of you, milor'," Madame Echec said her sarcasm plain as she bent to gather the fallen paper. She sat down and began to count aloud.

Highslip reddened. "You dare?"

"In for ze penny, but never leave ze table till you count up ze pounds, as my *cher* Papa would say," Madame Echec replied and continued. "900, 920 . . . 970 . . ." she said, coming to the end of the bills. "30 short?"

The swathed head turned and somehow all could tell that her wordless regard was accusing. Highslip flushed, fumbling in his purse once again until the shortfall had been remedied. She folded the money carefully, and swiveled to leave, sweeping from the room like a dark cloud as the crowd stared after her in amazement.

At the window, David silently applauded as the indistinct dark-clad figure stepped into a waiting hackney carriage. Sylvia had planned it perfectly from start to finish. Obviously she had known from the beginning that she could beat him, yet she had let him go. Bit by bit, the pieces of the puzzle came together, only the full picture was nearly as confusing as the parts.

As the carriage rolled out of sight, David sought Sylvia's brother, pulling him to a private corner to converse. "You meant it when you said that you could not play chess?" he asked.

"Aye," William said. "That is why your letter set me wondering, milord. 'Tis my sister who's the pawn-pusher, not I, but you'll not tell her I said so?" he asked anxiously. "Uncle never liked to have her skill noised about, thought it unwomanly and now as I've seen this Madame Echec, I know why. I have never seen so formidable a female."

"How long was your uncle ill?" David asked.

"Months," William answered. "Out of his head in pain, more times than not. Sylvia was a brick. Nursed him right up through the end."

"Played chess with him?" David asked, softly.

"I should say not. Uncle wasn't in no condition to wield a spoon much less a chess piece. After all she'd done for him, that foolish chess Will was doubly a shame," William declared. "To be truthful, with all the agony that chess has caused to those dear to me, I've come to despise the game. At least today turned out well. You may have lost the match, but it seems to me that you have had the devil's own luck today."

"The devil's own luck," David repeated, although his emphasis upon the words differed. It was increasingly obvious that Sylvia had been the correspondence chess-player. In fact, David reflected in growing bewilderment, it now seemed that she had rejected him twice. There had been no need for today's farce. All Sylvia had needed to do was to claim him, for she had already won his hand in forfeit through the post.

Was she so besotted by Highslip that she would eschew an offer of marriage to take up the earl's *carte blanche*? It made little sense, but what aspect of love did? Certainly, it was the only answer that David could find. He would make her see reason, he vowed. Bidding farewell to William, David started to seek out Petrov, only to bump into a pillar. *The first move*, David decided, *was to find his spare pair of spectacles.*

. . .

As the rain pummeled the moving carriage, Sylvia quickly shed her disguise, folding it into a parcel as they turned on to Piccadilly. She covered her hair with the large brimmed bonnet, pulling a light veil down to obscure her features just as the carriage pulled up near Devonshire House, as she had instructed.

She paid the driver, secure in the knowledge that he would no more be able to describe her than any of the crowd in the Cocoa Tree. Nonetheless, she turned up Stretton Street avoiding the more direct route to Berkeley Square, taking a roundabout way home. Soaked to the skin, she shoved the bundle of dark clothing into a dark corner of the mews to be retrieved later, then went around to the front door.

Sylvia entered to find her aunt and Caroline listening to William's account of the chess match. The circuitous walk had permitted her brother to precede her.

" . . . and she let him go, you say?" Aunt Ruby was asking.

"Not merely set him free," William declared, "humiliated him to boot. Made him get down on bent knee to propose, only to reject him."

"I cannot say but it serves the conceited wretch right," Aunt Ruby said with a sniff. "Still, I think the woman was the worse fool. Imagine, rejecting a purse like Donhill's and a title as well."

"They say that she must be something of a nabob herself," William said. "And I would concur. Her clothing was of fine quality, a type that I had often seen in the East when I was a boy."

"Nabob or no," Caroline said. "It was still rather cruel to cause him to kneel before her."

"Do you think so?" Sylvia said, her cheeks burning despite herself. "What about his cruelty to the other females who have challenged him to the ruin of their reputations?"

"I thought you were fond of Lord Donhill," Caroline asked, surprised at her cousin's vehemence.

"I have little respect for any man who could needlessly stake his entire future on the outcome of a game," Sylvia said, eying her brother significantly.

William reddened at the implied reference to his gambling losses.

"What a pity," Caroline sighed. "Still, Lord Donhill is free now, able to marry whoever he might choose. The matchmaking tabbies will be in alt." In consternation, Caroline clamped her mouth shut as she noted the growing gleam in her mama's eye.

"He has a title," Mrs. Gabriel purred, "and money."

Suddenly, Sylvia found she could endure no more.

"I am going upstairs," she announced, "to change into some dry clothing." No one paid her the slightest notice as she went past the main stairway. Sylvia swept out the doors to the garden, to stand heedless in the mist.

Memories stirred. Had she been needlessly cruel to David? He doubtlessly hated Madame Echec for his humiliation. Yet, Sylvia thought, lifting her chin proudly, he had dishonored her in a far more personal manner. David Rutherford had deserved what he had gotten and more, far more. There was no cause for regret.

Even so, as Sylvia slipped out to the mews to retrieve her bundle, she was honest enough to acknowledge that Caroline was partially correct. There had been no real purpose to cause him to abase himself other than petty revenge. Sylvia comforted herself with the fact that it would make no difference; David would never know Madame Echec's identity. As Sylvia made her way up the back stairs to the nursery, she heard her aunt haranguing Caroline, hoping to redirect the girl's affections toward Lord Donhill.

Strange, Sylvia mused as she reached the nursery door, how her daydreams had been played out with such exquisite irony. In the back of her mind, she had always known that David was hers for the taking. She would challenge him. He would lose, but declare himself the winner still, for her dreams would always end with his avowal of love.

It seemed one of Fate's crueler jests that Sylvia had released him from the bondage of his wager only, in all likelihood, to free him to marry another. David was now a prime catch who could look far higher than a dowerless girl who had nothing but a pretty face to recommend her. Even disregarding the absence of a marriage portion, Sylvia knew that one did not offer to wed a woman who was previously considered no more than mere mistress material.

There was a shout as Sylvia opened the nursery door. "Make way!" Miles warned as he rushed past her, Lord Donhill's dragon kite trailing behind him.

"Did you do your lessons?" she demanded, her annoyance rising as she saw his books open as she had left them.

"Not yet," Miles said, ignoring the danger in her voice.

"Now!" Sylvia ordered, wrenching the kite from the boy's hands. As she glared down at him, he watched in trepidation, his eyes beginning to glisten.

"You're holding it too tight!" Miles wailed, his lower lip trembling. "You're going to break it."

Sylvia bowed her head, unable to meet his tearful gaze for a moment as shame filled her. It was unconscionable to take her anger out upon the boy. After all, it was not his fault that she still loved David Rutherford, Sylvia thought miserably, as she set the fragile kite gently upon the shelf. "Sorry I snapped at you, my dear," she said, returning to his side and tousling his hair by way of an apology. "Finish your lessons now and perhaps, if the day clears, we may sneak out later and launch your dragon into flight."

"Don't wonder that you're peevish, the way Mama has you working. Why, you're soaking wet." Miles said, brightening at the promised treat, as he wiped away his tears.

Sylvia glanced down at her sodden gown. "So I am. I had best go change. There is still a great deal to do before tomorrow night. We want Caroline's ball to be a success," she declared, with false brightness.

"Don't care if it is, or it isn't. I won't get to see nothing of it anyway," Miles complained, his mouth drooping. "Mama says I'm to stay put in the nursery and not set foot downstairs."

"Come Miles, it is all grown-up nonsense anyway,"

Sylvia said. "Dancing and chitter-chatter and the like, nothing of interest to a fellow like you."

"'Cept the food. Cook won't let me down in the kitchen, says I'm underfoot but I can smell it all the way up here. It's torture I tell you, knowing I ain't gonna get a bite of it!"

"I shall make sure you get your share." Sylvia laughed. "Go to my room tomorrow night and stand by the corner window, the one that looks over the garden." Casting her eyes around the nursery, she sighted a paintbrush-filled basket in the corner. After emptying the brushes onto the shelf she detached the reel from the kite and tied the line securely. "I shall come to the garden. Then you lower the basket, and I shall fill it for you."

"The whole basket?" Miles asked with a delighted grin.

"The whole basket." Sylvia promised, raising her hand in solemn avowal, as a shiver caught her unawares.

"Get out of your wet things, Syl," the boy urged. "If you catch an inflammation of the lungs, you ain't gonna get me nothing tomorrow night."

Sylvia's laugh was punctuated by a loud sneeze. Hurrying to her room, she closed the door behind her before finally peeling off her rain-drenched clothing. After she had dried herself and changed her gown, she opened her reticule to remove the roll of bills, unfolding them carefully. A thousand pounds! She had held diamonds and rubies by the palms-full, but never had she held so much money at once.

Sylvia set the notes in piles by denomination as she counted them out. Less the five-hundred-fifty that William owed Hugo, she would have four-hundred-fifty pounds of her own. As Sylvia spread the chador out to dry, an idea began to take shape.

What had been done once could likely be done again. As Sylvia's father had proven long ago, there were fortunes to be made upon the chessboard. She was every bit her papa's equal at the Game of Kings. He had been more than proud when her skills began to surpass his own.

With four-hundred-fifty pounds as her stake, she could leave London and David Rutherford behind forever. As the mysterious Madame Echec she might travel once more, roaming wherever fancy and fortune took her. Hugo had been right in one respect. She had no wish to spend the rest of her days as her aunt's dogsbody.

In a gratifying twist of fate, the very man who had sought to shackle her was the unwitting impetus of her passage to freedom. Although Hugo would never know it, the earl had provided her with the means to release herself from servitude.

Sylvia folded the money carefully, then bent to pull aside the small braided rug before her bed. After prying up the loose floorboard, she placed the bills in her hidden cache. As she restored all to its former order, she could hear Miles singing a rhyming song, his high reedy voice penetrating the closed door.

Leaving him would doubtlessly be the most difficult thing of all, she thought, her throat tightening. Caroline would marry her Ivan. William had not truly needed her for years, but Miles would miss her. Even so, Sylvia knew that if her life as Madame Echec was to succeed, she must seize the strategic moment or else the opportunity would be lost.

The sun was beginning to break through the clouds as Sylvia went to stand at the window to contemplate the future. It would be a difficult existence, living forever behind a veil of secrecy, but the persona of the Madame Echec might enable her to have a life of her own choosing. A life of autonomy, she told herself, subject to no will but her own, limited only by her skill and wit. Yet, despite the possibilities of adventure and wealth as a mysterious mistress of chess, the days ahead seemed to hold little promise. For those days would be lonely, without family, without love.

Without David.

CHAPTER 10

"You look real pretty, Syl," Miles declared. "Almost better than the ladies at Astley's Amphitheater."

Sylvia grimaced at the comparison to the less than demurely dressed equestriennes at the famed riding show. "A high compliment, indeed," she said, knowing that in truth the boy meant it as the sincerest of accolades. "Will you dance with me, kind sir?"

Miles bowed and Sylvia took his hands, whirling him about the room. Her gown had been created for movement; the full skirt caught the air in a billow of creamy white lace. Beneath the frothy drapery a slip of jade green satin shimmered in a soft glow as she moved. Two rouleaus of white satin served the dual purposes of ornamentation and cleverly patching together two short lengths of the fabric that would otherwise have been insufficient. A corsage of the same white, set with a panel of lace, hugged her breast, while the full sleeve, slashed with lace, set off the alabaster expanse of her neck and shoulders.

"The coaches are beginning to come," Miles said as Sylvia loosed his hand. He ran to the nursery window to watch the guests arrive.

Sylvia hastened to complete her toilette. With all the last-minute preparations for the ball, there had been scant time to dress. Carefully, she pinned her hair into a coronet. The small mirror in her room told her that she had never looked better, but she could not completely erase the furrow of worry at her brow. Her small satin reticule held five-hundred and fifty pounds, payment in full to satisfy her brother's debt to Lord Highslip. Nonetheless she knew that discharging William's obligation would not be easy.

"Remember," Miles called. "I'll be watching the garden for you. I shall let down the basket."

"And I shall fill it," Sylvia promised, blowing him a kiss as she went out the door. "Just be waiting at my window."

...

"CAROLINE'S BALL IS CRASH," Petrov commented as he and David tried to negotiate his way through the sea of elegantly clad elbows.

"*Crush*," David corrected automatically, his eyes searching the crowd for a glimpse of Sylvia. "It is *crush*."

"Why do you repeat what I am saying?" Petrov asked. "Is you they come to see, David. You name is being on everyone's tongue tonight."

"How the mighty have fallen," David commented, his tones wry.

"I am thinking, was after you took her knight when the falling was beginning," Petrov said, proceeding to analyze the game.

"It was just a phrase, 'How the . . .' Oh never mind." David sighed, deciding that it was not worth a lengthy explanation.

Unfortunately, it seemed that the Russian was correct. As they made their way across the room, David could hear the barely suppressed titters, the sudden quiet as he approached, the looks, the hushed snatches of conversation. However, the whispers did not concern him so much as the fact that Sylvia was seemingly nowhere to be found. Suddenly, he saw her coming down the main stairway. She paused, scanning the room as if she were looking for someone. Her cat's eyes met his, touching him briefly, their anger like a razor's edge. Did she hate him now? David wondered, his heart sinking. Was that why she had chosen to bring him to his knees?

"David, is that you?"

Startled, David turned to find Brummel regarding him through his quizzing glass. "What is the matter now, George?" David asked, his voice sarcastic. "A spot on my sleeve? My cravat awry? Mud on my pumps?"

Brummel smiled in his usual caustic manner. "I must say, 'tis extraordinary. I cannot find anything amiss with your attire. I had quite thought that once the wager was done, you would revert to your former havey-cavey ways. In fact, I bet on it. And now, I find you looking most presentable and have lost a good ten pounds for it."

David glanced back at the stairway to find that Sylvia had disappeared into the crowd. "I am sorry to have cost you money, George, but I have learned that we can never go back to what was, however much we may wish it."

"I must salute your courage" the Beau said, changing the subject. "Hazarding the parson's partisans without your chessboard to shield you! Why every matchmaking mama in Town is here tonight to cry 'view halloo' and you, my lad, are the fox. You have eluded the matrimonial hunt long enough, by unfair means. They fully intend to bring you to ground now as you are lawful game."

"Hardly." David snorted. "What woman would wish to marry so sorry a specimen as I, beaten by a mere chit, if the description of the maid at the Cocoa Tree is to be believed?" Where had Sylvia gone? Was she even now, meeting with Highslip as she had promised? He had to find her.

"Do you actually think that any one of them gives a tinker's damn that some intellectual Athena can surpass you at pushing a pawn?" Brummel asked. "Your unfortunate experience only enhances you in feminine eyes, for there is nothing more appealing to the heart of the gentle sex than a proud man who has been humbled. They would heal your wound, heaven help you."

Petrov nodded. "He speaks truth."

David scanned the room anxiously, paying little heed to either of them.

"If you are looking for Miss Sylvia Gabriel, she has gone to seek refreshments, I believe," Brummel said with a sniff. "And never say I did not warn you before you proceeded upon the path to doom."

"Thank you, George," David said, hurrying off to intercept Sylvia. However, she was not to be found among the tables of lobster patties and cold meats. Nor, David realized with a sick feeling, was Highslip anywhere to be seen.

"Sylvia? I believe she was heading for the back garden for 'a breath of air' she said," William supplied upon being asked.

David surreptitiously slipped inside the almost empty room. The moonlight from the open doors illuminated the uncovered portion of the black and white marble floor. David crept toward the door, moving along the carpet area with silent swiftness toward the sound of Sylvia's voice.

"Have you had your fill?" she asked.

David hesitated, wondering just what he was about to interrupt. He hid himself in the shrubbery, not daring to go further.

"You forgot the cakes." Miles' voice came piping from above.

"Greedy goose!" Sylvia laughed. "I shall fetch you some cakes. Be waiting with the basket in another half hour. I am sure that what I have given you thus far shall tide you over."

"The ones with the cream," Miles called.

"Cream it is," she agreed.

David felt weak with relief. She was merely sneaking food to her young cousin. But before David could reveal himself, he saw a silhouette in the door.

"Sylvia?" Highslip stepped into the moonlight.

Sylvia moved into view, the glow upon the white lace of her gown causing her to look as ethereal as a beam of quicksilver.

"I am here, Hugo," she said.

David was surprised by the tone of her voice, cold and distant as the moon itself.

"So my love," Highslip said, advancing towards her. "When will you come away with me? Everything is arranged. You have only to pack your bags."

"Do you have my brother's vowels?" she asked.

Highslip pulled a scrap of paper from his pocket and waved it before her.

"I am prepared to discharge his debt," she whispered.

Highslip's laughed triumphantly, handing her the paper. She perused it carefully before tearing it to shreds. David began to realize that there had been far more to the earl's dishonorable proposal than he had understood.

As Highslip moved toward Sylvia, David started to rise from his hiding place. He fully intended to pull Highslip's hands from her and break every bone in the fop's body thereafter. But Sylvia had moved away and put the stone bench between them.

"I am afraid I shall have to upset your arrangements, Hugo." Sylvia said firmly. "There has been a change of plan."

"Do you think to cheat me of what is rightfully mine?" Highslip said, his eyes narrowing. "Your person, Sylvia. Or five-hundred-fifty pounds.

"Here!" She tossed her reticule on the bench and stepped back. "Five-hundred-fifty pounds, milord," Sylvia exulted. "The full sum of my brother's debt to you." She watched as he pulled the roll of bills from the mouth of the satin sack and counted it incredulously.

"Where did you get the money?" Highslip asked from between clenched teeth.

"That is none of your concern, Hugo," Sylvia said, airily. "Clearly, I have resources of which you are not aware. I will not be your mistress, Hugo, yours or any man's."

"Do you still hope for marriage, Sylvia?" Highslip sneered. "Let me assure you that any suitor of yours shall meet a fate similar to Colber's and Entshaw's. London is a dangerous city and one can never tell what might happen."

"No," Sylvia said softly, "I have no hopes of marriage."

"Not even to Donhill?" Highslip asked, his voice soft and deadly. "For you seemed to be rather fond of him on the Harwell terrace. He is free now that he has lost that damnable chess game. A thousand pounds it cost me. A thousand pounds!"

Sylvia controlled a frisson of fear at the stark mask of hatred upon Hugo's face. She forced herself to look at him directly. "Donhill is nothing to me, Hugo. Besides, as you yourself said over a year ago, who would be so foolish as to marry a female without a pennypiece to her name, however lovely she might be?"

"That is true," Highslip said, broodingly. "I love you, Sylvia, but I cannot marry you, you understand."

"Yes," she whispered. "I understand."

"I shall not let anyone take you from me," he declared, his eyes wild. "You are mine, Sylvia, mine or no one's!" He turned and walked from the garden. His footsteps echoed from the empty ballroom.

When she was sure that he was truly gone, Sylvia leaned against a tree, taking long, ragged breaths like a spent runner. She closed her eyes as she let the relief wash through her. For a moment, she had been afraid that Highslip would do her physical harm. Now, her course was plain. There was no choice. She would have to leave before Hugo vented his insane jealousy upon David or some other imagined suitor. Madame Echec was her destiny.

"He is quite mad."

Startled, Sylvia opened her eyes to find David standing before her, concern in his eyes.

"There is a leaf upon your shoulder, milord, and a twig in your hair," Sylvia said, her voice weak. "Doubtless, souvenirs from your listening post. If eavesdropping is your new avocation, let me warn you that it shall play havoc with your clothing. Or did you merely wish to apprise yourself of the current asking price for my favors? Do you now wish to raise your bid?"

"I owe you an apology, Sylvia," David said, worried at the wan look upon her face.

"So, pay your penance and be done with it!" Sylvia snapped. "As you have obviously heard, I am a dangerous woman. Association with me can adversely affect your health."

"I would like to help you," he began.

"Dear heaven!" she exploded. "Is this to be another of your infamous offers of help? First you help me climb back into polite society and thereby into Hugo's notice. Then you proceed to help me with my uncle's puzzle only to further complicate matters and lastly, you offer me *carte blanche*. I do not know if I can survive any more of your mode of help, milord." She took huge gulps of air, endeavoring to calm herself, but the burden of fear, anger and weariness had become too great to bear. She could no longer contain the sob that wrenched loose from her throat. Somehow, she found herself enfolded in David's arms.

"It will be all right, Sylvia," he whispered, soothing her as he would a child. "It will be all right."

Her sorrow was like a storm in its fury, wracking her body in a tempest of emotion until she stood limp in his arms, utterly spent. David held her, stroking her hair gently, murmuring quiet words of comfort. The knowledge that he had utterly misjudged her plagued him, but her words twisted like a knife in his breast.

Donhill is nothing to me.

Sylvia had evaded Hugo's attempt to force her into his bed this time, by dint of her skill. However, from what David had heard, it was clear that Highslip would not be so easily thwarted. She would have to be protected. Yet, David realized ruefully, Sylvia was correct in that he had already been far too free with offers of protection. Somehow, he would have to undo the hurt he had caused, move with care if he ultimately hoped to win her.

"Your linen is wet. All the starch is gone."

The calm tone of her muffled words caught him by

surprise. "The devil take my linen," he declared roughly. "Highslip is the problem that we must needs deal with."

At the mention of Hugo's name, Sylvia reluctantly disengaged herself from David's grasp, leaving his temporary haven. She would not allow him to put himself into danger for her sake.

"Highslip is my problem, not yours," she told him.

Her eyes gleamed fiercely, like a feline's in the dark. The strength of Sylvia's spirit was admirable, but David had no illusions as to her ability to deal with a demented man. "Do you think the money you won as Madame Echec will put him off for any length of time, Sylvia? 'Tis you he wants."

Sylvia gasped. David knew how she had humiliated him. "How?" she asked, despair filling her voice, wondering who else might be aware of her identity? "How did you find out?"

"No one else knows." He hastened to assure her, reaching out to steady her. He turned her hand, tracing the healed line of the scar gently. "'Twas this that gave you away, the wound where that dog bit you. Only I saw, so you need not fear. Once I knew you were Madame Echec, it was easy to surmise the rest. It was you that played the game by post, wasn't it?"

Sylvia nodded. "Uncle was far too ill, that last year."

"And you wrote the letters as well?" A nod confirmed his suspicions. "I sat up all last night reading them. Kept them all, you know. You mimicked your uncle's style well, but it was your thoughts, your voice in those last letters."

"I was all alone," Sylvia attempted to explain. "My brother was off at school and Uncle was dying," Sylvia said, turning away. "Although he encouraged me to play, he thought that prowess at chess was somewhat unsuitable for a female. Most men hate to be bested by women, so I did not dare reveal myself for fear of how you might react."

"True enough," David said, recalling his own feelings on the matter. "I was an arrogant fool. Will you, look at me, Sylvia?" He touched her lightly, turning him to face her once again. "Why did you refuse my offer of marriage?" he asked, searching her face. "Did you hate me so much because of that unfortunate offer I made that you would not have me, even as a prize?"

"It was because I could not hate you that I refused you," Sylvia answered softly. "Even though you did not know it, there were years of friendship between us, a friendship far too strong for my anger to break. When I saw you kneeling there, I knew that I could not force a marriage without love upon you. I could not harm you, however much you had hurt me."

Without love, David agonized, the words tearing at his soul. *Be grateful you fool*, he told himself. *You have acted like an utter knave, impugned her honor, be glad that she does not hate you.* He swallowed the bitter gall in his throat and seized upon the only thread of hope.

"Can we be friends again, Sylvia?" David rasped, his heart aching. Friends. At least it was a start. She cared for him. If she would let him into her life once again then he might be able to build upon that comradeship. "I am sorry that I hurt you. It is just that I was afraid that you would go to Highslip, concerned that he would do you harm. It was the only way that I could think of, short of marriage, to keep you safe, Sylvia. And unfortunately, in my position, I could not offer to wed you."

"You must have a very low opinion of my common sense, milord," Sylvia said, a warm feeling glowing within her at the thought that, without the wager, he would have married her to protect her from Highslip. *But the wager came first*, she reminded herself.

"I shall deal with Highslip," David vowed.

"You must take care! The man is deranged." Sylvia warned him.

"I protect my friends, Sylvia," he promised. "You needn't fear."

Sylvia looked at him sadly. Never before had "friend" seemed so painful a word. Doubtless, she would never be anything more to him. It was unlikely that she would be able to content herself with the crumb of friendship when she was starving for the whole cake. It would be exquisite torture, watching him court others as he surely would. Madame Echec was still the best solution to her problems. Once Sylvia removed herself from the scene, Hugo would no longer be a threat to either her or David.

"I too, owe you an apology, milord," Sylvia found her voice once more. "I should not have brought you to your knees, the other day."

"I am glad you did, else I would never have known it was you," David said. "You play remarkably well. In fact, I have reviewed that game in my mind over and over and I am stunned by that brilliant gambit you used midgame. You must publish it. A variation on your father's strategy, was it?"

"My own actually. I formulated the original Gabriel's Gambit," Sylvia said distractedly, his suggestion of publication disturbing. "I have no desire for notoriety. You will not tell anyone of Madame Echec's identity?"

"Of course not!" David exclaimed, taken aback. "Though I think it a shame that you hide your talent, I would not betray you. We are friends."

"Yes," Sylvia said. "Honor has been satisfied all around. We are friends."

There was a rustling sound behind them and they

turned. A basket was descending from the window above.

"Cream cakes," Sylvia sighed. "I shall fetch your cakes in a few minutes Miles," she called. "Wait at the window for me."

"I'm starving," came the reedy wail as the basket was withdrawn. "Come back soon."

"He shall likely be sick to his stomach in the morning," Sylvia commented as she and David crossed the garden.

"Every boy deserves a chance to gorge himself silly at least once in his lifetime," David said, pausing to let her through the door. From within the house came the distant strains of the orchestra, striking up a waltz. The partially empty floor gleamed invitingly. "Do you think Miles' sweet tooth would wait for a few moments? Would you dance with me, Sylvia?" he asked.

Sylvia hesitated. They had never waltzed together and she wondered if it would be wise.

"To seal our newly cemented friendship?" David cajoled softly.

It would do no harm Sylvia decided. Hugo would not see them dancing here in this secluded room. One last dance with David. It would be a memory to cherish in those empty years ahead. Wordlessly, she moved closer. David put his arm about her waist, taking up her other hand as they stepped into the cleared corner of the room and began to move to the rhythm of the distant music.

David knew that he was holding her far closer than he ought, but he did not care in the least. The satin of her sleeve brushed against his cheek and he breathed in the soft lilac scent of her hair, trying to fill the empty feeling within himself. He had been a fool, thinking that he would be satisfied to have her merely as a mistress.

Forever was what he wanted, with all that an eternal pledge implied; home and children and loving until that blonde hair was as silver as moonlight. But that knowledge had come too late. He should have sent Brummel and the wager to hell, gone after his heart when he had the chance. Now, he was on the brink of losing the most important match of his life, a novice playing against hopeless odds in a game that had no rules.

Sylvia leaned against David, the faraway music not nearly as loud as the beat of her own pulse. It was intoxicating to move so closely in tandem, joined in rhythm to a man that she loved absolutely. She closed her eyes, whirling in darkness, feeling the touch of his hand, the fluttering caress of his breath upon her cheek. She knew why the waltz had been condemned as the most dangerous of dances.

They spun around the floor, stepping in the pool of moonlight reflecting on the pattern of black and white marble as David led her to the music. He wished that he could command them to play on, that he could suspend time itself so that he could hold her in his arms this way forever. Black and white, black and white, the squares passed beneath them, black and white, black and white. Nearly dizzy with motion and desire, David looked down at the marble tiles, coming to an abrupt halt. Jarred, Sylvia opened her eyes and peered anxiously at David's stunned face.

"What is wrong, David?"

"Count the tiles, Sylvia!"

"What?" Sylvia asked in growing bewilderment.

"The black and white tiles," he said, his eyes aglow with excitement. "Help me roll up the rug so we can count the tiles. Think upon it. Your uncle's Will sends you immediately to London for your come-out-"

"-with a card room re-done not too long after Hugo

began to court me," Sylvia said breathlessly, realization dawning. "A chess puzzle set to be played…"

Together, they rolled the rug aside.

"Fourteen squares long," David said in disappointment. "There are too many."

"Look," Sylvia pointed to the center of the room. The moonlight shone full upon a patterned border. There within its center was a perfect square of alternating two foot black and white tiles.

"Eight by eight. A chessboard," David declared, his face nearly splitting with a grin. "Now call out the rhyme."

Sylvia began to recite slowly,

"' . . . When you seek to tread the matrimonial measure,

You shall recall these words with pleasure.

King's pawn black, king's pawn white,

Bishop's move black and black's move knight.

Knight to rook's forth move again.

Queen to rook's fifth, bishop's mate at end.

Seek the board and step at leisure.

And you shall uncover the Rajah's treasure.'"

David stepped upon the tiles in sequence. As he touched on the final square there was a click from behind him. He turned to watch open-mouthed as a panel in the wall silently slid ajar.

"Dear heaven," Sylvia whispered, grasping his hand. Together, the two stepped into the concealed room. The moonlight through the open door illuminated the glistening hoard of the Rajah's treasure. Sylvia recognized many of the valuables that her father had accumulated upon his travels. She reached for a velvet box, opening it to find her mother's diamonds.

David saw shelves filled with banded piles, all carefully labeled - deeds, certificates and notes undoubtedly worth a fortune in themselves. At the center of the room stood a small stand with a gold and silver chessboard upon it. The pieces were carved in semi-precious stone and were set in the configuration of a fool's mate. In the center was a piece of paper. David picked it up, shaking off an accumulation of dust before handing it to Sylvia. Beside the board was a tinder box and candle-holder. He lit the taper, holding the light aloft as Sylvia read.

"My dearest child." The paper in her hand trembled as she recognized the familiar scrawl. "I knew that you would solve the puzzle and hope that you will forgive an old man's interference. I love you dearly and would not have you shackled to a man such as Highslip. By now, I am sure that he has revealed his true nature and you are safe. Forgive me, Sylvia. It was the only move that I could make. My love always, Uncle Miles." Her voice trembled as she read his last salutation and the tears ran down her cheeks.

"Shall I find your aunt?" David asked.

"No," Sylvia shook her head, smiling ruefully. "I do not think that I could bear Aunt Ruby quite yet. 'Tis certain she would take one look at this hoard and advertise that I now have enough of a dowry available to secure a duke. However, my brother ought to know. 'Tis his fortune as well. You will likely locate him wherever the sweets were set out. And please bring back cakes for Miles."

As he went off to seek Sylvia's brother, David cursed his abominable luck, wishing that he had made his feelings plain prior to the treasure being found. The value of the contents of that secret room was beyond reckoning. Sylvia was now a very wealthy woman. Combined with her looks and wit, her newfound fortune would allow her to look as high as she wished, certainly higher than a mere baron who was something of a minor nabob. Why would she consider a man who had not valued her enough to offer her marriage when he had the chance, a man who had placed a drunken wager above love?

...

Lord Highslip sat in a corner of the grand ballroom watching for Sylvia's return. From his vantage point, he could see the door to the room leading to the garden. He waited impatiently, touching the wad of bills in his pocket once again.

Where had she gotten the money? Certainly not from her pinch-purse aunt. He could have sworn that her uncle had not left her a feather to fly with.

The door opened and David Rutherford looked around before hastily pulling it closed behind him. Highslip's expression hardened. "Rutherford," he whispered angrily to himself. "He must have supplied the money. He is free now, damn him, but he shall not have her. He shall not have my Sylvia." When Rutherford had disappeared into the room that held the refreshments, the earl made his move.

...

At the entrance to the hidden vault, Sylvia exclaimed with delight as she located familiar treasures, keepsakes that she had thought lost forever. Except for the tidiness, it was almost like exploring a pirate's cave, she thought, as she went deeper into the narrow chamber. The long, thin hidden room paralleled the exterior for its full length. She heard a sound behind her and turned eagerly, expecting to see her brother.

"Look what we have found, William," she said, the words dying on her lips as she saw Hugo, his eyes glittering like daggers in the semidarkness.

"Look, indeed!" He fingered the open jewel case, pulling out the diamond necklace. "So you have found your uncle's hoard at last. You are once again an heiress," he hissed softly, laughing at her expression of consternation. "Now there is nothing standing in the way. It appears you will marry me after all, lucky girl. You will come with me."

"Of course, Hugo," Sylvia said, realizing there was no getting past him in the confines of the narrow chamber. She prayed that David would find William and return in a hurry. There was a look in the earl's eyes that frightened her. He was beyond reason, beyond sanity. She tried to keep her voice calm, soothing as she picked up a rope of pearls and waved it before him. "It will take but a few seconds to gather a few things. We are quite rich now."

"Do you think to delay me?" Highslip took her by the shoulders and shook her. "I saw Rutherford. He was with you, wasn't he?" He shook her by the shoulders. "Wasn't he?"

"Hugo, it is not what you-" she began.

Without warning, his hand shot out, turning Sylvia's head with the force of his slap. She slid back, stunned, pulling a box of jade figurines to the floor with a clatter as she struggled to keep herself upright.

"You shall not cheat me this time, Sylvia. I will have you and your fortune." He steered her out of the vault and through the doors out into the garden. "By the time I am done with you, you will have no choice, you see." Hauling her by the hand, he pulled her toward the gate to the mews. She struggled against him, only to have him hit her once more.

She opened her mouth to scream.

Hugo laughed. "Scream and I will hit you again. It's a waste of time. No one will hear you, Sylvia. The racket from the ballroom will drown out any sound that you could make."

Desperate for a way to save herself, Sylvia noticed the basket hanging from the window and deliberately tripped. It was fortunate that she had not screamed. Miles would have come running and she was certain that Highslip would not hesitate to do the boy harm.

"Where are you taking me, Hugo?" she asked as loudly as she dared.

He dragged her up roughly.

"To my little love nest on Marybone Lane," Highslip declared. "That shall do for now. In a week or so, you shall be glad enough to go to Gretna with me. I doubt that Rutherford will want you then, even with a fortune in your pocket. I fully intend to make sure of you, my dear."

As he pulled her out to the mews, she could only hope that Miles had been listening.

. . .

It took David longer than he had expected to find William and return with him in tow. The young man entered the treasure room, clearly astonished at the accumulation of wealth. Sylvia, however, was nowhere to be found. As David started toward the garden to give her the plate of sweets, a small figure barreled through the door.

"Lord Donhill . . . was waiting . . . heard him talking.

He's taken her, Lord Donhill," Miles said breathlessly. "He's taken Sylvia."

"Whoa, child." David set the plate aside and knelt, taking the boy by the shoulders, trying to make sense of his frantic speech.

"Lord Highslip's got Sylvia," Miles said slowly, the tears coursing down his cheeks. "Went out through to the mews... heard it through the window."

"Where is he taking her?" David asked. "Do you know, Miles? Tell me exactly what he said."

The boy nodded, catching his breath, "'Marybone Lane,' he said. You've got to help her, milord... He's a bad 'un, I know it. Pinches the maids when they can't do nothin' about it... Don't want him to pinch Sylvia."

"He will not pinch Sylvia, Miles," David said, his jaw set in determination. "Not if I can help it. I shall bring her back, never you fear."

"This is famous! I cannot wait to..." William said, coming out of the treasure room. "I heard you talking and I thought you had located Sylvia."

"Show me the fastest way to the stables, Gabriel," David demanded.

"What's wrong?" William noticed his tearful young cousin. "Miles, what are you doing down here? If your mama catches you..."

"Lord Highslip has abducted Sylvia," David cut in. Miles tugged his arm pointing him to the garden gate.

"Highslip? But I thought..." William began.

"No time for thinking, William," Miles said, directing David to the garden gate. "You can get to the mews same as he did, milord. I'll show you. This way."

"Good lad! Close the door to the treasure room, William." David instructed as he headed out toward the mews to fetch his phaeton. "The last thing we need is to have the hoard discovered now. Get Petrov and tell him to help you craft some tale about your sister's whereabouts."

At the gate, Miles halted abruptly and looked up at David.

"You said to tell everything Lord Highslip said, 'n I forgot one part. . . He said that he will 'make sure of her.' How do you make sure of someone, milord?" Miles asked.

"Dear God," David muttered, breaking into a run and praying that he would find her in time.

CHAPTER 11

Sylvia put a hand to her aching head. As the room gradually came into focus, she saw Hugo's leering face at the foot of the huge bed that held her. She groaned, realizing that what had happened was not a bad dream but horrifyingly real.

"I was beginning to believe that I had hit you too hard," Highslip said, rising from his chair. "You were taking your time coming to."

Somehow, he made it sound as if her delay in returning to consciousness was an unpardonable social lapse on her part. "My apologies," she said, shifting upon the lumpy mattress to surreptitiously gain a sense of her surroundings. The pink and gold furnishings were in cloying bad taste and above the bed, a fresco of naked cherubs upon the ceiling were indulging in distinctly un-cherublike behavior. All around her the heavy scent of old perfume lingered, permeating the carpets and draperies. No particular genius was necessary to realize that this was a Cyprian's chamber.

Hugo was coming toward her, a mocking smile distorting the shape of his mouth. She pulled back to the corner of the bed, the metallic tang of fear mingling with blood upon her tongue. It was but a small comfort to realize that she was still fully clothed; no telling how long that state might last.

"So coy," Highslip sneered. "Are you this shy with Rutherford, Sylvia?"

The mention of David's name acted as an antidote to fear. He would come back and find her missing. Miles would tell him where she was. *Play for every minute*, she told herself remembering one of her father's cardinal rules. *In a timed game, keep your opponent off balance. Let him play the clock. Time?* She had no idea how long she had been unconscious. "Why did you hit me, Hugo?" she asked, deliberately erasing all expression from her face.

The non sequitur caught him off guard. "I did not expect you to remain quietly in the mews while I collected my carriage," Highslip said, seating himself close to her on the bed. But to his surprise, her countenance remained utterly calm.

"Quite true," Sylvia said, keeping her voice steady. "I find there is often difficulty with moves made upon the spur of the moment. One cannot think the consequences of impulse through fully. For instance, when I am discovered missing this evening, it will also be found that you have gone. Suspicion will, of course, fall upon you."

"And how would you have avoided that?" Highslip asked, feeling somewhat flustered. He had expected screaming, weeping, pleas for mercy. Instead, the woman sounded much as if she were a prosy Oxford don, lecturing him.

"Too much time has passed already," Sylvia said, choosing her words with care. "Doubtless, people will already be looking for me. If I had planned this, I would have returned to the ball immediately and mingled with the guests. That way, when the disappearance is discovered, I would be able to act as surprised as the rest, thereby averting any inquiry."

"Ah, but you are wrong!" Highslip declared, his lip twisting in a crooked smile. "Barely a half-hour has elapsed since we left and I have only to drive a few minutes to find myself at Berkeley Square once again. There are some advantages in having a mistress' residence so close. I fully intended to return to your cousin's ball, now that I have you safely hidden away. However, I cannot leave you to your own devices."

"You do not trust me, Hugo?" she asked, sarcasm creeping into her voice. It was a mistake.

He pulled her to her knees upon the bed. "I trusted you. You were pure, untouched but you forgot that you belong to me. Entirely to me. So beautiful," he whispered hoarsely, his lips nuzzling her throat. He pawed at her décolletage, ripping the fragile lace. "You will always be mine, Sylvia. Only mine." His fingers went round the slender white column of her neck, tightening in slow pressure. "Remember."

The sinister sound of his laughter whistled in her ear as his grasp tightened. The glazed, unfocused look in his eyes terrified her. He was utterly out of his head, perhaps insane enough to choke the life from her. "You would kill the golden goose before the egg is laid, Hugo?" she gasped as the room began to spin.

"Quite right." Highslip shook his head as if clearing it. "'Twould be unconscionably foolish to see you dead, before bed and wed." He cackled at his own wit, then stopped abruptly. "But how shall I restrain you? Rope?" He let her fall as he rose to rummage through a drawer. "Damme, she took it with her when I gave the bitch her *congé!*"

Sylvia's relief was short-lived. Highslip's eyes lighted upon a half-empty decanter of brandy. "Ah, there's an answer!"

Sylvia shivered upon the bed as he picked up the crystal, his eyes gleaming. She had to get him to leave, somehow. There was no telling what his maniacal whims might dictate next. "Liquor makes me sick to my stomach, Hugo. I shall only cast it up," she said with all the calm she could muster. He made a disgusted face and put the decanter down on the stand beside the bed, knocking down a small vial.

"Yes," he murmured, picking up the glass container. "This shall do quite nicely." He opened the stopper and put the vial to his lips, taking a swallow.

Sylvia tried to control her trembling body as he approached her.

"Have a drink, m'dear?" he laughed, a sly look upon his face as he shoved the vial under her nose.

Laudanum, she thought with a sinking feeling, recognizing the smell. Her uncle had taken it in his last months to ease the pain.

"How is it that you are still standing, Hugo, after drinking such a dose?" she forced herself to ask.

The question distracted him for a moment. "Oh, I am quite accustomed to the stuff. Takes far more than a little dribble to send me to the arms of Morpheus, but you m'dear will only require a few drops. Not too much mind, for I do not want a corpse in my bed later, merely enough to keep you from running off."

Yanking her hair, forcing her neck back, he held the bottle to her lips. "Drink your dose," he demanded "Or I shall have to knock you unconscious again. Take it in your mouth, a good swallow ought to do it!" He pinched her nose, forcing her to gulp.

Tears pricked at Sylvia's eyes as she felt the liquid go down her throat.

"That's it. Take your nepenthe and be glad of it, for I will allow you none later when it might dull the pain." He laughed in anticipation. "For I fully intend to punish you my girl, for your dalliance with Rutherford."

Hugo threw her upon the bed and for a moment she feared that he had forgotten his intention to return to Caroline's ball. "They shall be looking for me soon," her voice grated.

"So they will," he said, adjusting his hat as he headed to the door. "Wait for me, Sylvia."

"As if I have any choice," Sylvia muttered to herself as she heard the click of the lock, the sound of his retreating footsteps. She forced herself to rise with difficulty, her legs nearly folding beneath her as she tried to make herself to retch. She managed to cast up a little into the nearby basin, but obviously not enough. Her head was beginning to swim.

Unsteadily, she rattled at the door in the windowless room. Her sense of disorientation growing, she sat upon the floor trying to plan her next move. The candle on the table began to dance strangely becoming a nimbus of light that illuminated the brandy within the decanter until it glowed like amber.

Shaking her head, Sylvia tried to clear her mind, concentrating upon an imaginary game of chess. The pieces transformed themselves into people. The white knight wore David's head; the black king was Hugo. *Focus upon something*, she told herself, turning a head so heavy that it seemed to be made of stone. The fluid in the crystal container upon the table sparkled upon the glass facets. *Had Miles heard?* she wondered idly, but that had somehow become unimportant. *So pretty, the way the light was shines upon the liquid. Find a way out, must find a way out.*

A thousand thoughts spun out of control, some coming sharply into focus in a moment of profound clarity before whirling giddily out of sight. *So this was why people lived in bottles . . . Would be interesting if not for*

Hugo . . . He would kill her sooner or later, probably sooner . . . Utterly queer in the nob. . . She would never marry him . . . Uncle was right . . . Don't think about it . . . Focus on next move . . . David . . . Idiot to have hidden the truth . . . Foolish pride . . . Never to have said, "I love you," and damn the consequences. . . Hugo would return and . . . So pretty the light. . . On the cut glass . . . Cut . . . Glass. . . . A weapon . . . Glass cuts!

Sylvia reached for the decanter, its weight dragging down her hand. It was too heavy. "You must," she told herself. "You must." With supreme effort she smashed it against the footboard of the bed, noticing with detachment that she had cut her finger. She put the bloody gash to her mouth, sucking as she tried to gather her dissembled thoughts. Trembling, Sylvia chose a particularly wicked-looking jagged shard and ripped a piece of the pillow tick to wrap around it to guard her grip.

"Stay awake," she told the flushed face in the looking glass opposite the bed. Was that her? She stared at the dark circlet forming round her neck, recalling the strange look in Hugo's eyes while he had all but choked the life from her. *To think that she had once considered marriage to that madman. Aye . . . Dance with a fool . . . She was waltzing round with David . . . Whirling black and white. . . You are a rich woman now. . . .'Twere well it were done quickly. . . Where was all the blood coming from? . . . Oh yes, her finger . . . Out damned spot.* Sylvia surveyed the spots of scarlet on her jade dress. *Utterly ruined . . . Will not be ruined. . . Will, damned Will . . .*

Through the foggy haze, she heard the sound of approaching footsteps on the other side of the door. She leaned against the jamb, waiting for her chance. The key turned and the door swung open. "No!" she screamed, terror driving her in a rush of strength. "I won't let you!" Sylvia sprang forward with a cry sweeping her makeshift weapon before her.

"Sylvia," David caught her hand as the wicked piece of glass struck downward, barely missing his cheek. She struggled, her eyes wild as she snarled like a cornered cat. *What had Highslip done to her?* he wondered as he attempted to wrest the weapon from her hold. Her hair was disheveled; a streak of blood was smeared across her face. With growing rage, he noticed the marks upon her neck and the blood upon her skirts and ripped bodice. She reeked of brandy. "Hush, my Kali, hush!" he choked.

"Oh, you are not Hugo," Sylvia said, confusion creeping across her face.

"No, 'tis David." Although it was difficult to control his voice, he forced himself to speak calmly, running on in a nonsensical prattle to try to soothe her. "There is no need to cut my jacket. Mr. Weston would take it amiss, after all you have already ruined one. You should pay attention to the way you handle sharp objects Sylvia, you have already hurt yourself, you know. Let me help you."

"David?" She spoke in a rush, letting the shard slip to shatter upon the floor. "I thought you were Hugo, coming back to ravish me. I do not have to kill you then. You are my friend."

"Yes, sweetheart, I am your friend. You may wish to kill me and be entirely justified, but I suggest you wait until your wits are about you so that you may enjoy it," David said. "Where has Highslip gone?"

She turned her head and nodded to the door with a wince. "Went back to the ball. I suggested it. Divert suspicion, you know. Played him for time. Never noticed he was a lackwit. I am glad that it's you."

"Are you?" David asked gently, trying to control his rage. His hands had become slippery with blood, her blood. He mulled over her words while attempting to locate the source of the bleeding, sighing with relief when he found the open cut on her finger. He loosed his neckcloth.

"Another neckcloth gone for a bandage. Ruined anyway. . . all bloody." She sighed mournfully. "Always spoiling your clothes, David."

"You may destroy my entire wardrobe and welcome," David said, unwinding the length of white.

"So glad. Don't have to kill anyone now. Hard to get it right with shaky hands. Complex business…murder. Messy. Wrecked your clothes. Bled all over you," Sylvia babbled, staring at him wide eyed. "Ruined mine too. Better ruined clothes than ruined me."

There was a grim determination below the rambling chatter. Taking one look at her solemn face, David locked his arms around her, drawing her close.

"Feel so safe now." With a blissful smile, she nestled beneath his chin, closing her eyes, then opening them as she felt his body tremble "Are you chilly, David? You're shivering. Wonderfully warm, wonderful, I am!" She reached up holding a palm to his forehead. "You? You are sweating!"

"I was told that gentlemen do not sweat," David said softly, stroking a smear of blood from her cheek.

"Well you are! Might be sickening or something. Should take care." She brushed his hair back slowly. "Always wanted to do this. Perpetually in your eyes. Like a little boy."

Indeed, he was growing more than warm as her fingers caressed his skin. Like a friendly cat, she rubbed herself against him, murmuring words of concern. It was strange beyond measure that she was attempting to comfort him. He wanted to keep her in the circle of his arms and never let her leave. Ever. The utter trust in those eyes penetrated the heat, reminding him that he had to get her home and safe before he dealt with Highslip.

Reluctantly, David released her and set her at arm's length.

"Don't like holding me?" She asked sadly, her lower lip trembling.

"Untrue, Sylvia. I like holding you entirely too much," David said, his voice deep with emotion and desire. "You are flying high, my love and I would not take advantage."

"'Tis not drink, but laudanum, if you would know!" She declared, moving closer once more, putting her hands around his neck, kneading the tense muscles. "Wound tight as a watch, you are, David. Ought to relax. Here . . ." She removed his spectacles. "Your eyes. Like a woodland in March, all brown but a hint of spring."

Opium . . . her inebriated yet lucid behavior began to make sense. The pupils of her eyes were wide dark pools banded by green. "If I relax myself now, Sylvia, there will be the devil to pay." David smiled ruefully, putting his glasses back on. "I want to kiss you senseless."

"Sounds wonderful. I'm very close to senseless. Should be simple." She felt the chuckle rising through his chest, the movement of his ribs tickling against her as she moved closer still. She caught hold of a stray thought. "Did you call me 'my love?'" she asked, eying him glassily.

"I believe I did," David said, his lips drawn irresistibly to brush her forehead.

"Does that mean you love me? You know that I see two Davids now and you are both nodding?" she asked

"I love you," David said.

"I am so glad!" Sylvia declared. "Two Davids! Both in love with me! Which of you shall I kiss first?"

"Close your eyes and I'll solve the problem," David offered.

Sylvia's lids fluttered shut and his lips touched hers gently. Her kiss was tender, timid with innocence as his fingers tangled themselves in the silken coils of her hair. Honor warred momentarily with desire as David fought for control, but the temptation was too great. Desire won as soon as David tasted the velvety sweetness of her mouth. She moaned softly, pulling him tighter, closer, and his hand brushed aside the last of the remaining pins in her hair to let it cascade down her back in a flow of molten gold. When she opened her eyes at last, he saw a fire amidst that glowing green.

"David." He heard her whisper hoarsely. "Must go. . . he'll kill you. Entshaw. Colber. Monster. Must…" Her eyes lost focus, the lids slowly closing as she went limp in his arms.

David hoisted her up, her head cradled against his shoulder while he carried her down the stairs. He placed her carefully into the carriage, pausing to tuck a blanket around her. She stirred, whimpering and crying out softly in a fearful way that pierced his heart. Within a few minutes they were behind the Gabriel house at Berkeley Square.

Miles was waiting at the garden door. "Sylvia?" he asked, anxiously.

"Is sleeping on the seat," David said, swallowing his fury and smiling to reassure the boy. "Get William or Mr. Petrov."

Miles obediently ran and soon came back with both. "Where is he?" David asked.

There was no need to specify which he was meant. "Drinking and dining, behaving as if nothing is amiss, the blackguard," William said, "Shall I lure him out now?"

"*Nyet*, is good, let him be. This appearance is to be maintained for as long as possible. Use the servant's way to take sister upstairs," Petrov instructed. "Mine

Caroline will be meeting you up in her room. She will be making her cousin comfortable."

David lifted Sylvia from the seat, reluctantly handing her into her brother's arms. The carriage blanket slipped revealing her bloody torn gown.

"Sylvia was waiting at the door, ready to cut Highslip to shreds and nearly took me down instead," David told him, responding to the unasked questions in William's eyes. "She's a tigress, your sister."

"I will kill Highslip," William declared, tears forming as he stared at the blossoming bruises on his sister's neck. "I swear, I shall kill that bastard."

"No," David said, starting forward, "I have reserved that pleasure for myself. I feel I have earned that right."

William took one look at David's hard expression, his clenched fists and bloodstained clothing, before nodding his agreement and carrying Sylvia inside.

"The boy is out of the way. Bring him." David demanded.

"You will be listening to me, mine friend." Petrov put a restraining hand on his friend's shoulder. "Not here or now. It would be bad move, causing much scandal. We are convincing the guests that your Sylvia is resting, overdrawn."

"Overset," David corrected automatically, his eyes narrowing as he formulated his plan. "You are quite right, Ivan. Much as I would enjoy wiping the floor with the earl with half the Ton watching, I shall wait. Highslip will no doubt leave as soon as he thinks it safe. You let him go when he pleases, for I am certain he will return to Marybone Lane first. Follow him to make sure. I will be waiting there for his arrival. Then, I vow that every minute of fear, every drop of blood shall be paid for with a cent-percenter's interest. We will return to my rooms once the deed is done."

It was to be hoped that Sylvia would recall nothing,

David told himself as he took up the reins. Highslip, the tawdry room, her brush with death, would all be forgotten. If fate was in a kindly mood Sylvia had been too full of laudanum to remember the horror.

And the kiss?

Likely, she would never retain the memory of a kiss on the edge of insensibility. If she had indeed forgotten, it would remain his own private treasure, something that she would never remember and he would never forget.

...

IT WAS JUST PAST DAWN. David slammed his way into his apartments, roaring like a tiger on the prowl. "Petrov!"

Petrov set his teacup on the table with every appearance of calm.

"I waited, Ivan," David spoke from between clenched teeth. "It was nearly sunrise before I gave it up and I realized that something must have gone horribly awry. The devil take you, Ivan Dragomir Petrov!" David stalked across the room; his fist slammed down on the table, rattling the china, causing the tea to slosh into its saucer. "I drove to Highslip's rooms. There was a crowd gathered outside."

"So the body is being discovered?" Petrov nodded. "Is good."

David hauled Petrov up and grabbed him by his collar. "You had no right!"

"I am having every right!" The Russian said defiantly. "I am sorry to be depriving of your vengeance, but it was only choice. You would have been killing him."

David's answer was an angry glare. Petrov stumbled back as his friend loosed his grip.

"You know I am being correct," the Russian said wearily, taking David by the arm and pushing him into a chair. "Arrest of Highslip is meaning scandal for mine Caroline and her family, for your Sylvia, too. Are you wanting that? Is worth it to tear Highslip apart with bare hands, no jury or judge? Then you hang for murder?"

"What happened?" David asked.

"I offer Highslip choice. Sure imprisonment, scandal, or death by his own hand. He chooses pistol and I wait to make sure deed is done, stop quick to Berkley Square, then come here to wait for you."

"I heard someone in the crowd say that he shot himself because of debts," David recalled, his rage dissipating as the sense of his friend's reasoning penetrated his anger.

Petrov smiled. "Is good! Is exactly what we want all to believe."

"And Sylvia?" David asked, anxiously. "You went back to the Gabriel house, you said."

"No connection to Highslip. Entire town is talking of the Gabriel fortune." Petrov informed him with a sigh of relief. "They are believing our story, how all is discovered when room is cleaned for ball! Mine Caroline's mama is at sevens and eights. Is saying how happy she is for her niece and nephew, but really, she is tearing out her hair for how she has been treating them like poppers."

In his anxiety, David did not even bother to correct Ivan's English. "But Sylvia, man! How is she? You have not told me a blasted thing about Sylvia!"

"I go to Marybone Lane as soon as I am finding this out, but already you were gone, so I come back here to wait. Girl has devil of the head," Petrov responded.

"Caroline said that she has been, how you say? Shooting the dog."

"Shooting the cat, Ivan," David said, glumly, still feeling cheated and betrayed. Nonetheless, he had to admit the Russian was right. The scandal would have been enormous had David given the earl his just due.

"When I leave, Sylvia was sleeping. Maybe, you should be bringing her some of your man's amazing headache potion, David," Petrov suggested hopefully. "It might be helping."

"Excellent idea, just the thing," David said, seizing upon the excuse to ask after Sylvia. "I shall ask Harjit right away."

He started to rise, but Petrov put a restraining hand on his friend's shoulder. "Is too early to be paying calls. We just avoid a scandal, no? Do not wish to start another, I think.

David slumped back into the chair.

Petrov eyed his friend's tattered, bloody clothes. "Perhaps," the Russian said gently, "you are wanting to change and clean before you are going? And maybe, be getting some rest yourself"

David looked up at his friend. "I nearly lost her, Ivan."

"But you did not lose her," Petrov reminded him. "Now comes hard part. Now you must win her."

. . .

LATER THAT MORNING the two were tooling their way to Berkeley Square, a bottle of Harjit's miraculous remedy in hand.

"You were correct, of course, Ivan, to do as you did,"

David admitted reluctantly as they drove up Hyde Park Corner.

"I know. It was right move." Petrov accepted the apology with a shrug of his shoulders.

As he turned up Berkeley Street, David recalled Sylvia's words last night in Marybone Lane. Of course much of it would have to be discounted. She had been entirely top heavy as the result of the laudanum. "You are my friend," she had declared solemnly. It had been clear, though, that there had been far more than friendship in the way her arms had twined about him and more than friendship in those fuddled eyes and in that kiss.

How much would she remember, David wondered? Would cold sobriety prove that her feelings had merely been nothing more than gratitude and relief? He found himself hoping that the scene at Marybone Lane was entirely forgotten, as much for his own sake as Sylvia's. If Sylvia came down from the altitudes with her memory intact, his confession of love might very well come back to haunt him. The realization that his feelings were far more than mere comradeship could easily destroy their fragile *entente*. Yet, if she recalled nothing, would he have the courage to give voice to those feelings once again, in the clear light of day?

Unfortunately, it soon appeared that David would not have the chance to find out. Mrs. Gabriel took the proffered cure from David and firmly advised him that Sylvia was not up to company. The woman did take the time to point out the various congratulatory floral tributes that her niece had received, from a marquis, a wealthy earl and even a duke, telling David without words that he was now running a poor last in the titled suitor stakes.

With Highslip gone, however, Petrov had moved into first place in the race for Caroline's hand. Ivan gave David a look of apology as he accepted Mrs. Gabriel's invitation to stay.

As David took up the reins to his phaeton, he felt something hitting his hat. A marble rolled to the floor of his equipage.

"Lord Donhill!"

David looked up to see Miles hanging out the nursery window above. "Come 'round the garden way." the boy called.

David drove his phaeton round to the rear of the house and dismounted as the entry swung open. Miles put a warning finger to his lips, leading David inside by the hand.

"Sylvia said to be on the watch-out for you," Miles whispered. "Said Mama wouldn't let you in if you wasn't nothing less'n a belted earl." He led David up the back-stairs. "She ain't in the nursery no more now that she's plump in the pocket," the boy explained as he opened the door. "Go on. I'll stand watch in case someone comes up."

David entered, knowing that it was wholly improper.

. . .

"David, I thought you might try to stop by." Sylvia rose from a chair by the window. "I hate to cause you to sneak about, but I guessed Aunt Ruby might bar the door to you."

"I am but a mere baronet," he said, the rasp in her voice making him wish that he could have put the fear of the Devil in Highslip before the earl sent himself to Hell.

"She does not wish me to go into company quite yet." Self-consciously, Sylvia pulled the collar of her dressing gown higher upon her neck to cover the marks that Highslip's fingers had left. "For once, I can agree with her. I am told that they will fade."

"Are you otherwise well, Sylvia?" David asked, his voice deep with emotion. She seemed profoundly uncomfortable as she gestured him to a seat, looking everywhere but at him. How much did she recall of what he had said?

"As well as can be expected after swimming so deep in the laudanum bottle," she said, taking a chair opposite. "No significant pain to speak of." She raised a palm to brush the bruises on her face and looked away. "I have been trying to sort out what actually occurred last night, but the line between an opium induced dream and a blurred reality is difficult to discern."

A tear slipped down her cheek and David reached for her hand. "Perhaps you should allow yourself to forget," he suggested.

As she looked up at him, the speech that Sylvia had so carefully prepared deserted her. His touch brought back the memory of the way he had held her. Surely, no mere hallucination could be so complete, replete with the texture of his jacket, the clean smell of his hair, the taste of his lips. Had she actually invited him to kiss her? She wondered miserably. How could she have been so incredibly forward? Imagination or reality, the soul-searing memory of the way they had possessed each other when their lips had met was enough to put her to blush.

"I should not be here," David said stiffly, as the silence lengthened. Her discomfort was a palpable thing, apparent in her restraint, the flush that spread to her cheeks. There was so much that he wanted to say, but he was afraid to speak now. Pretty words had never been his forte and as he searched for the appropriate phrases to tell Sylvia the true depths of his feelings, his spirits began to ebb. Trite clichés, every one.

My life is empty without you. I need you. I love you. The tension increased in intensity until it was almost a physical pain to be so near her and not to gather her into his arms. But he could not bring himself to let go of her hand.

Sylvia was desperate to know the truth, had to find out if his declaration of love was a poppy induced dream. But how to ask? "I wanted to thank you, David," Sylvia began hesitantly, throwing the words into the gathering pool of frustration.

"What are friends for?" he asked. There was tension in his smile, sadness in his eyes.

"To be honest, David, I do not think we can remain friends." She forced herself to fully meet his gaze, trying to read his face, but found it utterly wiped clean of emotion.

"I understand," David's flat tones reflected his growing despair. He could only conclude that she had recalled last night and had taken him in disgust for his behavior. The game was over. It was time to lose gracefully. He rose dully, leaving go of her fingers, painting a last impression of those features in his mind. *I shall return to India*, he decided. At least he would thus be spared the pain of watching others court her. "I had best go now. I hope that you can forget what happened."

It was agony to watch him leave. Sylvia had hoped that he would make the first move. In matters of love the man led the game, that was the rule. She struggled with her pride, knowing that if she did not play a gambit of her own, she might very well lose him forever. David's hand was reaching for the door when she found her voice. She was not her father's daughter for nothing. Sometimes it was necessary to risk all upon instinct.

"Perhaps I don't want to forget," she said softly. At

first, Sylvia thought that he had not heard her plea, but slowly, he turned. "Please David. Stay."

"Why?"

The word was stark, but there was a crack in his impassive facade that sparked Sylvia's hopes. The jade and lapis chessboard upon the stand near the window caught her attention. William had brought it upstairs, wishing to please her. "It will pull you out of the doldrums," her brother had said, his expression rife with guilt.

Sylvia rose and crossed the room to take David's hand, pulling him to the chessboard then motioning for him to be seated.

"You want me to play chess with you?" David asked, utterly bewildered. Was the drug still affecting her behavior?

"You think me addled, no doubt," Sylvia said as she slid her king's pawn forward.

To his surprise, she then reached over and moved his pawn as well. "I am beginning to suspect so," David said, watching as she moved her king's rook pawn.

"I think I am, actually," she said as she put his knight into place. "It is time to put all the pieces upon the board." Sylvia took a deep breath and plunged forward. "Did you say that you love me, David Rutherford?"

At that question, his mask vanished, replaced by a look of agony. The moments seemed to lengthen interminably as she awaited his answer.

"Yes."

"And did I tell you of my feelings?" Sylvia asked eagerly, joy welling up inside her at the wealth of longing he expressed in that single syllable.

"I did not credit anything you said or did." David sputtered. "You ...were drugged after all."

"And just what did I say or do?" Sylvia asked, a smile tugging at her lips as she advanced a pawn desultorily.

"Nothing," David prevaricated, still unsure as to exactly how much she remembered..

"Do you call that kiss you gave me 'nothing'?" Sylvia laughed.

"'Twas you that initiated the kiss," David retorted defensively.

"Now I recall. You were being damnably honorable while I was acting horribly brazen." She picked up his bishop, set it into position and then went back to her side of the board to advance her pawn yet again.

"The drug," he reminded her. Her moves thus far had been ridiculous. He turned his attention from the board to her face. For once, her countenance was an open book and what he saw written there caused his heart to soar.

"No, David," she said, shaking her head. "It was not the drug that caused me to act so, although the laudanum might have served to let loose the truth. I remember that kiss, David, every second of it until I slipped into darkness. If you never kiss me again, there shall never be another to match it and that I could not bear. You see, I love you. I think I always have, from your letters and certainly, from the time I first met you." She set the final piece in place, forcing herself to meet his questioning gaze, wondering if she would find the answer she hoped for. "Now, 'tis your move."

David looked at the array on the board before him. "A fool's mate?" He asked. "Why?"

"I once made a foolish statement that I would not wed a man who could not best me at chess," she explained softly.

"You do not think I could trounce you in a fair match, woman?" David asked, joy welling within him. She loved him. He felt as if a great weight had been loosed and he was floating like one of Sadler's balloons. The statement upon the board could not have been plainer. She had set herself up for a loss in one move. "This is cheating, Sylvia. Shall we play a real game and see who comes up the winner?"

"No!" Sylvia said emphatically. "I find myself coming round to Lord Byron's opinion. Life is too short for chess and I have no wish to play this particular game by the rules anymore. If you move correctly, you shall have the rest of your days to match yourself against me. I warn you though, this will likely be the last time I shall deliberately lose to you."

"A challenge to a lifetime tournament. How can I resist?" David rose, smiling as he came round to her side and took her hands, raising her to her feet. "I say you 'check.'" One hand touched her shoulder, moving her close, while the other reached over to the table, slipping his queen into position. "You do know what this means?"

The depths of her emerald eyes were sparkling as she toppled her king.

"Mate?" Sylvia asked hopefully, her hands reaching out to straighten his wayward neckcloth.

"Most definitely mate," David said, his fingers gently tracing the outline of her lips. "And a forfeit. We cannot forget the forfeit, my Madame Echec." He bent to claim his prize.

...

Lord Donhill and Sylvia had been awfully quiet for a very long time. Miles cracked the door silently, his eyes rolling in exasperation as he saw the two of them locked in a tight embrace. The boy wrinkled his nose as he shut the door to resume his lookout post and ponder the strange ways of the adult world.

ALSO BY RITA BOUCHER

Re-releasing soon...

Miss Gabriel's Gambit
The Would-Be Witch
The Devil's Due
Lord of Illusions
The Scandalous Schoolmistress
A Misbegotten Match
The Poet and the Paragon

ABOUT THE AUTHOR

Rita Boucher is the author of seven novels, including Miss Gabriel's Gambit. If you'd like to send her a message, please feel free to write her c/o Oliver Heber Books @publisher@oliver-heberbooks.com

www.ingramcontent.com/pod-product-compliance
Lightning Source LLC
LaVergne TN
LVHW031538060526
838200LV00056B/4556